"My father seems quite vexed with you,"

Imogene whispered, trying to focus on her goal while her fingers kept moving over the keys of the piano. "Do you know why that might be?"

"I have never done anything to offend him," Vaughn murmured back. "Why would he take me in dislike?"

She wished she knew. Vaughn Everard seemed the perfect fellow: clever, talented, handsome, charming. How could anyone take him in dislike? Certainly dislike was the farthest thing from her mind. "There's some problem."

"Can you arrange a meeting?"

"He's so busy. I can't be sure of catching him."

"But won't you try, for me?"

Her mother rose from her seat, wandered closer, eyes narrowing. Vaughn straightened.

"And now, the crescendo," Imogene proclaimed, throwing herself into the music. She finished the piece with a flourish, and Vaughn Everard joined her mother in applause. But his head was cocked, his dark gaze on her as if he hadn't truly seen her before.

Books by Regina Scott

Love Inspired Historical

The Irresistible Earl
An Honorable Gentleman
The Rogue's Reform
The Captain's Courtship
The Rake's Redemption

*The Everard Legacy

REGINA SCOTT

started writing novels in the third grade. Thankfully for literature as we know it, she didn't actually sell her first novel until she had learned a bit more about writing. Since her first book was published in 1998, her stories have traveled the globe, with translations in many languages including Dutch, German, Italian and Portuguese.

She and her husband of over twenty years reside in southeast Washington State. Regina Scott is a decent fencer; owns a historical costume collection that takes up over a third of her large closet; and is an active member of the Church of the Nazarene. Her friends and church family know that if you want something organized, you call Regina. You can find her online blogging at www.nineteenteen.blogspot.com. Learn more about her at www.reginascott.com.

REGINA
SCOTT, 1959

*The Rake's
Redemption*

Love Inspired

38212005746265

Main Adult Paperback

Scott, R

Scott, Regina, 1959-

The rake's redemption

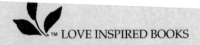

Recycling programs
for this product may
not exist in your area.

™ LOVE INSPIRED BOOKS

ISBN-13: 978-0-373-82940-8

THE RAKE'S REDEMPTION

www.LoveInspiredBooks.com

Printed in U.S.A.

And we know that in all things God works for the good of those who love Him, who have been called according to His purpose.

—Romans 8:28

To the heroes who leap without looking, trusting
in their skills and their Lord, especially Larry
and Edward; and to the Lord, who loves me
even when I look twice.

Chapter One

London, England, spring 1805

Where was he?

Lady Imogene Devary stood at the edge of the crowded ballroom, up on the toes of her white kid evening slippers. She hadn't even had a chance to dance, yet her heart was pounding in her satin-covered chest, and she could barely catch her breath.

Where was he, the stranger who had appeared at her door the past three days? Her father, Lord Widmore, had refused to see him each time, most recently so loudly the miniature of her little brother had clattered against the wall. Why did the stranger so concern him?

She peered about, twisting this way and that. The sounds of the ball brushed against her: the rise and fall of a hundred conversations, the strains of a string quartet, the dull thump of slippered pumps on hardwood and the laughter of flirtation. The Mayweathers had rented the prestigious Elysium Assembly Rooms for their annual ball. A dozen fluted columns marched down the center in Grecian elegance, and two crystal chandeliers hung from the gilded, domed ceiling above. Ladies in satins and velvets strolled past, and gentlemen nodded at Imogene in greeting. She knew almost every one of the nearly three hundred guests. How could a stranger escape notice?

Had he seen her pacing him in the ballroom when she'd first spied him earlier? She'd been shocked that anyone her father refused to acknowledge would be allowed entrance to such a fine occasion. So where had he gone now? Had he ensconced himself in the card room like her mother? Evaporated like a wisp of her imagination? Was she never to learn the truth?

And we know that all things work together for good to them that love God, to them who are called according to His purpose.

Yes, she had to hope in that verse. She had a purpose in spending her time searching the ballroom when she ought to be finding herself the perfect suitor. She loved her father too much to see him harassed. Hadn't they suffered enough? Or perhaps the stranger thought their suffering made them vulnerable. She squared her shoulders. That fellow would learn the Devary family was made of stronger stuff.

But perhaps she would not be able to convince him tonight. She puffed out a sigh and lowered herself to her heels. If she could not find him, she would have to determine another way to wrest some pleasure from the remainder of the evening. Tomorrow she could question Elisa about the guest list, perhaps identify him that way. She'd simply thought she would be better at this espionage business.

Her good friend Elisa Mayweather certainly had a talent for going unnoticed. She had pressed her back against the creamy white wall, and Imogene was certain she was strategically placed so that a column hid her from her imperious mother. As if to be certain no one would recognize her, she fluttered an ivory fan before her long face, embroidered satin skirts swinging with the motion. Another friend stood sentinel beside her.

Imogene hurried to join them. "Why aren't you dancing?" she asked, noticing their tight lips, their deep frowns.

Elisa snapped her fan shut and leveled it at a group of men crowding the far corner. "She's doing it again."

Kitty Longbourne sniffed, dark eyes narrowed to slits that made her resemble her nickname. "Rotten beau-snatcher."

"What, not you, too?" Imogene whirled to join her glare to theirs. "Freddie Pulsipher has lived in your pocket the past year. Don't tell me he's defected."

"Defected and forgotten me entirely," Kitty said, her normally dulcet voice closer to a growl. She shook her pale skirts and lifted her chin as if she were well rid of the boy.

"That is the outside of enough!" Imogene started toward the group. Elisa snatched at her shoulder to pull her up, fingers biting into the lace on Imogene's short sleeves.

"Where are you going? You can't accost her!" Elisa's wide brown eyes begged Imogene not to cause a scene.

But Imogene wasn't about to stand along the wall like some hothouse palm and bemoan her fate. She might not be able to find that stranger tonight, but she could help her friends.

She patted Elisa's hand. "There, now. I shan't kick up a dust. But someone must put a stop to her."

"This is her first Season," Elisa said, dropping her hand. "She was only presented to the queen two weeks ago. Perhaps she doesn't know the rules."

"I understand she was raised in the back of beyond," Kitty agreed with another sniff, this time of decided superiority.

Imogene had heard the rumors, too. The girl was an orphan with only three male cousins for guardians. That might have been enough to put Imogene in charity toward her, except her rival was also a beautiful heiress, with her own title no less, and the respected Lady Claire Winthrop was her sponsor. Where the young gentlemen of London were concerned, those factors conspired to make Samantha, Lady Everard, very popular indeed. But that her friends should be ignored while every gentleman danced attendance on the upstart—well, *that* was something Imogene would not tolerate.

"I don't intend to rip out her hair," Imogene informed them, to which Kitty muttered, "Whyever not?" Imogene shook her head. "But something must be done. Look, this set is ending, and the musicians are likely to take a short break. I for one plan to have a partner when they strike up the music again." Before her friends could say another word to dissuade her, she lifted her white skirts and swept across the room.

Her way was impeded immediately. Couples promenaded past, gazes entwined. A collection of dowagers debated the latest fashions. Distinguished gentlemen gestured with crystal goblets, intent on making their points on politics.

But by far the largest single group, at least three deep, was clustered in the corner. Imogene couldn't even make out the lady at the center. That truly did seem excessive. A girl on her first Season should expect a loyal group of followers but not at the expense of every other young lady on the *ton*.

Imogene put on her prettiest smile and tapped the

rear gentleman on the shoulder. Short as she was, it was difficult to tell his identity from the back, but she recognized him the moment he turned.

"Mr. Wainsborough," Imogene informed him, "I am quite vexed with you."

He blinked blue eyes as if suddenly finding himself transported to the farthest reaches of the Empire. "Lady Imogene, I have no idea what I could have done, but I most sincerely beg your pardon."

Imogene raised her chin. "You are forgiven, so long as you march yourself over to Miss Elisa Mayweather and ask her to dance."

"Miss Mayweather?" He glanced around the room, and Imogene nudged him to the left so he could see Elisa standing against the wall. He looked back at the crowd of gentlemen, then returned his gaze to Imogene as if begging for mercy.

She narrowed her eyes at him. He slumped in defeat. "Of course. Delighted. Your servant, Lady Imogene."

She waited only until he was on his way before tapping the next nearest fellow. "You, sir, are no gentleman."

He jerked around, sandy brows up in surprise. "Why, Lady Imogene, what do you mean?"

Imogene put her hands on her hips. "Here you stand while my good friend Kitty Longbourne pines away for a moment on the dance floor."

"She's pining?" His head turned as if he expected to see Kitty reclining on a divan with a cold compress on her forehead.

Imogene caught his coat, pointed him toward Kitty and gave him a push. "Go on, now. There's a good lad."

As he started off, she pulled up her long gloves and tapped the next fellow.

By the time the musicians started tuning up again, she had succeeded in peeling away all but five of Lady Everard's admirers, and every girl who needed a partner had one for the next set. All Imogene required was one for herself. She put her hand to the closest broad shoulder. The man turned.

And Imogene froze. She recognized the platinum hair held away from his lean face in an old-fashioned queue at the back of his neck, the sharp angles of cheek and chin. Instead of the black cloak that had enveloped him the last time he'd called, he wore a tailored black coat and breeches with a black-striped waistcoat and an elegantly tied cravat. Those dark eyes had looked merciless as the footman had sent him away for the third time. Now they were merely curious.

"There you are," she exclaimed. "I believe you wanted to dance."

One pale brow went up. "Forgive me. Have we met?"

"We must have met," Imogene insisted, taking his arm and threading hers through it. My, but he was strong; his arm felt like a mahogany banister under hers. "How else would I know you wished to dance?"

His mouth quirked. "How else indeed." He glanced over his shoulder at Lady Everard, then settled Imogene's arm closer. For a moment, she had the oddest feeling of being trapped. It shouldn't have felt so pleasant.

"Very well, then, my dear," he said, voice low and warm, like the purr of a tiger she'd seen in the Tower zoo. "Let us rise with the notes of the song and dance upon its joy."

The phrase sounded familiar, but she couldn't place it. In fact, as Imogene strolled with him toward the line of dancers, she was very much aware of another sound, for her heart had started drumming again.

Vaughn Everard stood across the line from the young lady who had accosted him. It wasn't the first time he'd been approached. He was a published poet, and some ladies imagined they had been his muse or understood his character because they'd read his work. A few even sought him for his reputation as a duelist, as if they thrilled to flirt with danger. A frown was often enough to send them scampering back to their mamas.

But not this young lady, he sensed. The look in those light jade eyes was challenging, and even the chestnut color of her curls, springing on either side of her creamy cheeks, seemed to crackle with energy. The grin on her peach-colored lips could only be called mischievous. Couple all that with a lush figure that showed to advantage in her simple, high-waisted white satin gown, and he found himself quite disposed to dance.

She looked to be a little older than his cousin Samantha, perhaps nineteen or twenty. Certainly younger than his twenty-six years and just as certainly a lady, or the high-stickler Mayweathers would never have allowed her to join them at their stuffy little ball. He had only been invited, he was sure, because he was one of three guardians to a beautiful young heiress making her debut in London Society. The Mayweathers coveted a relationship with the new Lady Everard. They were willing to suffer her ne'er-do-well cousin if necessary.

But why had this young lady insisted on a dance? She was watching him as if she wasn't entirely sure what to do with him as he bowed and she curtsied to the first measures of the music. Testing her, he kept his gaze locked with hers until they had passed shoulder to shoulder in the center of the lines. She did not look away, but her cheeks turned the same delectable color as her lips as she moved back into place.

When she placed her hands over his for the turn, he let his fingers caress her palms. She raised her pointed chin but did not jerk away.

Interesting. If she was bent on an assignation, she should be responding in kind. If she was a green girl, she'd be dashing from the set in embarrassment. As it was, her assessing look said she didn't intend to fall for nonsense. For some reason, that made him want to behave like a gentleman for once.

And that would be a mistake.

He had no right to the title; his grandfather and father had made that abundantly clear. And his purpose at this ball had no noble motive. He'd been sure his quarry would attend, yet he'd searched every room, and Robert Devary, the Marquess of Widmore, was nowhere to be found.

It had been the same everywhere he'd gone. The marquess was never home to callers, never at his club when he'd been expected, never at his solicitor's place of business, Tattersall's Horse Emporium or even Parliament when it was in session. Vaughn had hired a boy to follow him; the lad had never returned.

He'd lurked across the street from the house; his lordship went out the back. He'd loitered in the alley near the stables; the fellow escaped out the front! He'd even tried stalking the corridors of Whitehall, hoping to catch the marquess between meetings with the Admiralty or the War Office, where he advised on matters with the French, and still the man managed to avoid him. And the other members of government looked less than kindly on questions raised about their colleague.

But if he couldn't solve the mystery of the marquess tonight, at least he might discover more about his pretty partner. When they reached the end of the line and were forced to stand out for a cycle, he said, "You, madam, are a cipher."

She batted her cinnamon lashes. "Me? What of you, all in black? Are you a wraith, sir, flitting about the ballroom in search of prey?"

"If I was I would certainly search you out."

"Ah, but somehow I thought you were out for something larger, an earl or a marquess, perhaps."

Did she know? How could she? The reason for his quest was a closely held family secret, and even his family had been known to try to dissuade him from approaching the marquess. "You wouldn't happen to have one in your pocket, would you?" he asked. "It would make my work much easier."

She spread her hands as if to display her shiny gown to him. "No pockets, alas. And what would you want with an old marquess anyway?"

She had no idea. He leaned closer. "At the moment, I couldn't care less. Come now, admit it. We've never met."

Her light eyes twinkled as she dropped her arms. "Really, sir, I should take offense that you don't remember me."

Vaughn smiled as he straightened. "Forgive me. Any lady whose beauty outshines the stars should be impossible to forget."

Her smile grew. "There now, you see what a charming gentleman you can be when you put your mind to it?"

Vaughn took her hands and pulled her back into the

dance. "A momentary aberration brought about solely by your presence, my dear."

Still, he tried to treat her with the utmost civility as they progressed back down the line. It was hard to recall his purpose in London with her gazing at him that way. She smiled with her whole body—eyes alight and crinkled around the corners, chin lifted, body leaning forward as if she were about to impart a delightful secret. He found himself leaning forward just to hear it.

The set ended far too soon for him. As the music faded, ladies curtsied and men bowed. He didn't want to move, didn't want the moment to pass, didn't want to return to his dark pursuit of hunting a killer and making him pay. For these few precious seconds, he could pretend he was a typical young gentleman dancing with the loveliest lady in the room.

But he had never been typical. As if even the Mayweathers understood that, a tall, hawk-nosed female he knew to be the matriarch of the family was bearing down upon them.

"Lady Imogene," she said in a booming voice guaranteed to draw attention. "A moment of your time." She seized the girl's arm as if to ensure obedience.

Imogene. It suited her. Nothing in the common way like Jane or Ann. Vaughn bowed, mouth tipping up in a half smile. Lady Imogene frowned, and he could have sworn she tried to pull away. But her hostess was having no part of it. She visibly tightened her grip on the lady's arm and dragged her to safety.

Vaughn shook his head, turning away. Lady Imogene's mother or sponsor might be remiss in her duties, but her friends were clearly more attentive. They recognized the danger he posed, even if the lovely Lady Imogene was oblivious. They thought they knew him.

They were equally oblivious. The real Vaughn Everard lay deep inside. Only one man had ever known him, and that man was now dead.

He had to applaud his cousin Richard for trying, however. Vaughn hadn't even crossed the floor to the door before his older cousin caught up with him. A former sea captain, Richard Everard moved with the assurance of a man used to command, though he looked the consummate gentleman in his evening black. Unfortunately for Richard, Vaughn had never been good at accepting commands.

"What was that about?" Richard demanded, taking Vaughn's arm and drawing him aside. Around them, ladies in fine gowns strolled past, favoring them with coy smiles.

Vaughn ignored them. "There's better sport to be had. Care to join me?"

Richard shook his russet head, though he released his grip. "I feared you'd found sport here, as well. Claire recognized your partner before I did, but I thought Samantha would go looking for your sword when she saw you dancing."

Trust Richard's lovely betrothed Lady Claire Winthrop to notice anything untoward. She was Samantha's sponsor after all. Samantha, however, was far less interested in propriety when it came to those who held her loyalty. In that, as in so many things, she was like her father, a fact guaranteed to endear her to Vaughn. Every burst of fondness he felt for her only reinforced his mission. He had to learn the truth behind her father's death, even if it meant hunting the marquess to ground.

"Neither Samantha nor your lady love have cause for concern," Vaughn assured Richard. "It was only a dance."

"Was it?" Richard took a step closer. "Claire cannot like your methods, and neither can I. As far as we can tell, Lady Imogene Devary is an innocent. You cannot use her to punish her father."

He felt as if all the members of this fine company had turned and shouted in his direction. "What did you say?"

Richard's dark eyes, so like Vaughn's, gazed down at him. "You didn't know who you were dancing with, did you?"

Vaughn still couldn't believe the implication. "Devary? Related to the Devarys who hold the Widmore marquessate?"

"His daughter," Richard said. "His only surviving child. From what I've seen, he dotes on the girl. As close as you were to our uncle, I'm surprised you didn't know."

Of course he hadn't known. He would have used the dance to far greater advantage had he realized she was connected to the enemy who may have killed Arthur Everard, Samantha's father.

"The marquess may have been Uncle's closest friend," he told Richard, "but he never had much use for me. I've not met his wife or daughter." He cocked a smile. "Of course, I could say that about half the better families in London."

Richard straightened as if believing him. "Just remember your promise. We wait for Jerome before accosting the marquess."

Vaughn smiled. "I promised to wait until Samantha was presented to the queen to avoid any hint of scandal. She was presented two weeks ago. Widmore is mine."

Richard shoved in front of him. His cousin was the tallest of the family, and being a captain hadn't helped his diplomacy. "You will not touch the marquess until we talk to Jerome," Richard commanded. "My brother is still the head of this family."

Vaughn gazed up at him from under his brows. Richard might have the longer reach—and he certainly had experience in using the blade, having fought pirates on his travels—but Vaughn was fairly certain he could beat his cousin if it came to a duel. Richard would hesitate before wounding a man, particularly a member of the family. Vaughn wouldn't.

"Do what you must, Cousin," Vaughn said. "I know where my duty lies. Do you?"

He returned to the ballroom then, at last seeing his path clearly. The Marquess of Widmore might refuse to give him the time of day, but Vaughn thought he stood a good chance of convincing the man's daughter otherwise. He had yet to meet a lady who didn't swoon at a well-placed verse, a lovesick smile. Much as he abhorred dragging an innocent into this business, his duty lay in solving the mystery of his uncle's death. And Lady Imogene Devary, he very much feared, had become the key.

Chapter Two

Imogene watched her mysterious stranger stride away, the crowds parting before him. Even if she could have escaped the tenacious grip of her hostess, she could hardly chase after him; she'd already made a spectacle of herself by insisting on a dance. And she hadn't even learned his name!

"That was very foolish," Elisa's mother scolded, scanning the room. "Where is your mother? I'm certain she'll have something to say about the company you keep."

Imogene stilled. Mrs. Mayweather knew the man. Of course she knew the man! She'd invited him. But she didn't seem particularly pleased by the fact. Her hostess's face was an unbecoming shade of red that clashed with the rust-colored velvet of her ball gown. Each tightly wound gray curl, the lift of her hawkish nose, the compression of her already thin lips shouted righteous indignation. Small wonder Elisa tended to hide behind columns.

"I'm sorry if I offended you," Imogene said. "Naturally I assumed anyone you invited would be an acceptable partner."

The red faded, leaving Mrs. Mayweather as pale as fine muslin. "Certainly we only invite the best," she said, dropping her grip on Imogene's arm. "I cannot help it if some families have members who distain their honor."

So he was dishonorable? She ought to have expected it. Certainly her father's reaction to him had made him seem dangerous, dastardly. But that had not been her impression as they'd danced. The fire in him burned through the polite malaise of the other lords and ladies. Like a hearth on a cold day, it called to her. Oh, he was an outrageous flirt, holding her gaze and fingers far longer than needed, but nothing about his demeanor or conversation spoke of an evil lurking inside.

Lord, please help me know the truth!

"And what family would that be, precisely?" Imogene asked.

Mrs. Mayweather frowned down at her. "You didn't know? My dear girl, you have been most shamefully used. That...that creature was none other than Mr. Vaughn Everard, who dares to call himself a poet. Surely you've heard of him."

Certainly she'd heard of him. She had all three volumes of his poetry in her bedchamber, the pages dog-eared from repeated reading. *That's* why she'd recognized his phrase about dancing! But wait. "Everard?" she asked, stomach tightening. "Then is he related to..."

"Lady Everard," Mrs. Mayweather said, making the last name sound like something she'd found clumped to the bottom of her shoe. "Indeed, he is her cousin. I tried with the greatest tact to suggest that she leave him home, but she would hear none of it. They say she wears his heart about her neck like her pearls."

He was also one of Lady Everard's followers? Imogene could only feel disappointed in him; from his beautiful poetry she'd somehow thought he'd be more discriminating. In fact, for a moment on the dance floor, she'd wondered whether she'd finally found the suitor she'd been praying for—someone who could help her protect the family name, as her father's only living child.

But why was he interested in her family? How had her father even become acquainted with one of London's most infamous poets?

"Now, then," Mrs. Mayweather said soothingly, evidently taking Imogene's silence for shocked propriety, "we'll say no more on the matter. I'm sure any of the other fine gentlemen will be only too happy to partner with you for the next set."

Imogene thanked Mrs. Mayweather and watched her bustle away, but dancing was the last thing on her mind. She had only one goal now. How could she meet Vaughn Everard again and learn more?

In the shadow of one of the alabaster columns, Vaughn watched Lady Imogene. She'd managed to escape her diligent hostess, leaving the woman in charity with her if the smile on Mrs. Mayweather's face was any indication. Now she flitted about the ballroom, talking to this young lady, that gentleman, a bee buzzing from flower to flower.

She was obviously as good at talking her way out of a scrape as she was getting into one. Yet why would the Marquess of Widmore's daughter—beautiful, wealthy, charming—ask him to dance? He could find a way to put the question to the lady, along with other questions on his mind, but still he hesitated. He knew his best chance in meeting the marquess lay in charming Imogene, but he had never countenanced using others for personal gain. He'd seen firsthand the pain and devastation that followed.

Besides, that smile was too knowing, too confident, and he had a feeling that jade gaze could pierce flesh and see inside him. Yet if she had seen inside him, she would never have asked him to dance. No, he'd been handed an opportunity to gain the attention of the Devary family. He'd be a fool not to take it.

Keeping her ever in sight, he moved around the edge of the ballroom. He tensed for a moment when the affable Lord Eustace bowed over her hand, but she sent him off with a wave and a laugh that sparkled as brightly as her gaze. She didn't intend to dance, then. Odd. Why would one of the most beautiful and eligible women in the room refuse to take the floor, except on his arm? He ought to feel honored, yet he couldn't believe honor had been her motive.

Her friend saw him before Lady Imogene did. With her coal-black hair and hawkish nose, the young lady now standing beside the marquess's daughter was a Mayweather, he guessed, although one of the prettier ones. Her brown eyes widened, and she stopped in mid-sentence to flutter her ivory fan in front of her face. Lady Imogene turned, then blinked.

Vaughn bowed. "Lady Imogene, your servant. You asked me to dance earlier. I thought to return the favor."

Her brows went up as if she had not expected him to know her name. "Mr. Everard," she replied. "I fear dancing with you was so thrilling I haven't been able to retake the floor since. Perhaps a promenade instead?"

Her smile told him his face had betrayed his surprise that she knew him, too. It seemed her previous invitation had not been all innocence. But a promenade would give them more of an opportunity to be alone, or at least as alone as was possible in a crowded ballroom. He offered her his arm. "Charmed."

"Imogene." The word was a mere whisper of anguish from her friend. She, at least, was concerned about the damage to Lady Imogene's reputation. One interaction could be poor judgment. Two might mean poor character.

Imogene reached out a hand and patted her friend's. "Never fear, Miss Mayweather. I'm fairly certain Mr. Everard doesn't bite. And I'll be back before you know it."

With a dazzling smile that almost made Vaughn rethink his strategy yet again, Imogene put her hand on his arm, and they set off around the ballroom.

Thank You, Lord!

Imogene nearly said the praise aloud. She'd been quizzing her friends about this man, until even Kitty and Elisa were teasing her about her sudden *tendre* for the fellow. She could not tell them that it was hardly *amour* that moved her.

Oh, he was handsome enough with that white-gold hair like a yard of the finest silk and those impossibly deep brown eyes like melted chocolate. And one could hardly fault his address, standing tall and lean and so very sure of himself. He took each step as if claiming the polished wood floor for England.

But what she needed to know was his character and background. Surely they would give her some notion as to his business with her father. How wonderful that she'd been given this opportunity!

"How do you know my father?" she asked just as he said, "Is your father in attendance?"

Imogene laughed. He smiled, a warm, open smile that invited her closer, promised it was meant for her alone. Too bad it disappeared as quickly as it had come.

"Forgive me," he said. "Ladies first."

"My father wasn't able to join us," she said, answering his question. "I didn't know you were acquainted."

She waited, hoping for similar honesty. He turned slightly toward her, lips poised to respond, and she sighted Mrs. Mayweather headed in their direction, eyes narrowed. "Oh, dear."

He must have seen the danger, too, for he expertly steered Imogene away. Once they had put a row of columns between them and their hostess, he said, "Your father and my uncle were good friends."

Friends? Had she ever been introduced to an Everard old enough to be his uncle? Her confusion must have been written on her face, for he clarified. "Arthur, Lord Everard. You must have met him."

Imogene shook her head. "I'm sorry. I don't recall. What does he look like?"

"Tall, lean, fair-haired—a great deal like me, actually."

Imogene beamed at him. "Forgive me. A gentleman that handsome would be difficult to forget."

He chuckled, then stiffened and guided her behind the dowager's circle. The older ladies batted their eyes and waved their fans as he passed, and he nodded and smiled encouragement to them.

On the opposite side of the circle, his cousin, Lady Everard, looked far less encouraging, her pretty face scrunched up in confusion. She had thick golden hair, worn up high and cascading down her back, and dark brown eyes that must run in the family, for they were very like his. Every girl in the room would be wondering how to copy that gown—clear muslin over an underskirt spotted in gold so that it sparkled as she moved.

"I fear our promenade will end all too soon," he murmured to Imogene. "Do me the honor of answering two more questions."

"Anything," she said, then chided herself on her eagerness.

"First, do you remember what your father was doing the night of March third?"

What a singularly odd thing to ask! Whatever issue he had with her father must have something to do with that day. Imogene thought back. Had they been in London yet? Her father had been intent on getting them all there from their country estate. Business, he'd said, that could only be conducted in London.

Vaughn Everard was leading her toward the main entrance to the ballroom now. Framed in the doorway, her mother glanced about, obviously in search of her. Mrs. Mayweather stood beside her, foot tapping against the fine wood floor.

"I don't remember," Imogene said in the rush. "What's the second question?"

"May I call on you tomorrow?"

She was so surprised she actually stopped, pulling him up short. The movement was enough for her mother to spy her and start in her direction.

"Cousin Vaughn," Samantha Everard said behind them, her voice surprisingly hesitant for her usual confidence in the social scene. "You promised me the next dance. Have you forgotten?"

His body turned dutifully as he released Imogene, but his gaze remained on hers, waiting. She could almost see the hope.

"There you are, Imogene," her mother said, coming

up to her and taking her arm. "It's been a long evening, dear, and I'd like to retire."

Samantha Everard's fingers were reaching for her cousin's wrists even as Lady Widmore's wrapped around her daughter's. Before Imogene could answer him, they had parted, and she knew they would not be given the opportunity to talk again that night. She glanced at him twice as she walked with her mother to the door, but if he returned the look, she didn't see it. Imogene felt a sigh of pure frustration escape her.

Her mother waited until they were seated in the carriage on the way home before requesting an explanation. How could Imogene refuse? Elisa Mayweather might be burdened with an overbearing mama, but Imogene knew how fortunate she was in her own mother. She hoped she'd look so lovely when she reached her mother's age. Lady Lavinia Devary, Marchioness of Widmore, had hair that was a distinguished shade of silver, but her face was as unlined as Imogene's, and she carried herself with an elegance her daughter envied. Even now, confronted with Imogene's possible indiscretion, she was more concerned than censorious.

"Darling," she said, reaching across the coach to take both of Imogene's hands. "Why the interest in Mr. Everard? Surely you know his family is considered scandalous."

Imogene frowned. "Are they? Why?"

Her mother's voice was stern though her look remained concerned. "The former Lord Everard was not a gentleman, despite his title. I refused to allow him entrance to our home even though your father considered him a friend."

Her mother was usually determined to see the best in everyone. Lord Everard must have done something terrible for her to take him in such dislike. But at least Mr. Everard had been right in calling her father and his uncle friends. "And do you find Mr. Everard so scandalous, as well? Is that why Father refuses to see him?"

Her mother squeezed her hands. "I have heard he has dueled, but I had nothing to do with your father's decision. Still, I trust his judgment."

"I wish I did. Something's wrong, Mother. I can feel it."

Her blue eyes were sad. "You are a loving daughter, Imogene, but you needn't worry for him."

Imogene leaned forward. "How can I not worry? He doesn't talk to me anymore. He's seldom home. It's almost as bad as when Charles died."

Her mother paled, as if even hearing the name of her lost son hurt. Imogene hurt with her.

"Your father is a very busy man," she said, releasing Imogene's hands, "called to serve the king in many areas. With Napoleon threatening to invade at any time, do you think something as small as a misguided poet could concern him?"

Imogene sighed. "Perhaps not, but he continues to refuse Mr. Everard entrance, even when he's perfectly capable of receiving him. I'd like to know why."

Her mother turned her gaze to the window. "There are a great many questions about this life that remain unanswered, Imogene. You would be wise to grow accustomed to the fact."

She knew her mother was right. She'd never understood why her younger brother had died, why her mother had lost all the other older sisters Imogene might have had. She called Imogene her little gift from the Lord. Didn't the fact that Imogene alone had survived and thrived mean God had some purpose for her life?

Something more she was meant to do than simply dance through each Season with no thought but to her own pleasure?

I know You do, Lord! I know I was meant to save my family. Surely You have a greater plan than for all to be lost when Father dies someday. Show me the man You mean to help me gain approval to carry on the title of Marquess of Widmore!

She tried to ask her father about the problem as soon as they returned home, but Jenkins, their head footman, reported that he was still away. She hadn't been willing to broach the subject with the marquess earlier without knowing a name. In truth, many people rapped at the door of the Marquess of Widmore: widows seeking redress from the War Office, or the Admiralty where he advised on French tactics, émigrés related to their French ancestors to request aid in rebuilding their lives in England, solicitors and land stewards needing decisions on the family investments.

Her father refused admittance to any number on a given day, depending on his plans and mood. Recently he'd been particularly difficult to pin down. He had little time for his family; he certainly had no time for strangers.

But Vaughn Everard was no longer a stranger. She had danced with him, walked with him, seen his dark eyes brighten in admiration. From his works she was certain he had a refinement of spirit that was nothing short of amazing. Why would her father have taken him in dislike?

She has missed her opportunity to find answers to-night, but that didn't mean she had to give up. She hurried upstairs to her room, hoping for a few moments alone.

She and her mother shared a ladies' maid, not because they couldn't afford one for Imogene but because her mother insisted on it. Imogene thought her mother enjoyed whispering suggestions in the maid's ear as to what gown would best suit Imogene for a particular occasion and how she should wear her hair. With Bryson busy helping her mother first, however, Imogene had time for a little more research on Vaughn Everard.

She started with Mr. Debrett's *The Correct Peerage of England, Scotland and Ireland.* The two slim volumes listed every member of England's most notable families. The Everard barony was one of the newer entries, unlike her father's. He was the tenth Marquess of Widmore and likely to be the last, unless she succeeded in her plan. There were no male relations as far as anyone knew, and unlike the occasional barony and dukedom, marquessates could not be inherited by the female line. When her younger brother Peter Devary, Viscount Charles, had died a few years ago of a fever, her father had been even more devastated than Imogene and her mother, and Imogene knew that the inevitable end to their family name and heritage was part of his sorrow. If only she could find a suitor well-positioned enough to petition to have the title recreated in him!

But what was this? The book made no mention of Samantha Everard. According to it, Lord Arthur Everard had no issue. Imogene thumbed back to the title page and checked the date: 1802, only three years ago. Why hadn't the publisher known about Lady Everard? She couldn't be adopted—only heirs of the blood stood to inherit a title.

Imogene returned to the Everard page. It listed the

heir presumptive as Jerome Everard, nephew of the late Lord Everard, with his brother Richard after him. And there—Imogene cradled the book and allowed her finger to linger on the name—was Vaughn Everard, with no wife noted. His father had been the third son of the first Baron Everard and the brother of the second.

That made him first cousin to Samantha Everard. Although it was not unheard of for first cousins to marry, particularly to keep a title or fortune in the family, it was still an uncommon practice. And with every gentleman in London gathered around her, Lady Everard had her pick of suitors. Surely she could spare her cousin.

Imogene heard the door open quietly behind her and set the book back on the shelf, wondering why she felt guilty. Bryson paused only long enough to curtsy respectively, then hurried to do her duty. The maid had raven hair held tightly back from her face and a long pointed nose. She chose to keep only the darkest dresses her mistress offered. When Imogene was little, she had once drawn Bryson as a raven.

Now the maid went to shutter the windows on either side of Imogene's bed, her dress solemn against the soft blues of the room. She had closed the shutter on one side, each movement sharp and precise, when something rattled against the glass, and she recoiled.

"What is it?" Imogene asked, moving closer.

The maid turned to her, wide-eyed. "There's a gentleman down in the garden. He seems to be throwing rocks!"

A gentleman? Who would be able to slip past the carriage house and stables, to avoid the notice of the footmen and butler? Frowning, Imogene ventured toward the window until she could peer down into the small garden below. In the light spilling from the windows above, she could see the carefully clipped hedges, the wrought-iron benches near the flowers, the stone-lined path to the stables beyond.

Someone was standing there, face turned up to her window, black cloak swirling around him like smoke from a blaze. Fingers shaking, she raised the sash.

"But, soft! What light through yonder window breaks?" Vaughn Everard called up. "It is the east, and Lady Imogene is the sun. Arise, fair sun, and kill the envious moon, who is already sick and pale with grief that thou, her maid, art far more fair than she."

"I'll fetch Jenkins," Bryson said, backing from the window.

Imogene caught her arm. "Stay a moment. We're in no danger." As her maid frowned at her, Imogene called back. "Really, Mr. Everard, you resort to the Bard? I thought you were a man of inspiration."

He swept her a bow, one arm wide. "I divined your room correctly, didn't I? But alas, your beauty halts my tongue. My words could only be cursed as praise too faint."

"A likely story," Imogene said. "I do believe, sir, that you are lazy. You think to win me over with words alone."

Straightening, he pressed his hand against his chest. "You wound me, my lady. Tell me what I must do to prove myself."

"Go ahead," she whispered to Bryson, who fled the room as if Imogene had put a brand to her skirts. To Vaughn she said, "Present yourself to the front door tomorrow at two, sir."

He dropped his hand. "Alas, a dragon guards your bower, fair maiden. I have been refused entrance too many times, as I think you know."

"And you, sir, pride yourself on your swordsmanship, I hear. Surely a dragon is no match for you."

She thought he smiled. "Swords are messy. A whispered word from you might do the trick."

Below, she heard the kitchen door open, saw a brighter light cut across his figure along with the shadows of Jenkins and one of the under footmen as they marched toward him.

"Consider yourself invited, Mr. Everard," she called. "I shall expect you tomorrow at two. Do not be late."

"I shall fly to your side," he promised. With a swirl of his cape, he dashed off into the night, the staff right behind.

Imogene set down the sash and leaned against the glass, her breath quickly fogging the pane. Vaughn Everard was coming to call on her tomorrow. This time she intended to make sure he was allowed entrance, if she had to take on her father herself.

Chapter Three

Vaughn wanted to return to the Devary home the next day as soon as it was considered decent. Though he generally rose and retired whenever the mood struck him, spending his days and nights as he pleased, he knew the fashionable ladies of London usually did not receive guests until after noon. So he presented himself at the door at exactly two, as Lady Imogene had requested.

The house was becoming familiar after his many attempts to speak with the marquess. It was wide and squat with far too many furbelows around the windows and door, as if a wedding cake had taken up residence on a corner near Park Lane. He would have wagered the marchioness had approved the purchase, for surely no gentleman worth his salt would choose to live in such a house.

Though the day was bright, with the sun spearing through clouds and brightening the gray stone pavement, Vaughn's mood was considerably darker. Even something so simple as a request to call on Lady Imogene had required him to enact a Cheltenham tragedy, resorting to Shakespeare, no less! A few moments away from the garden last night, and he was wondering again whether there was another way besides charming the lady to gain a moment of her father's time.

So he'd tried accosting the Marquess of Widmore at White's after convincing a gentleman friend of Jerome's to bring him in as a guest, but the lord had not been on the premises of the heralded gentleman's club on St. James's. Discreet inquiries had only served one purpose: to garner Vaughn the attentions of Lord Gregory Wentworth.

Though he was the heir to the Earl of Kendrick, Lord Wentworth was a toad, his only purpose in life to curry favor with those more rich and powerful. Vaughn supposed he was handsome enough with his sandy hair pomaded back from a chiseled face and a cleft in his chin, but the fellow had no opinions save an extreme overestimate of his own worth. Because his family estate lay next to Samantha's home in Cumberland, he seemed to think he ought to be good friends with the Everards.

But by far his worse fault, in Vaughn's mind, was the affectation in his speech, recently acquired, according to Samantha. Lord Wentworth tended to clip off his sentences, as if his life and deeds were too grand for mere words to describe. Vaughn had little use for anyone with such a lack of appreciation for the beauty of language.

"Evening, Everard," he had greeted Vaughn last night, strolling up to him through the clusters of gentlemen already crowding the club. His ingratiating smile set Vaughn's back up even further. "Lost the marquess, eh?"

"If he is lost, he can be found," Vaughn assured him, turning for the door.

Lord Wentworth angled himself to block Vaughn's path, his shoulders too broad in his evening coat of navy superfine. "Heard as much. Might know where."

Vaughn eyed him. "Then pray share your knowledge."

Lord Wentworth glanced both ways as if to be sure the other members of the club were engrossed in their various pursuits, then leaned closer, eyes lighting. "I'll learn more about the marquess's plans. You put in a good word for me. Agreed?"

Vaughn very much doubted the marquess would accept his recommendation. But much as he disliked the fellow before him now, he was in no position to refuse help. "I'd be delighted to receive any information you care to pass along," he'd said with a bow. He hadn't been surprised to hear nothing more from the man this morning.

And so it would have to be Imogene. The lilt of her voice last night had betrayed her eagerness to have him call, to pursue their acquaintance. He felt the same eagerness, but he buried it deep. She was attracted to nothing more than the idea of him—a poet, a swordsman. Reading more into it was dangerous to them both.

He reached for the knocker on the purple lacquered door and noticed the tremor in his hand. Nervous? Him? He flexed his fingers and gripped the brass, bringing the rod down once with finality.

A footman opened the door immediately, head high in his white-powdered wig, iron gaze out over the shoulder of Vaughn's crimson coat. Only a twitch of his lips suggested he remembered seeing Vaughn there before.

"Mr. Vaughn Everard to see Lady Imogene Devary," Vaughn said, squaring his shoulders.

The footman did not move from his place blocking the doorway, his black coat and breeches making him a dark shadow clinging to the wood. "I regret that her ladyship is not at home to visitors."

"I think you will find you are mistaken," Vaughn said.

The footman didn't even blink. "The lady is unavailable, sir. Good day."

He started to swing shut the door. Not this time. Vaughn stuck his shoulder in the gap, crowding the fellow backward. "I suggest you speak to your mistress. She will not thank you for turning away a caller she specifically requested."

A flicker of uncertainty crossed the footman's face, but he held his ground. "Very well, sir. If you would wait a moment, I will see if I can locate Lady Imogene."

Vaughn waited. On the stoop. Like a penitent, not worthy to breathe the rarified air of the marquesses of Widmore. He took a step back and eyed the stone decorations around the door and windows. Easy enough to put his hands there, his toes there. How would Lady Imogene react if he climbed through her withdrawing room window and plopped himself down on her sofa?

Before he could find out, the door swung open again. "Lady Imogene will see you now," the footman said to the air over Vaughn's head, and he stepped out of the way to allow him entrance.

He was here! Imogene had recognized that husky purr, equal parts elegance and danger, at the bottom of the stairs. She'd been waiting, listening for it, using any excuse to loiter near the door. And she'd been highly tempted to seize the vase of lilies her mother had arranged on the table at the top of the stairs and throw it at Jenkins's back if he'd kept Mr. Everard waiting another second.

But Mr. Everard mustn't know she was eager to see him. After confirming to Jenkins that Mr. Everard was expected, she flew from the landing to the withdrawing room and perched on the settee before the footman opened the door the second time. The room was a perfect frame for her new apricot-colored day dress for the walls were a pale green and peaches blossomed in the pattern of the carpet at her feet. On the ceiling, cherubs floated on clouds above a sunset sky. Even the furniture, done in satinwood with white-on-white upholstery, favored the reddish tones that always made her chestnut curls gleam.

She arranged her silk skirts carefully, picked up a book (not of his poetry—that would be far too obvious) and pretended to be absorbed. She counted each tread as the footman approached and found herself holding her breath when Jenkins paused in the doorway.

"Mr. Vaughn Everard to see you, Lady Imogene. Your mother will join you shortly."

Despite her best efforts, the book tumbled into her lap and her breath left her chest in a rush. As if he knew it, Vaughn Everard sauntered into the room and swept her a bow. Oh, but he knew how to use the moment to effect. His lean arm was wide, the lace at his cuffs fluttering in his crimson sleeve; his head was bowed, allowing the sunlight from the window behind her to anoint his pale hair with gold. When he straightened, his dark gaze sought hers, as if every moment apart had been an agony. Imogene was highly tempted to applaud his performance.

"Mr. Everard," she said instead. "How delightful of you to call. Won't you have a seat?"

He settled himself on one of the white-on-white chairs. Goodness, but his legs were long. From his polished black leather boots up his tan chamois breeches, they stretched nearly to the tips of her apricot-colored slippers. She clasped the book closer.

"Thank you for receiving me," he said. It was the expected response, but the depth of his voice told her he meant it.

Imogene smiled at him. "Well, I did promise. I knew I could get Jenkins to let you in."

His lips turned up just the slightest bit, as if reluctantly, but something inside her rose with them. "To what heights have I risen that the fairest of the fair should do battle for me?"

Imogene shook her head. "Hardly a battle. I heard you at the door."

His smile lifted. "Listening for me, were you?"

She mustn't give him that impression. She waved a hand. "Voices carry all too easily in this house. It was built to humor my French grandmother, who loved her music." She glanced at the door but heard nothing of the swish of her mother's skirts approaching. "We only have a few moments. Perhaps you'd care to tell me why you're so intent on calling on my father?"

His pale brows went up. "Very well. I believe he may know more about my uncle's last moments."

Of course! She'd read in the paper that Lord Everard had passed away, and that's why his daughter had come to London. But why would her father refuse to see his nephew? Perhaps he did not realize that this was Mr. Everard's purpose in calling? Did her father not know of the relationship between this man and Lord Everard? "You were close to your uncle?"

"He was father and mother to me. At times it seemed he was the very air I breathed."

She could hear the emotion in his voice, though she thought he meant to hide it behind his fanciful words. She tried to imagine losing both her mother and father, and her spirit quailed. It had been bad enough losing little Charles.

"I'm so sorry," she murmured. "I'm certain if Father knew something of value he'd be only too happy to tell you."

The smile remained on his handsome face, but it seemed suddenly stiff, like a mask on display. "No doubt. But I'll rest easier once we've spoken. Is he home, by any chance?"

Imogene started to explain that he'd been called to the Admiralty that morning, but her mother appeared in the doorway.

"Ah, Mr. Everard," she said, sailing into the room in her day dress of palest silk. "To what do we owe this pleasure?"

Vaughn rose and bowed, and Imogene couldn't help noticing that the movement didn't have quite the same flair as the bow he'd offered her. "Lady Widmore, your servant. I believe you know that I made your lovely daughter's acquaintance last night at the Mayweather ball. She utterly charmed me, and I could not survive a day without paying my respects."

Imogene's mother glanced her way, smile regal, but Imogene saw the slight narrowing of her eyes. Oh, but her mother meant to have words with her when he left. "Yes, Imogene is much sought after this Season. The knocker is rarely silent. But then I am her mother. I must take pleasure in her popularity."

"Pride can easily be forgiven," he replied, taking his seat as she sat beside Imogene on the settee, "when it is so amply justified."

At his look, Imogene felt her cheeks coloring. "Mr. Everard was asking after Father, Mother. I don't believe we expect him home until later."

"Much later," her mother confirmed, posture straight. "If you meant to speak with him, I fear you have made the trip for nothing, sir."

Vaughn smiled at Imogene. "A trip is never wasted when a gentleman finds himself surrounded by beauty."

Imogene felt her mother's gaze on her. "And poor Imogene often finds herself surrounded by callers. I fear she has little time to herself."

It was a pointed hint. A gentleman would beg her pardon, excuse himself immediately. Vaughn merely crossed his long legs at the ankles.

"But dear lady, how could you be so cruel as to deprive us of our source of inspiration, of light? Even the farmer welcomes the bees hovering about his flowers."

If anything, her mother's back was even stiffer. This was getting ridiculous, and it was getting Imogene no closer to her goal of discovering the source of her father's antipathy for the fellow. She racked her brain for a way to converse privately with him.

"Do you enjoy music, Mr. Everard?" she tried.

She was certain of his answer. What poet wouldn't enjoy the strains of a well-played song?

"I take pleasure in the sound of a pianoforte or a violin played with precision," he allowed. There was the slightest crease between his brows, as if he wasn't sure of her direction. She had to make this work. She very much doubted she'd get another chance to see him again otherwise.

Lord, help him to follow my lead!

"Then you must come hear my latest composition," Imogene told him. She stood, forcing him to his feet while her mother went so far as to frown at her. "I'm not quite certain I'm happy with it, and I'd very much like your thoughts."

"Delighted," he replied.

"If you'll just excuse us a moment, Mother," Imogene said, heading for the door.

She heard the whisper of silk as her mother rose. "No need, my dear. I find myself quite curious about this new song, as well."

Imogene puffed out a sigh, but she kept going.

Vaughn caught up with her easily, pacing her down the corridor and stairway for the music room. With her mother right behind, there was no time for any but the most commonplace of topics, and she thought by the stiffness of his responses that he was as frustrated by the whole affair as she was.

The music room was just off the main entry, a small, north-facing room with misty gray walls and fanciful white curls festooning the coffered ceiling. She went straight to her piano and seated herself on the bench. "Would you be so kind as to turn the pages for me, Mr. Everard?"

He stood behind her. If she had leaned back, she would have rested against him. She kept her spine straight, her gaze on the sheet music in front of her.

"It starts slowly, like this." She began playing the piece. She already knew it by heart, she'd written it after all, so she didn't have to keep her eyes on the music. Still, she looked up only long enough to be certain her mother had taken a seat on one of the gilded chairs near the fire.

"You see how it drifts along here?" She nodded toward the music.

Vaughn bent closer, putting his face on a level with hers. She could feel the heat of him so close, his breath as it brushed against her curls. "Encouraging and lilting, much like the beginnings of a courtship," he said.

Oh, but her cheeks would give everything away if he continued to speak to her like that. "My father seems quite vexed with you," Imogene whispered, trying to focus on her goal while her fingers kept moving. "Do you know why that might be?"

"I have never knowingly done anything to offend him," he murmured back. His long-fingered hand reached past her, almost as if he meant to embrace her, then she realized he was following the notes more closely than she was and was preparing to turn the page for her. "Why would he take me in dislike?"

She wished she knew. Vaughn Everard seemed the perfect fellow: clever, talented, handsome, charming. How could anyone take him in dislike? Certainly dislike was the furthest thing from her mind. "There's some problem."

"Can you arrange a meeting?"

This section of the music was *allegro,* and she launched herself into the complicated runs. "He's so busy. I can't be sure of catching him."

His whisper caressed her cheek. "But won't you try, for me?"

Her mother rose from her seat, wandered closer, eyes narrowing. Vaughn straightened.

"And now the crescendo," Imogene proclaimed, throwing herself into the music. Her mind moved faster than her fingers. Vaughn Everard seemed so right, the very man she'd been searching for since she'd made her debut last Season. Only the perfect husband would do for the Marquess of Widmore's daughter. She had a family name to uphold, after all. But was she mistaken in Mr. Everard's character?

If her father knew Vaughn Everard was a scoundrel, as his refusal to see the poet implied, Imogene would be wrong to help him, to welcome him any further into their lives.

Lord, help me know the truth! Show me Your will in this!

She finished the piece with a flourish, and Vaughn Everard joined her mother in applause. But his head was cocked, his dark gaze on her as if he hadn't truly seen her before. It made her want to preen and disappear at the same time.

"So, what do you think, Mr. Everard?" she challenged.

He bowed, as if she'd done something magnificent like beat Napoleon single-handedly. "I found the piece intriguing and its execution intoxicating. You are a gifted musician, Lady Imogene."

She was coloring again. This time, her mother's smile was genuine. "Yes, she is. Not many recognize that, Mr. Everard."

"I suspect it's because Mr. Everard has talents of his own that he's quick to recognize them in others," Imogene said.

His mouth quirked, but he did not manage a smile. "My talents pale before the work of a true artist. To show my gratitude for your gift, may I take you driving tomorrow?"

Imogene couldn't help glancing at her mother. She knew how she wanted to answer. She'd have sacrificed her music for a month for a bit more time to study the poet. But she was fairly certain her mother was going to find an excuse to refuse.

"Well, Imogene," her mother said, "don't keep Mr. Everard waiting. I believe your afternoon is free tomorrow."

Imogene knew her mouth was hanging open and

hastily shut it. With a grin, she turned to Vaughn. "I'd be delighted to join you, Mr. Everard. Say three?"

"I shall count the moments until then," he said. He took her hand and bowed over it, then did the same for her mother before striding from the room. Her mother's sigh at his retreating back matched Imogene's.

Imogene blinked. "Do you approve of him, Mother? I thought you disliked the Everards."

Her mother patted her shoulder. "I find them presumptuous in the extreme. But I have not known you to be so willing to share your compositions, and I've never seen a gentleman caller more attuned to you, more appreciative of your abilities. For that, Mr. Everard deserves at least one other opportunity to impress me."

Chapter Four

Imogene barely had time to congratulate herself on gaining another opportunity to become better acquainted with Vaughn Everard before she and her mother were besieged by callers. Elisa and Mrs. Mayweather stopped by to compare impressions from the ball the previous night; Kitty and the elderly cousin who was sponsoring her arrived to chat. Various gentlemen Imogene had met this Season and last paid their respects and angled to take her driving or walking. She put them off with encouraging excuses. At the moment, she had enough on her hands trying to determine why Mr. Everard and her father were on the outs.

Her mother had already retired to her room to change for dinner, and Imogene had just opened her book in the withdrawing room when Jenkins brought her one last caller. She managed a smile as Lord Gregory Wentworth bowed over her hand.

"Lady Imogene, radiant."

She wasn't entirely sure he meant the compliment for her or whether it was a compliment at all. She rather thought any radiance had seeped away over the long afternoon. But he flipped up his navy coattails, took the chair nearest her and leaned back as if well satisfied with his ability to flatter.

Because of his good looks and future earldom, any number of young ladies had set their caps at him, but Imogene had never been sure why. Lord Wentworth, she feared, was rather lacking when it came to charm and intelligence—fatal flaws in a suitor. Unfortunately, her opinion had not prevented him from calling with determined frequency.

"And how did I earn the honor of your presence today, my lord?" she asked now.

"Hoping for a word with your father," he drawled, "but of course couldn't leave without greeting you."

"How kind." She ought to find something useful to say, but she truly didn't want to encourage him.

He tipped up his chin. "Have mutual friends, you know. Everard. Good chap."

Imogene tried not to frown, but she found it hard to imagine the two men having anything in common. "Oh?" she said. "How are you acquainted?"

He preened as if he knew the heights to which he'd risen. "Known his family for years. Uncle had the estate near ours in Cumberland."

So there was actually a connection between them? Why, she could use that to her advantage. *Thank You, Lord, for providing this opportunity!*

"How fortunate," she said, smiling at him with considerably more warmth. "And what do you think of Mr. Everard?"

He shrugged. "Bit wild, but loyal. Clever. Your father wouldn't think so highly of him if it weren't true."

Imogene cocked her head. "My father thinks highly of him?"

Lord Wentworth blinked, paling. "Doesn't he? Good

friends with the fellow's uncle, you know. Why dislike the nephew?"

Imogene leaned closer. "So my father favors him?"

"Are you saying he doesn't?"

They gazed at each other a moment, and Imogene was certain her face must mirror his for confusion.

Her mother joined them just then, and he climbed to his feet and bowed to her. Imogene spent the next few minutes in conversation about the weather and the latest offerings at the Theatre Royal and other such nonsense, all the while stifling an urge to reach across the space and throttle Lord Wentworth with his pretentiously tied cravat.

What did he mean making up stories about Vaughn Everard? They couldn't be friends; surely Mr. Everard would disdain the man's pomp, his belittling clipped sentences. In fact, it sounded as if Lord Wentworth knew less about the poet than Imogene did. Otherwise he'd know there was some difficulty between Mr. Everard and her father.

The topic must have remained on his mind as well, for he brought it up again when he took his leave a short time later.

"Hope I didn't give impression I follow Everard," he said with a bow over her hand. "Opinions would be swayed by your father's, whatever they are."

"So I've heard," Imogene said brightly. "A great many people are swayed by my father."

He looked at her askance, as if begging her to explain. It was a shame she couldn't put the fellow out of his misery and clarify her father's opinions on the matter, but the marquess's attitude toward Vaughn Everard was growing more mysterious by the moment.

* * *

"You seemed a bit cool to our guest," her mother said after the footman had seen him out and she and Imogene had repaired to the dining room. Her smile was gentle as she sat across from her daughter, the seat at the head of the table conspicuously empty. "Has he done something to offend you, dearest?"

Imogene could think of any number of annoyances but none that rose to the level of offense. She pushed her peas about on her gold-rimmed china plate. "No, Mother. I just find him a bit tiresome."

"Unlike your Mr. Everard."

Imogene fought a smile. "Very unlike him."

"And why do you think you find him so interesting?" her mother persisted, reaching for her crystal goblet.

A reason suggested itself, but she shoved it away. It was far too soon to claim her heart was engaged, and she still had doubts that Mr. Everard would meet her criteria for a husband.

"Outside this business with Father, I'm not sure I know," she replied, abandoning her peas and gazing at her mother. "When I brought up the matter of his interest in Father last night, he asked me about the third of March. Do you remember anything significant about that date?"

A slight frown marred her mother's face in the light of the silver candelabra on the table. "March third? I believe that's the night we arrived in London. What is the importance to Mr. Everard?"

Imogene motioned to Jenkins to come take her plate. "It appears to be the day his uncle died," she said, thinking about their aborted conversation at the dance. He'd asked her where her father had been. Then she hadn't been sure. But if March third was the night they arrived in London, she knew what her father had been doing, and his actions only deepened the mystery.

Her mother offered her a sad smile, nodding to the footman to remove her plate, as well. "Ah, significant indeed. I understand Mr. Everard and his uncle were close."

"Very," Imogene assured her. "He seems genuinely hurt by Lord Everard's passing. I suspect Mr. Everard has great sensitivity."

Her mother's lips quirked as the footmen began bringing in the second course. "So it would seem. But the other gentlemen this Season are not so very lacking. I'm sure a number of young ladies find Lord Wentworth, for instance, quite presentable."

"And I rather suspect he agrees." She sat straighter, coloring. "Oh, Mother, forgive me! That sounded waspish. I don't know what's gotten into me today."

Her mother's look was assessing. "I fear it isn't just today. I want the best for you, Imogene, but do you think perhaps you have set your sights too high?"

Imogene raised her chin. "I am the Marquess of Widmore's daughter. I thought I was *supposed* to set my sights high!"

Her mother patted the damask cloth beside her as if she longed to pat Imogene's hand. "I did not mean to suggest you marry the ragman, dearest. However, you seem to have high expectations of your suitors, so high that I fear no man, not even Mr. Everard, can live up to them."

Imogene shook her head. "I would think that intelligence and charm are not too much to ask."

Her mother smiled. "I would agree. Lord Eustace has those, yet you refused him out of hand last Season."

Imogene remembered the enthusiastic man who had

offered his heartfelt proposal on bended knee. "Lord Eustace is no more than a friend, Mother, and unfortunately addicted to whist."

"David Willoughby, then," her mother insisted, lifting a spoonful of the strawberry ice they had been served. "Handsome, charming, the heir to a barony. He looked crushed when you refused him."

"He hasn't darkened the door of a church since he reached his majority," Imogene informed her, digging into her own ice. "I won't have a man so lacking in devotion."

"And Sir George Lawrence? He certainly attends services and supports any number of charitable causes."

Imogene shuddered, swallowing the cool treat. "He also picks his teeth. With his nails. After he's eaten enough for a regiment. He'll die of gout before he's thirty. I have no wish to be a widow."

Her mother sighed. "You see? No one is perfect."

Vaughn Everard's face came to mind, brightened by that genuine smile she'd seen at the ball last night. His poetry proclaimed him a man of intelligence and creativity. His actions spoke of a devotion to family, of determined perseverance. But she thought she was only seeing the edges of his character.

She dropped her gaze to her lap and was surprised to find the fingers of her free hand pleating the silk of her skirt. "I know no one's perfect, Mother. But none of those gentlemen you mentioned stirred my heart. Surely I am allowed to feel something tender for the man I'll marry."

"I would like that for you, dearest," her mother murmured, "but not every bride can claim a love match, despite what the novels tell you. There are many other good reasons to wed—security, position, children."

Saving her family from penury. Oh, but she mustn't say that aloud. She wasn't sure she could pull it off, and telling her mother she had a plan to prevent them from losing the marquessate and all its attendant income would only get her hopes up.

"I understand, Mother," she said. "Please know that I will do my duty. The man I accept will be a credit to the name of Devary and the House of Widmore, I promise. I will settle for nothing less."

Vaughn's afternoon was far quieter, a fact designed to cause him no end of difficulties. There was nothing he liked less than indolence. He needed action, challenges, something to keep his mind and hands busy. When Uncle had been alive, they'd never lacked for diversions—wagering on impossible odds, cheering horse races and pugilistic displays and closing the gaming tables in the wee hours of the morning. He wasn't sure when those things had begun to pale—it had begun some time before his uncle's death, he believed—but he found he had little interest in them now.

So he sat in his room in Everard House and stared at the empty parchment in front of him. The windows were shuttered, the fire banked low. He'd had the new valet he shared with his cousin Richard remove the clock so its steady ticking would be no distraction. Everything was conducive to starting his next poem, but he found the words had dried up. It was as if everything meaningful to him had turned to dust the day Uncle had died.

He leaned back in the chair at his writing table, fixed his gaze on the pattern of the wallpaper and traced each leafy green frond back to the center. Why couldn't he order his thoughts? Other men seemed to concentrate so easily, to shift their attentions when they wished. He found himself concentrating to the point of shutting out everything else or being unable to make his mind settle on a single topic. Even now, it flitted from problem to problem, never solving anything, merely teasing him with possibilities before moving on.

For a time after Uncle had died, only vengeance had sustained him. His cousins had been concerned for his state of mind. He'd seen the looks flashing between Jerome and Richard when they talked about what had happened the night Uncle's body had been returned home. If he dwelled on that day now, he'd likely go mad.

He pushed back his chair and went in search of game.

Everard House ought to be crowded with him, his cousins Richard and Samantha and Lady Claire Winthrop in residence, to say nothing of his cousin Jerome and his new wife, who were expected any moment. Yet sometimes days went by without more than a chance meeting in the corridor. The others were all intent on making Samantha the toast of London, and that meant taking the girl out where she could be seen.

Today, for example, Samantha and Lady Claire, as they had all begun to call his cousin's sponsor, were just returning from some event when he reached the stairs and gazed down into the entryway. The marble-tiled space looked remarkably empty since they had removed the massive statue of a naked Eve holding out a golden apple, one of Uncle's mad whims. Samantha seemed entirely too small, her dainty features as animated as the hands she waved in front of her sky-blue spencer.

"But he asked to call," she was saying breathlessly. "I thought surely you'd advise me to encourage him."

"Anyone else, certainly," Lady Claire replied, handing her feathered bonnet to the footman. Vaughn had been unsure of Richard's betrothed at first. The color of her thick, wavy hair might be as warm as honey, but her blue gaze could be as cold as ice. And it didn't help that she had thrown over Richard for a wealthy viscount years ago. He had come to realize, however, that a loving heart beat beneath those fashionable silk gowns, and her devotion to Samantha was unquestionable.

His cousin puffed out a sigh as she allowed the footman to take her bonnet. "I'm only trying to fulfill Papa's will!"

"And with considerable style," Vaughn called down.

Her face brightened as she looked up at him. "Cousin Vaughn! You're home!"

"An astute observation, infant," he replied with a smile as he descended the stairs. "And as you appear to be home as well, what say we find ourselves some mischief?"

She grinned as he reached her side. "What shall it be? Boxing? Fencing?"

Lady Claire raised a brow. "Entirely without imagination. Pugilism would ruin your gown, and you've already beaten him twice with the blade."

Three times, but he was not about to admit to their bout the other morning in the stables. "I allow her to win. It inspires confidence."

"Ha!" Samantha made a face at him. "Damages your consequence, you mean."

"Regardless," Lady Claire said with a twinkle in her eyes, "as we need time to prepare for a ball this evening, perhaps a short game of skittles in the library."

Vaughn nearly made a face at that. Was this what he had fallen to for entertainment—swinging a little ball on a chain so it collided with a set of pins? Where was the adventure, the excitement?

"Lovely!" Samantha exclaimed with a clap of her

hands, and he felt compelled to bow her and Lady Claire ahead of him to the library. He'd promised to support the girl in any way possible, after all. She was doing them a favor.

Uncle had written his will oddly. The law required the only legal child of his blood, Samantha, to inherit the title and the bulk of the Everard legacy—lands in six counties, shares in more than a dozen ships and money in the Exchange. But Uncle had left a sizable bequest to each of his nephews provided they help Samantha achieve three tasks. The first, being presented to the queen, had been accomplished two weeks ago, thanks to the help of Lady Claire.

The other two were more difficult. Uncle's reputation for wildness had caused any number of families to close their homes to anyone named Everard. The will required Samantha to be welcomed in those homes. Vaughn knew he wouldn't be much help there. Between his loyalty to his uncle and the duels he'd fought the past two years, he'd managed to lock those doors and set up an oak barricade across them. Only Samantha's bubbly personality, beauty and barony would open them.

The final task he disliked the most of all. Samantha was to garner no less than three offers of marriage from eligible gentlemen. She'd already received one from an old family friend, a boy she'd known for ages. She'd refused, and the lad had been recalled home before he could press her further.

Of course, Vaughn had also offered, more in jest than anything else, though her sponsor seemed determined to count it. Samantha had known better than to accept. Though she seemed equally fond of him, she saw the similarities between him and her father and feared them. He'd always said she was a clever minx.

The next half hour proved just how clever. She won the first game handily, and he was hard-pressed to win the second. All the while she cast him glances under her golden lashes, smile playing about her rosy lips as if she knew what he was thinking. Unfortunately, he was certain his sweet little cousin might run crying from the room if she knew the darkness that sometimes threatened him.

As if he suspected Vaughn's mood, Richard, who had wandered in during the second game, stayed behind when Lady Claire took Samantha away to change for the ball.

"I understand you're pursuing Lady Imogene," he said, taking Samantha's spot across the table from Vaughn.

Vaughn continued to set the polished wood pins back in their positions on the board. "If you know only the single song, pray stop harping."

He thought his cousin might react to the goad. In fact, a small part of him wanted a reaction, perhaps even an argument. Anything was better than staring at that blank page upstairs where his muse lay stillborn. But Richard crossed his arms over his chest, straining the shoulders of his brown coat.

"You can't dwell on the past," he said. "It will eat away at you."

Vaughn knew Richard spoke from experience. He'd courted Lady Claire when they were both too young and he'd watched her wed another. Only when the now-widowed Claire had chosen to sponsor Samantha had the two worked through their differences.

"Easy for you to say," Vaughn returned, aligning a pin into the triangle. "Your past is now your future. For me, there will be no second chance. Uncle is dead."

"We'll see him again someday," Richard countered.

Something black boiled up inside him. "Men of faith go to heaven. By your theology, Uncle and I are headed somewhere else entirely."

Richard's long arm shot out, clasped his shoulder. "Only if you choose it. Uncle had a change of heart before he died. I see no reason not to hope for you."

Vaughn glanced up at him, feeling the concern coiling out from Richard's grip, seeing the worry in that tense face. With one finger, he hit the closest pin and watched as all the others tumbled, as well. "Only if your God has a sense of humor," he said, though he felt his gut twist at the joke. He very much feared that nothing he could do would earn him a place beside his cousins when this life ended.

Richard looked ready to argue, his bearded jaw set. Vaughn rose and turned his back, striding from the room before his cousin could call him back or call him to task. He needed light, he needed air. He needed something to focus his mind!

A picture kindly presented itself, sharp and clear, and he knew exactly how to fill that waiting page. He took the stairs two at a time, shoved through the door and threw himself into the chair. The words flew from the quill, powerful, purposeful. Only when he'd filled that page and three more like it did he stop to marvel at the flow.

That the poems came so easily should not have surprised him. All he'd needed was a little inspiration. And it seemed his mind had finally deigned to fix itself on a point on the horizon: a shining star named Imogene.

Chapter Five

Imogene was ready when Vaughn Everard called for her the next day. She was once again loitering near the landing, but she took her time descending the stair to his side. It would never do to let a gentleman think she was longing for his company or that she admired him in his high-crowned beaver, bottle-green coat and spotless boots. She tried not to blush as he took her hand and declared that the angels in heaven must be weeping for their inability to match her beauty.

But she couldn't help exclaiming over his carriage.

It was a newer class, a "chariot" she believed she'd heard, in a shade of lacquered blue that complimented her lighter blue spencer and the velvet ribbons that crossed her white bonnet. Every sleek line said speed and power. The perfectly matched snowy-white horses waiting at its head looked capable of flying, and even her under footman holding them seemed awed by his task. She glanced at the seats in the compartment behind the high driver's bench.

"I prefer to handle my own horses," Vaughn said as if he'd seen her look. "I was hoping you'd join me up front."

Imogene grinned at him. "I was hoping you'd ask."

That smile appeared, so fleeting and yet so warming. She wondered what she'd have to do to make it remain.

He handed her up into the seat, a padded-leather perch surrounded by a brass rail, then went around to take his place beside her. Up so high, she could see down the street, across the park in the center of the square and through the trees to the more trafficked street beyond. As she glanced around, however, she noticed that the space for the footman or tiger at the back was empty, and her under footman showed no sign of climbing aboard as he released the bridles at Mr. Everard's nod.

Of course, sitting up on the driver's bench, everyone could see her as well, so her reputation would not suffer—at least no more than would be expected sitting next to this man.

He clucked to the horses and set them off at a good clip, the rushing air tugging at her bonnet. His hands held the great beasts lightly, and he easily threaded the horses through the traffic on Park Lane. A little thrill ran through her. She was driving with the famous Vaughn Everard! Would he speak of love, of great historical events, of the French massing on the farther shore of the Channel, ready to devour England?

"Fine day for a drive," he ventured, gazing out over his horses.

She stared at him. Oh, she must have misunderstood. He was merely warming up, like a musician tuning his instrument before a concert. "Exceptionally fine," she agreed, waiting for the opening bars of his solo.

"And your mother is well?"

No, no, no! That wasn't how the ride was supposed

to go. He couldn't be as endlessly polite as her other suitors. She'd go mad. "Exceedingly," she clipped.

"How are you enjoying your Season?"

Imogene turned to him. "Well, it was all going tremendously well until you turned into a dead bore."

He blinked at her, then grinned, and her heart danced. "Forgive me. I should have known better than to try to impersonate a gentleman. I promise to improve once we reach the park. Which would you prefer, the carriage path along Park Lane or the one down to the Serpentine?"

The Park Lane route was the more popular, she knew. She'd been driven there by more than one suitor. The path down to the Serpentine, however, was less frequented. Gentlemen were rumored to hold trysts among the trees. She'd never driven that route.

"The Serpentine path," she said, settling back in her seat. "And I'll be much more in charity with you if you give me a chance at the reins."

With a laugh, he turned the horses, and they entered Hyde Park.

The carriage path wound across the northernmost lawn and into the trees surrounding the wooden walls of the upper powder magazine. Imogene had always found it odd that the army would think Hyde Park a good place to mix and store gunpowder, but she supposed having the magazine out among the trees protected the populace and the crowded buildings of London from accidents.

Today the way toward it lay empty, but she could see crowds beginning to gather as the fashionable made their afternoon descent on the park. Couples strolled along the footpath to Kensington, carriages paused along Park Lane and gentlemen on horseback headed for Rotten Row to the south. Closer to hand, however, it was only her and Mr. Everard. As if he realized it, he slowed the horses. "Perhaps it's time we spoke of more important matters."

The light of the lovely spring day seemed to dim. This was not a pleasure drive, after all. He wanted information from her, and she must make her report. "You asked after my father," she said. "Particularly what he was doing on March third."

"Have you remembered something more about that day, then?"

She could hear the hope in his voice and chanced a glance at his face. His gaze was fixed on his horses, but she didn't think he even noticed the actions of the snowy pair.

"A little," she admitted. "I talked with Mother about the day. She reminded me that on March third we'd only just arrived in London. I know we spent the evening settling in and seeing everything unpacked."

"Then your father was at home."

She thought he sounded relieved. "For the evening, yes. I understood we were to make an early night of it, but as I was preparing to retire, I heard a noise from the gardens and looked out the window. Father was leaving on his horse. I assumed it was a summons from the War Office, and he simply didn't want to overtire our coachman, who had just driven us to London."

"Possibly," he said, but his look had darkened.

The air felt cooler. She rubbed the arm of her spencer. "You think he went somewhere else, don't you?"

He clucked to the horses as they took the turn through the tall trees past the magazine, the sunlight through the leaves striping his face with light and shadow. "My uncle fought a duel the night of the third. He lost, and we lost him forever."

So that was how Lord Everard had died. "And you think Father was a witness."

"I think he was there, yes. I'd like to hear his account of the event."

Imogene put her hand on his arm and felt the tension in it, beyond what it should have taken to guide the team. She had friends who had lost loved ones—a mother to childbirth, a brother in the war. She knew each had a way of grieving all their own. Some cried, some were blue for weeks and others attacked life as if hoping to wrest every ounce of joy from the moment, never sure whether it was their last. She rather thought Mr. Everard fit the last category.

"It's hard when someone you love dies," she murmured. "When my brother Viscount Charles passed on I felt so confused. He was just a boy—he hadn't even started to live! I didn't understand how God could take him, particularly after He'd taken all the others, too."

"Others?" He glanced her way, seeking clarification.

Imogene withdrew her hand and dropped her gaze as she smoothed down her muslin skirts. "I would have had three older sisters had they lived beyond their birth."

"I'm so sorry."

Other people had said those words, to her father, to her mother, to her. Never had she heard such emotion behind them, as if he understood the pain of loss better than most, as if he understood how that loss had hurt her.

"So am I," Imogene assured him, raising her gaze. "And I regret that your uncle left you, too."

He managed a parody of a smile. "These thoughts are entirely too melancholy for such a lovely day. May

I only say that I have no doubt where you will spend eternity, Lady Imogene. Surely so pure a spirit must rejoice with the angels."

It was a pretty compliment, one she might expect from a poet, but the sentiment did not ring true. As if he meant to distract her, he held out the reins. "Now, perhaps you'd care to demonstrate how well a pure spirit can drive."

She knew she must be a sad trial to her mother because the gambit worked. Imogene stared at him, hopes rocketing skyward. "Truly?"

His eyes widened. "Tell me this won't be the first time."

She laughed at the trace of panic in his voice. "Not at all, sir! I've driven our gig to church at our country estate, and Father even bought me my own pony cart."

The reins inched closer to his chest. "A chariot is a much larger vehicle."

"Obviously," she replied with a grin. "But with you here to advise me what could go wrong?"

One corner of his mouth lifted at that, and he offered her the strips of leather.

Imogene slipped her gloved hands over his, relishing the strength, the confidence with which he held the team. As he released the leather into her care, she felt the tug of the horses, the weight of responsibility for their guidance. A tremor started in her arm, and she forced herself to stiffen. She could do this. She was the Marquess of Widmore's daughter.

Vaughn must have remained a little nervous for his horses, for he edged closer to her on the seat until his leg pressed against her skirts and she could feel the warmth of his body. Suddenly it was much more difficult to concentrate.

She took a deep breath. The scent of something clean and crisp drifted over her. Funny, she would have thought he'd wear some exotic cologne, but he smelled more of spring and sunlight. She wanted to close her eyes and breathe him in.

This would never do! She mustn't be caught wool-gathering while driving! She had a duty—to the horses, to him, to the other people in the park.

The horses trotted on, completely comfortable with their surroundings and seemingly oblivious to the change in leadership. She was tempted to whip them up, send them pounding down the path, but that was never wise in Hyde Park. They might meet another carriage around the next turn or come across a pedestrian. She had to be careful.

"What a splendid pair," she told him instead. "And how well matched. Their gaits are as one."

She didn't dare glance Vaughn's way, determined to drive well, but she could hear the smile in his voice. "Our Master of Horse will be pleased to hear that you approve. They were each rejected at Tattersall's for being too unruly to pull a carriage or serve as a gentleman's mount. I thought differently, and he proved my point."

"They're darlings," Imogene assured him. "Anyone who thought otherwise clearly lacked vision. What are their names?" She nearly closed her eyes again, this time in mortification. Did gentlemen name their carriage horses? She'd never been introduced to a team.

But he didn't seem to find fault with her question. "Aeos on the left and Aethon on the right."

"From the legend of Apollo's chariot pulling the sun," Imogene realized. And how like a poet to choose such names.

"You know your Greek mythology."

Imogene smiled. "Father insisted on it. He said there was no reason I couldn't be as well educated as any gentleman."

"And better than most," he agreed. "The Ring is coming up on your left. We'll need to swing around it. Give Aethon his head."

She could see the group of trees coming up and the fence that circled the remains of the old riding circle. She eased up the pressure on the left set of reins, but Aethon kept pace with his teammate. She frowned.

"May I?" Vaughn asked.

She thought he meant to take back the reins, and her spirits sank. But he leaned closer and cupped her wrists, gloved fingers glazing the bare skin between her sleeves and her gloves. A tremor shook her again, but it had nothing to do with concerns about her driving skills.

"Like this," he said, voice purring beside her bonnet. She felt the strength as he drew back her hands. Together they guided the pair, through pressure and tension, around the trees and out onto the shaded path. The air felt cool as he pulled away, and Imogene drew in a breath, surprised to find she had been holding hers.

"Nicely done, Lady Imogene," he said. "The next thing you know, you'll be driving the mail."

She highly doubted that, though a part of her preened. She'd heard that some gentlemen dressed like coachmen and even bribed the mail coach drivers to let them take a hand at the great coaches. "Have you driven a mail coach?" she asked.

His gaze was once more out over the horses. "When I wish to drive hard, I don't need to borrow a coach. And I don't need the approval of others to assure myself of my skills."

That must be nice. She'd put in a great deal of effort over the years to win her father's approval. Now it seemed as if he'd forgotten her entirely. "But you must belong to a club," she said. "What about White's? Surely you're a member there."

He stretched one leg with a grin. "They dislike fellows who rarely lose."

"One of the other gentlemen's clubs, then."

"Same faces, same rules. As you said, a dead bore."

Imogene glanced his way. His polished boot was high on the footrest, his gaze out across the trees and pathways, a smile playing about his lips.

"Do you belong nowhere, sir?" she teased.

The smile disappeared. "To nothing and no one, Lady Imogene. Count on it."

He was trying entirely too hard. Had she goaded him into it by calling his earlier conversation boring? Surely he cared about something; his poems were evidence of that. He saw things—in nature, in people—that others missed. He must belong to someone.

Perhaps he could belong to her?

The thought came unbidden, but she couldn't dismiss it. She imagined a great many ladies had thrown their lures at him, yet apparently he was immune. It seemed he had a devotion to his cousin, Lady Everard, if the rumors were true, but he was here with Imogene now. Was she the woman to make Vaughn Everard settle down at last? He was clearly arrogant enough to think it impossible. She was just arrogant enough to try!

They were nearing the stone cottage of the Keeper's Lodge, hidden away behind a picket fence and high hedges. Soon they'd be surrounded by other carriages and more people. She puffed out a sigh. She didn't want the rest of the world. She knew she'd have to give him up soon enough, but right now she wanted to spend more time with him, unwrapping each layer like a birthday present swathed in tissue. She was certain that what lay beneath was nothing short of perfection.

But as they rounded the curve, she could see other carriages approaching, and she wasn't quite ready to maneuver Aeos and Aethon among more horses.

"I think perhaps you should drive now," she said, reluctantly offering him the reins.

"If you insist," he said, his smile returning and warming her.

She thought he would whip them up, set the horses at a good clip again, but he kept the team at a walk, as if just as loath to rejoin society. Perhaps that was why it was so easy to spot the other couple as Imogene and Vaughn crossed a little-used path meandering over the lawns.

The man was tall and lean, his hair, now white with advancing age, peeking out of his high-crowned beaver. Imogene recognized the tailored navy coat, the tasteful gold buttons. She wasn't close enough to see, but she knew that each one was stamped with a D for Devary. The woman beside him was buxom, and her crimson gown was cut to emphasize the fact, displaying a large beauty mark below her neck. Her bonnet, however, was veiled, the black lace tucked under her chin, and Imogene couldn't make out her features. As she watched, her father took the woman's gloved hand and pressed a note into it.

Imogene must have made some noise because Vaughn slowed the horses to a stop at the edge of the path.

"That was your father," he said, and she thought she heard accusation in his voice.

"Yes, it was," she replied. "He was supposed to be in Whitehall this afternoon, but I must have misunderstood." *A very great deal,* she added silently, unwilling to believe the evidence of her eyes.

"I can see the matter concerns you. Allow me to reunite you with your father so you can discuss it with him."

"No, please, that isn't necessary," Imogene said, but he flicked the reins and began to turn the team on the path. She could feel her face heating. What could she say to her father? And how would he feel to find her driving in a secluded part of the park with the man he refused to acknowledge?

"I'm afraid," Vaughn said, eyes once more that merciless black, "that I must insist. We've both been denied a conversation with your father, and I plan to rectify that."

For some reason, the usually responsive chariot felt harder to turn, but Vaughn knew it wasn't the horses. Lady Imogene sat beside him, fingers tugging at the ribbons of her bonnet, body hunched forward as if to protect herself from attack. She didn't want to confront her father, fearing they'd stumbled upon some indiscretion. And Vaughn could not tell her that he suspected far more than an illicit liaison was involved.

He hated hurting her, hated that he'd pulled her into this mess. But if he could get answers from the Marquess of Widmore now, Imogene would be free. She wouldn't have to sully her reputation by spending more time with him; she could return to her Season and find the right gentleman to marry. If some part of him protested that he might be that gentleman, he wrapped it in chains and sank it deep. His duty lay in uncovering the reason behind his uncle's untimely death. Besides, he could never be a suitable match for a woman like her. She deserved better. He righted the chariot and set the horses back toward the other path.

By the time they reached the spot where her father had been waiting, his partner had gone and his lordship was a distant figure on the way to Kensington Palace. Vaughn slapped the reins, and Aeos and Aethon sped in pursuit. Lady Imogene clamped one hand to her bonnet as if fearing the rushing wind would whip it off, but she said nothing more to dissuade him from his purpose.

Indeed, her silence goaded him. What—had he developed a conscience? It shook a fragile finger at him now, warning that nothing good could come from his actions. He had to let go of the past and move into the future.

How could he? Uncle had been the only one who had ever truly cared about him, who had seen that darkness inside him and still wished his friendship. Vaughn didn't understand why his uncle hadn't come to him with his troubles, why he'd gone to the duel alone. To walk away from the murder, to pretend all was well, went against everything Vaughn believed in. And there was still the concern that England itself might be in danger from the marquess. Three weeks ago, a man connected to the marquess had warned Richard that Widmore meant to topple the crown. Vaughn wasn't sure what to believe, but he had to learn the truth.

The marquess must have heard them coming, for he stepped to one side of the path and glanced back. At the sight of the carriage bearing down on him his head came up, and he turned from the path and set off across the grass, long legs eating up the yards.

Oh, no, it would not be so easy to escape this time.

How could Vaughn not suspect him when the man went to such lengths to avoid him?

"My lord!" Vaughn called, urging the horses forward and narrowing the gap.

The marquess didn't pause.

Lady Imogene glanced at Vaughn. Her pretty face was puckered, her brows down in a frown as if she couldn't understand why he was so intent on pursuit. Something of his despair must have shown on his face, for she turned front once more, cupped her hands around her mouth and cried, "Father, wait!"

The marquess halted and turned, and Vaughn thought he sagged in resignation. But as the carriage drew to a stop beside him, the man's frame was as upright as ever and a pleasant smile lit his lean face.

"Imogene and Mr. Everard. What a delightful surprise to see you out on such a lovely day."

Vaughn was very nearly struck dumb. How could the man stand there and speak of commonplaces? He had to know Vaughn had been hounding him from pillar to post. Vaughn glanced closer.

The Marquess of Widmore had always been a striking man, with a slender body, elegant features and assessing gray eyes. Though his lips were thin, they were often curved in a smile, lighting his face. Now his tailored coat seemed too large for his frame, as if his energy had worn him thin, and Vaughn detected a tremor in one hand as the marquess stood gazing up at them.

"Father," Imogene greeted him, fingers worrying in her lap. "I'm surprised to see you here, as well. Mother and I were under the impression that you were in Whitehall."

Something flickered behind those gray eyes, but his smile remained. "And so I was, but matters grew too heated. I felt the need for some fresh air and privacy to clear my head."

Another gentleman would have begged his pardon for intruding and whisked Imogene away. Vaughn had too many questions to accept dismissal.

"I'll only take a moment of your time, then," he promised. "Perhaps you'd care to drive with us. We could return you to the War Office when we're done."

The marquess took a step back from the carriage, as if even now determining how he might escape. "I fear I have an appointment in Kensington. Another time, perhaps."

Vaughn was more concerned another time would never come. He handed the reins to Imogene, who raised her brows.

"If you'd be so kind," Vaughn said.

She clutched the leather, wide-eyed, but nodded, and he jumped down to land beside her father.

"Forgive me for detaining you," he said to the marquess, positioning himself to keep the man between him and the horses. "But I need answers. As it seems you are the only one who can give them, we must talk. Now."

Chapter Six

Imogene watched a frown settle on her father's face. No one had ever talked to the Marquess of Widmore that way, she was sure. Certainly she'd never have attempted it. Yet Vaughn Everard stood with booted feet firmly planted, one placed in front of the other as if he was ready to fence. His head was high, his shoulders in his bottle-green coat solid. And his tone demanded obedience.

From anyone less than her father. "Mr. Everard," he said, each word precise, "I had a great fondness for your uncle. Do not presume upon it."

Imogene swallowed at the rebuke. Vaughn pulled his hat from his head, and the sun gleamed on his platinum hair. But neither his manner nor his words said he was penitent.

"It is because of that fondness that I appeal to you," he replied. "I believe my uncle was murdered."

Imogene gasped, then covered her mouth with her hand, slapping herself in the face with the reins in the process. She flinched, and Aeos and Aethon shifted in the traces. As if to comfort her, her father took a step closer to the carriage, forcing Vaughn to turn to meet his gaze.

"I understood the authorities ruled it a duel," her father said, frown deepening.

Vaughn's hand sliced the air as if he threw off such a ridiculous notion. "A duel with no seconds? No opponent who will acknowledge his part?"

Her father shrugged. "As you said, your uncle died as a result. Perhaps his opponent feared reprisal. That would not be unheard of."

He implied that Vaughn would seek vengeance. From the tension in him, Imogene could almost believe it.

"If it was truly a duel that my uncle consented to fight," Vaughn said, "his opponent would have nothing to fear from me."

"I'm sure it would comfort him to know that," her father said. "But your reputation precedes you, Mr. Everard. What is the current count, six duels fought and won?"

Six duels? Her mother had mentioned he'd dueled, but did that mean he'd killed six men? No, it couldn't be! He must have pinked them, drawn first blood with only a scratch. That would satisfy honor on both sides.

"I fight only when necessary," Vaughn said, easing the tightness that had gathered in her chest at the thought of men dying.

"Perhaps," her father allowed. "In any event, I know nothing of use to you. Your uncle didn't confide in me." He took another step back, closer to the horses.

Vaughn paced him, quick as a dancer. "And what of Repton and Todd? Will you deny knowledge of their deaths, as well?"

More dead? The tightness returned, threatening to squeeze the breath from her lungs. She'd thought he only wanted assurance that his uncle had died well. What had she stumbled upon? She clutched the reins, and Aeos shook his head in protest, setting the tack to jingling.

"I have no idea what you're talking about," her father said. "And I am losing patience."

"As am I," Vaughn told him, closing the gap between them. Imogene thought her father would stand his ground, but he retreated until he was standing by Aethon's hind quarters.

Vaughn pursued him. "You make a good case for your ignorance of my uncle's affairs, but you cannot disclaim knowledge of Chevalier."

Chevalier? Monsieur Chevalier, her dance master? Imogene hadn't seen him that Season, but she'd assumed he was teaching other young ladies the latest steps. What could he have to do with all this?

"Henri Chevalier?" her father asked with as much surprise.

"The same," Vaughn spit out. "He attempted to murder my cousin to prevent her from coming to London. He claims you paid him to do it."

Imogene stiffened. What a preposterous story! "And you believed him?" she demanded of Vaughn.

Vaughn glanced up at her with a frown as if he'd forgotten she was there. Imogene met him look for look. He might be a poet, but he'd have to spin a better story than that if he was going to accuse her father of all people of murder.

"You see?" her father said, forcing all gazes back to him. "My daughter understands the folly of your questioning. Why would I pay a dance master I haven't seen for more than a year to murder your cousin, who I barely know?"

"You sent Chevalier to us," Vaughn replied, but Imogene thought his voice was calmer, as if her doubts had given him pause.

"At her sponsor's request. Lady Winthrop told me that she wished the dance master to attend Lady Everard but that he had a better paying position. Because of my friendship with her and your uncle, I intervened. If you have doubts as to Chevalier's motives, perhaps you should question Lady Winthrop's instead."

Imogene knew her frown must match Vaughn's. Lady Claire Winthrop was a good friend of her mother's, despite the fact that the lady was closer to Imogene's age. She was also betrothed to Vaughn's cousin Captain Richard Everard. What possible reason could she have to harm the very girl she was sponsoring or the family she hoped to marry into?

If her father wished to point out the flaws in Vaughn's argument, he seemed to be making headway, for the poet stepped back. "I cannot doubt Lady Winthrop's affection for my family," he said. "Nor do I understand why you would wish Lady Everard harm. I only know that all roads of inquiry have led to your door. Because I believe you held my uncle in esteem, I am giving you a chance to explain."

He made the request sound like a challenge. Would he throw down his glove? Demand her father choose a weapon to defend himself? Despite her best efforts, she must have tugged on the reins, for both horses shuffled their feet and the seat shifted beneath her as the carriage wobbled.

Neither man paid her any attention, their gazes locked, their faces set.

"Your devotion to your uncle's memory is commendable," her father said, "but I fear it's addled your wits."

His eyes narrowed, and Imogene had never heard his voice so hard as he said, "Arthur Everard is gone. His thoughtless actions brought his death upon his own head. I suggest you accept that fact."

"Never!" Vaughn's fists were clenched at his sides. "He didn't shoot that ball into his own chest. Someone killed him. I will not rest until I know the truth."

Imogene hurt for him. How he must have loved his uncle that the unexplained death brought such pain! She could understand his need to know why; she'd certainly asked God the same question when Charles had died. But blaming her father wasn't going to help matters.

Her father seemed to agree. "If you cannot envision a better way to spend your time, Mr. Everard," he said, "perhaps I should give you one."

He reached out and slapped Aethon on the rump.

It all happened so fast Imogene couldn't have acted to save herself. Even as she gasped, the white horse reared, cracking the traces, and one set of reins flew from her fingers. She clutched at the air, but the leather slapped the ground as the horse rushed forward, dragging Aeos with him.

The force of their run slammed Imogene back in the seat, and she grabbed at the brass railing of the driver's bench to keep from falling under the whirling iron-bound wheels. Each bump across the grass rattled her bones, her teeth. She clung to the single set of reins, wrapped them around her fist and tugged hard.

The horses ignored her.

Fear crawled up her back and settled in her heart. She could not imagine what her father had been thinking, but she knew she had only one hope of rescue as the horses headed for the trees.

Lord, help me!

* * *

Vaughn's hat fell from his fingers as Aethon reared and started to drag the carriage forward.

"Are you mad?" he demanded even as he raced after it. Over the rattle of tack and the crack of iron on rock he thought he heard the marquess laugh. Then there was no time to think, only to act.

Fortunately, that's what he did best. Before the carriage could pick up speed, he launched himself at the back. His fingers snagged on the brass of the tiger's perch, and he clung to it, feet dragging along the ground. Someone was going to owe him a new pair of boots after this! Fingers tightening, he hauled himself up onto the perch.

The carriage careened to one side and nearly bucked him off. Blood roaring louder than the wind, he pulled himself upright and hooked first one hand then the other onto the roof. The curved lacquered wood heaved like a ship in a storm. He could see Imogene's head, bobbing along with the carriage as if she were no more than a little girl's porcelain doll.

She was much more than that to him. He would not allow her to be harmed.

Fingers clamped to the brass on either side, he pulled himself up and crawled along the wood until he could swing himself beside Imogene.

Her bonnet was hanging down her back; her face was white. But she held on to Aeos' reins as if it meant her life. Perhaps it did. She didn't even glance at Vaughn as he slid in beside her.

"Easy," he said, leaning closer. "Let me help."

She jerked a nod as if speaking was too much. He wrapped his fingers around hers. Together they turned the left horse, forcing Aethon to match him. The pair veered in a circle, the momentum pressing Imogene against Vaughn. For a moment he fancied he could hear her heart drumming over the sound of the horses' hooves, over the pounding of his own heart. He put his arm around her to steady her and held her tightly.

The horses slowed, walked, then stood. The carriage rolled to a stop at nearly right angles to the team. Another few seconds, and the chariot would have tipped over. Vaughn released Imogene and watched as she took a shaky breath.

"Really, Mr. Everard," she said. "You go to great lengths to put your arm around me."

Vaughn chuckled at her wit, even after nearly losing her life. She met his gaze with a watery smile, then burst into tears.

He put both arms around her then, holding her close and murmuring comfort. He couldn't have said afterward what words he used, but they had seemed right at the time. All he felt was an overwhelming gratitude that she was safe.

After a time, she pulled away and wiped at her eyes with her fingers.

"I fear I am no proper gentleman," he said, hoping to coax a smile from her. "I have no handkerchief to offer you."

She sniffed. "Then I'm no lady, for I have no idea what happened to mine." She sighed. "Nor do I know why my father would do that. I expect he thought I could handle the horses, but surely he knew your carriage might be damaged or your team injured."

The marquess hadn't cared about the carriage or horses. Despite Imogene's protest, Vaughn thought he hadn't cared whether his daughter was hurt either, and the fact chilled him. The Marquess of Widmore had gambled Imogene's life on the possibility that Vaughn was honorable enough, and quick and clever enough, to catch her. It was a slimmer chance than he could have known.

"Thank you," she murmured in the silence. "You saved my life. That was an answer to a prayer and the most heroic thing I've ever seen."

She would have him a saint in a moment. "I had to save my horses," he said. "They've come to mean a great deal to me."

She beamed at him as if he'd said something remarkably clever. "Of course they have! I just thank God for giving you the presence of mind to act."

Yes, Lord. Thank You for saving her.

Where had that thought come from? He hadn't prayed since he was a child and his grandfather had sat beside him and ordered him to speak to the Lord. Grandfather seemed to think he had to guide Vaughn in everything, including prayer. He'd impatiently corrected the words Vaughn had said aloud over folded hands before retiring. Grandfather had had a firm conviction in how one approached the Almighty and who was allowed to do so, and Vaughn challenged both.

Beside him, Imogene bowed her head and closed her eyes a moment. Her peachy lips twitched as if moving to words from her heart. Her curls were wild about her face, her cheeks still bright from the excitement. Her innocent devotion held him pinned to the seat, unable to look away. It was almost as if he could see the love glowing about her, her faith in the One who could keep her safe, meet every need.

Even for a sinner like him?

No, that was too much to ask. He knew that, had been told that in word and deed too many times. Before she could open her eyes, he jumped down from the seat and went to check the horses. Stroking their glossy flanks, telling them how proud he was of them felt no more foolish than wishing to be someone he wasn't.

"Are they all right?" she called from the driver's seat.

Though they still trembled from their exertions and Aethon's eye showed white, Vaughn knew the horses had sustained no lasting harm. "They'll be fine," he replied. He walked the circumference of the carriage and squatted to inspect the axles. The chariot was also undamaged. Too bad he couldn't say the same for his state of mind.

He retrieved the other pair of reins, threaded them back to the bench, then climbed up beside her. She smiled at him. "Perhaps," she said, "you should take me home. You can handle the reins."

He ought to do just that—take her home and refuse to see her ever again. Just being with him endangered her life. That had never been his intent, but it had been the consequence nonetheless.

He reached out and touched a strand of chestnut hanging beside her face. "You might want to put your bonnet back on. I wouldn't want your mother's worst thoughts of me confirmed."

One hand flew to her curls, but her eyes widened. "Mother! Oh, what shall I tell her?"

He was fairly certain she was thinking beyond the incident and the current state of her coiffure. "Perhaps the less said the better," he replied, gathering up the reins with care.

She nodded. "You're right. In any event, I can't find an explanation for half of what happened this afternoon, even to my own satisfaction. Thank you again, Mr. Everard."

Vaughn grimaced. Growing up there had been a few too many Mr. Everards in the household, with his cousins Jerome and Richard also being raised by Uncle after their parents' deaths. "Perhaps," he said, "after what we've been through, you could call me Vaughn."

Her cheeks darkened even further. "I'd be honored, but only in private, Mr….Vaughn. I wouldn't want your family to think I had designs on you."

They were far more likely to think he had designs on her, but he decided not to say so.

"It's an unusual name, Vaughn," she continued, fingers curling her hair back away from her face. "I don't recall hearing it before."

"It was my mother's maiden name," he supplied, watching in fascination as the chestnut strands fought her efficiency. He'd had his gloves on when he'd touched them a moment ago. Were they as smooth as satin, as sleek as mink?

"When did you lose her?" she asked around the hairpin she'd stuck in her mouth.

"She isn't dead," he replied. When she frowned, he felt compelled to explain. "She was an actress at Covent Garden. My father married her without Grandfather's permission. Because they were both of age, there was nothing Grandfather could do about it except insist that she go live on the Continent. She left right after birthing me."

He was almost thankful that the bonnet was now back in place, for it obscured her face for a moment. "At least she made sure you were raised in a good family," she said with a certain primness.

He nearly choked on the emotions that leapt up inside him. "She waited because she knew Grandfather would offer her more money to leave me behind. And the only thing good about my family was going to live with my uncle and cousins."

The horses were fretting again, and he knew he had to master his emotions before he set the pair off once more. "If you're ready, I'll see you home."

Her hand darted out and stilled his.

"I'm very sorry, Mr. Everard." Her voice was more than contrite; it trembled with sorrow, as if she could imagine such an odd upbringing as his and truly hurt that he had been subjected to it. "I didn't mean to pry. I'm very glad you had your uncle's affections, and I'm very sorry my father wasn't able to answer your questions to your satisfaction."

"Thank you," he replied, fully aware of the inadequacy of those words. In fact, he'd never had such trouble formulating a reply. Her kindness continued to open old wounds, ones he had thought scarred over long ago. Yet each time she opened them, her very presence and understanding helped them heal.

He didn't want them healed. Not now. Now they fueled his desire to avenge his uncle. Without them, he'd be all too tempted to go on with life, and that would be a betrayal of his uncle's memory.

Besides, she couldn't know how thoroughly her father had answered his questions and confirmed his suspicions. The marquess acted like a desperate man. He might protest his innocence, but Vaughn could all but see the blood dripping from his aristocratic hands.

More was here than met the eye. Vaughn simply wasn't sure what to do about it or about the lovely Lady Imogene and the feelings she was raising in him.

Chapter Seven

Imogene's bonnet might be back in place, her curls safely tucked inside and her hands folded once more in the lap of her muslin gown, but her spirits refused to calm as Vaughn returned her home. She simply could not reconcile the father she knew with the man they'd met this afternoon.

It had been years since she'd shared the kind of closeness with her father that they had enjoyed before Charles's death, but she still felt secure as to his character. Her father had always embodied his beliefs: love of family, devotion to country, care for the less fortunate. So why had he met that veiled woman in an unfrequented part of the park, alone? What had he given her? Why would he break off his conversation with Vaughn Everard in such a dramatic fashion?

By the set of Vaughn's mouth, Imogene thought he considered her father's actions reckless, that the marquess had endangered Imogene's life. There had to be another explanation. Her father loved her. When she was younger he had always taken an interest in her activities, joining her in the schoolroom to quiz her about her studies, helping her perfect her French over dinner conversations, listening with a beatific smile, eyes closed, as she played her latest composition. Now his efforts for king and country consumed him. If she saw him, it was often in passing in the corridor. She couldn't think of a single meaningful conversation they'd had in the past two months.

She knew Napoleon was breathing down England's neck, and every man was expected to do his duty. She also knew her duty lay in upholding the family name, in marrying well, in conducting herself as a model of Christian womanhood.

Isn't that what You expect, too, Lord?

So how was she to respond to what she'd seen? Vaughn seemed to think her father knew more about Lord Everard's death than he was willing to confess, that her father had wanted to harm Lady Everard, as well. She meant to extend to her father the benefit of the doubt. She would continue to believe him innocent of any wrongdoing until she had proof otherwise.

As Vaughn turned the chariot off Park Lane, she realized he had been just as silent, having said nothing since stopping to retrieve his hat. Very likely he was allowing her time to settle her emotions, and she knew he must have much on his mind, as well.

"Forgive me," she said. "I haven't been very engaging company."

He offered her a smile. "On the contrary. I could never claim the afternoon was a dead bore."

Imogene smiled in spite of herself. "It certainly wasn't. But instead of answers we've only succeeded in raising more questions. For instance, who are Repton and Todd?"

"It appears to be of no consequence at the moment, as your father does not recall their circumstances."

Was he going to be tight-lipped now, as well? How was she to discover the truth? Was it Vaughn's veiled accusations that troubled her father, or was it something more? Imogene bit back a sigh. "And Monsieur Chevalier?"

"Is currently residing at the Bow Street Magistrate's Office. I suggest you apply to him if you have questions."

Very likely he thought she wouldn't dare approach the office or any prisoners housed there. "Then is there nothing more we can do to learn about your uncle's death?"

He slid a glance her way, mouth tilting up. "We?"

"Certainly, Mr. Everard. I promised you I'd help, and I stand by that promise."

He reined in the horses in front of her home. "I cannot impose myself on your good graces any further."

"It is no imposition," Imogene insisted as Jenkins and one of the under footmen came down the steps to assist. "After today I am in complete agreement with you that my father owes you an explanation for his actions."

"Unfortunately, your father thinks otherwise," he said.

Imogene made a face as the under footman positioned himself beside the team and Jenkins stood next to their seat, waiting to help her down. "So it would seem. I wish I knew someone close to him who could advise us, but my father is far too busy to cultivate close friendships. From the sound of things, your uncle was the last."

He seemed to be focused on wrapping the reins around the brake. "Someone in Parliament, then, in Whitehall."

Imogene shook her head. "I would have no idea who to recommend. Mr. Dundas the Secretary at War, Earl Camden the Secretary of State for War and the Colonies and Lord Barham the new First Lord of the Admiralty know him well, I'm sure, but I doubt they would part with anything of use to you, and they will have even less time to spare than my father. I'll simply have to speak to him as soon as I see him."

His hand came down over hers, held it tightly. "I must ask you not to do that."

Imogene glanced at him with a frown. His jaw was tense, his profile tight, but she thought she saw some other emotion deep in his eyes. "He's my father," she said. "He wouldn't hurt me. He couldn't."

He withdrew his hand. "As you say." Before she could argue further, he jumped down and came around. Jenkins's look tightened as well, but he stepped aside to allow Vaughn to help her from the chariot, then preceded them to the front door to open it.

Vaughn held her at the chariot a moment. The breeze had freshened, and a pale lock of hair brushed his cheek. She itched to stroke it back into place, but she held her hands clasped in front of her.

"Thank you for all your help, Lady Imogene," he murmured. "If you have need of me, you have only to send word."

Imogene blinked. "That sounds suspiciously like a dismissal, sir."

He inclined his head. "I know how many other suitors vie for your time, your standing on the *ton*. I would not presume to intrude further."

He *was* dismissing her! This would never do! The change in her father was somehow connected to Vaughn

Everard; she was sure of it. Didn't she and Vaughn both deserve answers?

Imogene cocked her head. "Mr. Everard, I was under the impression we were becoming friends. Have I done something to offend you?"

"Never," he assured her. "But you must realize how unlikely our friendship would be."

She frowned. "Why?"

He tugged at his cravat, which had lost some of its perfection from his exertions. "We don't move in the same circles."

So that was the problem. "I am not unknown to the literary set," Imogene told him, nose in the air. "My father was much impressed with the poet Mr. Coleridge's ideas, and we've exchanged letters since he went to Malta."

His smile seemed reluctant. "Commendable, I'm sure. But that isn't what I meant." He paused to meet her gaze, and she felt herself slip a little further into those dark eyes. "I am not considered an appropriate companion for a young lady. A great many households refuse me entrance."

"Because of a penchant for poetry?" She waved a hand. "Ridiculous! You are better off without them."

He shook his head. "Oh, to see the world through your eyes." He leaned forward until they were nearly nose to nose. She caught her breath at the pain on his face.

"I am a scoundrel, Imogene. Some would say a rake. I thought I could use your good opinion to reach your father. I have failed and endangered your life in the process. For your sake, we end this now."

"Has anyone ever told you," Imogene said, "that you can be very charming when you're so intent?"

He reared back. Another man might have toppled over, but he caught himself. "Did you hear nothing I said?"

"That rubbish about being a scoundrel? Certainly. I am not hard of hearing, sir. I'm simply trying to determine whether you think to lie to me or yourself."

His look darkened. "I do not lie, madam."

"Then you are mistaken. I have not had the opportunity to meet many scoundrels, it's true, but I would think part of the breed would be an endless selfishness, the ability to put oneself and one's goals before all others. Surely you would agree that is also a requirement for a rake."

He took a step back from her. "As I demonstrated by using you to get to your father."

"Which you just confessed."

"Because I no longer have need of you."

"Don't you?" Imogene closed the distance. "Only after I promised to speak to my father on your behalf did you attempt to dismiss me. And was that not, sir, because you were concerned for my safety?"

He held his ground. "That concern still stands. After your father's actions today, I cannot feel comfortable embroiling you further."

"And is that the decision of a rake?"

He puffed out a sigh. "You persist in seeing a hero."

"Of course!" Imogene reached out for his arm. "Because you are a hero, whether you like it or not. Now, why don't you join Mother and me for tea?"

He removed his arm from hers but slid his hand down to cup her fingers instead. "I shouldn't keep my horses standing. And do not go into raptures about my devotion to the beasts."

Imogene dimpled up at him. "If you insist, though I do find it commendable."

"And I find you utterly enchanting." He bowed over her hand and pressed a kiss against her knuckles. The gentle pressure stopped her breath, made her heart start beating faster. His dark gaze drifted up to hers. "When may I see you again?"

She wanted to dance up and down the pavement in triumph. But she was the Marquess of Widmore's daughter. Such displays, however gratifying, did not become her. "Do you like the opera, Mr. Everard?" she asked instead.

"A great deal," he replied, releasing her and straightening. "And I believe we agreed on Vaughn."

Imogene grinned. "Of course. Then perhaps you could join us this evening at the Opera House on Haymarket, Vaughn. I'll endeavor to have more information for you then."

What an astonishing woman! Vaughn shook his head in admiration as he guided the horses through traffic on the way back to Everard House. After today it should have been apparent to her that he was considerably beyond the pale, yet she saw him as a champion. With her gazing up at him, full of hope, full of faith, he felt himself stand taller, wanting to be that hero. The vision matched what he'd once dared to dream. Was it too late to reclaim that dream?

And when had the marquess lost his own standards? Once, he'd been a champion for both England and France, working beside Uncle to protect the innocent aristocrats threatened by the Terror, helping England stay strong against French incursion. At a con-

fused fourteen, Vaughn had idolized the man along
with Uncle.

And he had needed someone to look up to then, having just been expelled from Eton for dueling and ordered by his father to live with Uncle. His devoted *père*
had been so embarrassed by the whole affair he hadn't
even gone to the school to fetch Vaughn, instead sending a junior partner of the family's solicitor firm, letter in hand.

"You have pained me for the last time," his father
had written, the strokes sharp with agitation. "I am
only thankful your grandfather has gone to his just reward and didn't realize how far you have fallen from
the ideals he set. I can think of one fitting punishment.
Go live with my brother, Lord Everard. His bent is as
dark as your own. Perhaps you will take a lesson from
him and change your character before it is too late. If
not, at least you will have company down that barren
road of regrets."

And so he'd gone to live with Uncle. Arthur Everard's
deeds had already become legend. He'd been a privateer
like Grandfather before the elder fellow's elevation for
rescuing a noble lady from pirates. But unlike Grandfather, who had sailed with the notion of protecting England from its enemies, Arthur Everard had captained
his ship like he did everything else, for the adventure
of it. He'd taken one look at Vaughn, standing in the
entryway of Everard House, trunk at his feet, sword at
his hip, gaze daring anyone to look closer, and clapped
him on the shoulder.

"You've an itch under your skin, don't you, boy?"
he'd asked. "A spirit inside you urging you to ride, to
run." He had motioned to the sword. "To fight. And
keeping it silent takes too much energy."

Vaughn had stared up at him. His uncle had the same pale hair, the same dark gaze. Could he, as Vaughn's father had intimated, have the same longings? "How did you know?"

"Because I have the same spirit," his uncle had confirmed. "And I can tell you the answer isn't trying to contain it—it's to set that spirit free and fly with it!"

Vaughn's heart had been his uncle's from that moment. Wherever Arthur Everard went, whatever he did, Vaughn was at his side, even if that meant going places no fourteen-year-old boy should ever see.

But never with the Marquess of Widmore. That had stung Vaughn then, though now he thought he saw the wisdom in the decision. Uncle was always delighted to tell Vaughn about his adventures with his old friend afterward, but the marquess had drawn the line about including a youth in any of their plans.

"He's too unpredictable," Vaughn had heard the man tell Uncle once over goblets around a crackling fire in the Everard withdrawing room. "I am not convinced I can control him. I have a hard enough time controlling you."

The marquess had laughed then, and Uncle had laughed with him, but Vaughn couldn't help wondering. In the end, had Uncle proved too difficult for the marquess to control? Was that why his uncle had been killed? Or had the marquess himself become the force of chaos that destroyed Uncle in the end? Had Uncle, like the dance master Henri Chevalier, who claimed to work for the marquess, realized treachery was afoot and challenged his friend? Chevalier had admitted being an agent for France—directed by the marquess he claimed. Was he telling the truth? Or had Vaughn misunderstood everything?

He reached Everard House in time to see a hired carriage pulling away. The two footmen tugging a trunk into the house gave Vaughn a clue as to the new arrivals. Leaving his horses to the care of a trusted groom, he took the steps two at a time.

He found both his male cousins in the library. Jerome and Richard seemed to feel right at home in the neatly organized space. Vaughn always wondered when the well-stocked bookcases would close in on him. But he strode to meet his cousins, and Jerome rose from his seat by the fire to shake his hand.

"Vaughn, looking well. No new holes or scratches, I see. Samantha must be keeping you too busy to duel."

His raven-haired cousin looked even better, Vaughn thought. Jerome had always carried himself with confidence, some would have said the Everard arrogance, but now he seemed settled in his own skin, as if the world was just as he had ordered it. His clear blue eyes seemed warmer, his smile deeper. Vaughn thought his new bride Adele might have something to do with the changes, and he envied his cousin.

"It isn't Samantha who's keeping him busy," Richard said as Vaughn disengaged. "I wrote you about Chevalier. Vaughn has been stalking the Marquess of Widmore."

"Odd," Vaughn said to Richard. "It seems we have more than one Everard intent on literary fame. I may be a poet, but you're remarkably set on telling tales."

Richard's dark eyes narrowed.

Jerome held up a hand. "Peace! I need to be aware of what's happening so we can decide the best course of action." He turned to Vaughn, lowering his hand. "You know you and I are in agreement that the marquess is involved somehow in the troubles plaguing us. What have you learned?"

"I finally caught up with him today," Vaughn admitted, thinking back on the altercation in the park. "He disavowed all knowledge of Uncle's death, any involvement in the deaths of our valet Repton or Samantha's footman Todd. He dismissed Chevalier's allegations of treason out of hand."

Jerome frowned as he retook his seat and waved Vaughn into another. "Could we have been mistaken?"

Vaughn refused the offer of a chair and went to stand by the fire instead, feeling the warmth brush against his thighs. "I would be tempted to think so, save for two things. One is how we found the marquess."

"We?" Richard interrupted, freezing in the act of sitting across from his brother.

In for a penny, in for a pound. "I was driving with Lady Imogene Devary."

Jerome raised his brows and glanced at Richard for confirmation. "The Marquess of Widmore's daughter?"

Richard crossed his arms over his chest, leaning back. In their navy coats and fawn trousers, his cousins looked like two finicky gentlemen of fashion, ready to pass judgment on him for his challenge to the ordinary.

"The same," Richard told his brother. "She seems to have taken a shine to our cousin."

"I am honored by her friendship," Vaughn insisted, then continued, ignoring Richard's snort. "We came across him by accident—in an empty corner of Hyde Park with a lady."

Jerome shook his head. "Sadly, he would not be the first to attempt a tryst in the park."

"Indeed," Vaughn agreed. "However, even though

the lady was veiled, I recognized her. It was Eugenie Toussel, the French émigré."

"The one rumored to spy for France?" Jerome asked with a frown.

"The same. He could have been using her to pass secrets to confuse the French," he offered in an attempt to consider all possibilities. He owed Imogene that much, at least.

"Or communicating with old friends who would prefer not to acknowledge an English connection," Richard mused, stroking his russet mustache. "The marquess has French ancestors, if memory serves."

"His mother," Jerome agreed. "Enough of a connection to the Old Regime to make him useful to the War Office in the current crisis. Too much to make Prime Minister Pitt inclined to offer him a cabinet post."

"I tend to share the Prime Minister's suspicions," Vaughn told them both. "When I pressed too hard with questions today, he startled my horses and I had to contend with a runaway team."

Jerome grinned. "He should have known better. With your skills, controlling your horses couldn't have been difficult."

"His actions were dishonorable," Richard added, "but hardly lethal."

Vaughn knew his smile was grim. "Except I wasn't at the reins at the time. I wasn't even in the chariot. The person in danger was Lady Imogene."

Jerome stiffened, and Richard whistled. "He risked his own daughter?" the captain asked. "Is he mad?"

Vaughn felt chilled by the thought. "I don't know," he said. "But it's one explanation for his negligence."

"I can think of another," Jerome said. "Desperate men take desperate actions. We may have been right about the marquess. And we may have him on the run at last."

"He'll be even more dangerous then," Richard said. "Unfortunately, we still lack any real evidence to approach the magistrates."

"Agreed." Jerome turned to Vaughn. "It seems we must continue our quest, Cousin. What do you advise?"

Vaughn raised a brow in surprise. Always before, Jerome strategized, Richard criticized and Vaughn acted. He wasn't sure what it meant that his cousin actually asked his opinion, but he liked the feeling. He straightened away from the fire. "The marquess will be more wary of us—particularly me—in future. I doubt we'll be given another opportunity to question him."

"Then we'll have to find another way to get the information," Richard said.

Jerome nodded. "It seems he's too good at deception. Our best hope lies with Lady Imogene. Vaughn, can you continue this friendship without risking her safety?"

Vaughn had wondered as much. He'd been ready to walk away this afternoon if it meant keeping her safe. But the look in her eyes, her sweet argument, the way she saw the good in him made him long for one more moment in her company. "I won't see her harmed," he vowed.

Jerome nodded again. "Then see what you can learn from her, even if that means spending every waking moment together."

Chapter Eight

Imogene had reached the conclusion that in Vaughn lay her best hope of proving her father innocent. She had gone over the events in Hyde Park again and again and dissected her discussions with Vaughn. He seemed to think her father was involved in any number of scandals. She had no idea how he'd reached such conclusions, but she was certain he was wrong.

Unfortunately, she had little to go on to uncover the truth. She knew a man accused generally brought authorities to attest to his innocence and character as well as witnesses to the alleged crime. She didn't think Vaughn was willing to listen to her protests that her father was a fine man. And the only witness to any crime, so far as she could tell, was the same fellow who was apparently accusing her father: Monsieur Henri Chevalier. How could she manage a moment with the dance master?

Although the Lord had encouraged his followers to visit the poor, the sick and the imprisoned, she didn't think her mother would be quite so understanding of a trip to Bow Street to see a man awaiting trial for attempted murder. And if Imogene was to be ready to go to the opera tonight and see Vaughn again, she certainly didn't have time to convince her mother, have the carriage prepared, go and return.

But she could still do some good. Accordingly, she convinced Cook to make up a basket of bread, mutton and a bottle of lemonade; added her own note requesting an explanation of Monsieur Chevalier's claims; and presented it all to Jenkins with the plea that he deliver it to the criminal.

Her normally obedient footman gazed down at her. "Does his lordship approve of this?"

Imogene stood taller. That only brought her to the chest of his tailored black coat, but it made her feel a little more authoritative. "My father is entirely too busy to be bothered with such insignificances, as is Mr. Prentice."

At the mention of the Devary butler, the footman's steely gaze narrowed. Imogene continued on, undaunted. "Monsieur Chevalier has given good service over the years. I'm certain Father would approve of supporting him in his time of need."

Jenkins still looked less than sure, but he left a short time later, and Imogene was able to spend a few minutes at the piano before dinner. The footman returned with the note just before dashing off to lead the serving. Her former dance master had scribbled a response in pencil at the bottom, and the dirt on the parchment attested to the filth of his surroundings.

"Pray for me that I may be forgiven for my misdeeds," he'd written. "And be careful. Your father has designs above his station, and you will need to protect yourself and your mother."

Imogene frowned at the words. As a marquess with his own estate and considerable political power, her father had one of the highest positions in the land. What could possibly be higher? Was he in line for a cabinet post after all? Was that why he spent so much time at Whitehall, to convince his colleagues he was dedicated to the role? But surely such a thing could not be considered above his station, so why would she need to protect herself, much less her mother, from such an honor? And how could that be associated with the Everards?

Was Monsieur Chevalier mistaken, as well? Then where had the rumors about her father started? It seemed someone had reason to point a finger his way. Who? Her father was a strong personality; she was certain more than one lord smarted from the sting of his disdain for an ill-placed comment, a poorly conceived proposal. Could someone be trying to implicate her father in some conspiracy as revenge?

The only person who seemed to have answers was Vaughn Everard. She was fairly certain he knew more than he was letting on. The only way to prove her father's innocence was to stick to Vaughn's side until she learned everything.

And then she'd bring the entire matter to her father.

She dressed with care for the opera that night, choosing a white satin gown with a Vandyke collar of stiffened tulle. Satin rosebuds of the palest pink meandered down the front and edged the hem and train.

"You look lovely, dearest," her mother said with a quick kiss on Imogene's cheek when they met in the entryway for their cloaks. She tucked an errant curl back into the pearl-studded bandeau around Imogene's head. "I told Bryson your hair would look splendid near your face. The style highlights your cheekbones."

"Highlighted cheekbones, a true sign of character," Imogene teased. She glanced up the stairs. "Has Father returned home by any chance? I was hoping he might join us this evening."

Her mother turned away. "Sadly, his presence was required in Whitehall. He sent word that we were to go without him."

Imogene followed her mother out to the waiting carriage, but she felt frustration accompanying her. All this business could be entirely swept away, she was sure, if she could just talk to her father, hear him explain the situation in his cultured voice. And how delighted Vaughn would be if she actually had an answer for him!

He was a bit of a puzzlement, she thought as she settled in the carriage beside her mother. He was all confidence and brash swagger, yet at moments he seemed to doubt his worth. When he was intent on flirting, his voice was husky and his words colorful; she could almost smell the flowers blooming from the prose. But in a moment of crisis, his sentences were short and crisp, each word as precise as a scalpel, his manner as brisk as the military officers who called on her father. Which was the true Vaughn Everard?

She spotted him immediately after she'd taken her seat next to her mother in the Devary box. Five rows of boxes like theirs stood on either side of the opera house, stacked on top of each other like layers on a cake. The rafters above and the pit below were thronged with people, their voices rising in cacophony against their gilded surroundings.

Vaughn was standing at the side of another box along the curve of the second row, pale hair bright against his evening black. A sigh of appreciation escaped her before she could think better of it. Goodness, but she needed to guard her thoughts!

As he shifted, she caught sight of his companions.

Lady Samantha Everard had been joined by two other women. Imogene recognized Lady Claire Winthrop and the man on her left, Captain Richard Everard. She wasn't sure of the other.

Her mother must have noticed the direction of her gaze, for she leaned closer to Imogene. "I see the eldest Mr. Everard has returned to town. That must be his new bride."

Imogene nodded, but the dark-haired beauty in the other box could only hold her attention a moment. She was far more interested in what Vaughn was up to. His head turned slowly from side to side as he gazed out over the audience. He was looking for someone. Could it be her?

"Imogene," her mother murmured, raising her lace-edged fan and opening it with a snap. "You are staring."

Imogene forced herself to look away. "Forgive me."

Her mother waved the fan in front of her face. Between the numbers in attendance and the great lamps along the boxes, the opera house was already becoming warm. "I believe Mr. Everard has completely captured your imagination."

At least her mother hadn't said he'd captured Imogene's heart. "I suppose he has. But I doubt I'm the only one."

"Very likely not," her mother agreed, and Imogene felt the comment like a blow. "Time will tell if he is sincere in his courtship. Indeed, I believe time to be your best ally when it comes to a gentleman like Mr. Everard."

Imogene frowned as the house lights began to be extinguished and the audience quieted in anticipation. "Why do you say that?"

"Because Mr. Everard seems to be one of those gentlemen who craves variety and adventure. They love the heady pursuit of a young lady, but they lack the ability to form the consistent abiding love and commitment required of a marriage."

Imogene leaned back in her seat, unsure which was making her more uncomfortable—the hard wood or the fact that Vaughn Everard might have a serious flaw in his character. Some part of her persisted in hoping he might be the suitor she needed.

"I thought you wanted me to be less stringent in my requirements for your future son-in-law," she replied.

"I think you can relax your requirements for position and demeanor, yes." Her mother tapped her fan against her amber bodice. "But it is the heart that counts, Imogene, the character of the gentleman. Never forget that."

Imogene found it difficult to think of anything else as the music began. Usually the rich sound, the stirring solos, kept her enthralled, spurred her to compose something of equal value. Tonight, she barely heard any of it.

She had assumed Vaughn's character was as good as his poetry. She hoped her convictions shone through her compositions. But by his words, it seemed Vaughn thought his character irreparably damaged. Certainly her mother was concerned about him. And Imogene still did not understand her father's mind.

She had to admit, though, that while she was used to being guided by her parents' opinions in particular, she could not agree with any of their assessments. The more she considered the matter, the more her convictions grew. Vaughn Everard was not beneath her notice; he came from an aristocratic family, and the current generation seemed set on being upstanding members of society.

And that business of him being a rake she dismissed

out of hand. A rake didn't race after speeding carriages to rescue young ladies at a disadvantage. A rake didn't speak of family members with fondness. If he had been a rake in the past, he certainly was on the road to redemption.

You can do that, Lord. You know his heart, his intentions. And You know mine, as well. Show me what I should do to help my father and him.

She was a little surprised when the lights rose for intermission. Conversation blossomed around them, and a rumble and scrape rose from the pit. It seemed she'd been woolgathering through the entire first act! She glanced around, blinking, and her gaze lit on a box a few doors down from theirs. The lovely face of the lady was unfamiliar, but the beauty mark high on her neck, displayed to advantage by a deep-cut gown of rich emerald velvet, was all too recognizable. She was the woman who had met the marquess in the park that afternoon—Imogene was sure of it. Was her presence why her father had refused to attend?

And was the fact that Imogene noticed her a sign that she was meant to confront the woman, perhaps learn the truth?

"The company is in fine form tonight," her mother said, and Imogene turned to her in time to see her wipe a tear from her cheek with a lawn handkerchief.

"I'm glad you enjoyed it, Mother," Imogene said, managing a smile though her mind was a hive of buzzing possibilities.

A tap on the door signaled the arrival of their first visitor. Imogene brightened, ran her fingers into her curls and sat straighter. But she couldn't help slumping when the footman announced Lord Wentworth.

Her mother held out her hand, and he bowed over it. "My lord, how nice to see you."

"Lady Widmore, Lady Imogene, charmed," he returned, straightening. His smile said he knew how delighted they must be by his company. His evening coat was of azure superfine that brought out the blue in his eyes. She found herself wondering what her mother thought of *his* character.

"But where is your husband?" he asked now. "Wanted a word with him."

Imogene regarded him, noting the sheen of perspiration along his brow. The opera house had grown heated during the performance, but she thought something else had made his temperature rise. Interesting. This was the second time the gentleman had come seeking her father. What business could they have that would cause him to sweat?

"It's the war," her mother lamented. "Great men are always in demand at such times."

"Indeed," he agreed. He fingered the pocket of his gold-embroidered waistcoat as if yearning to consult his pocket watch. "Expect him to join you later?"

"Very likely not," her mother said and turned to gaze out over the pit in clear dismissal.

He shuffled his feet, clearly at a loss. Imogene had pity on him. "And how are you enjoying the opera, my lord?"

"Eh?" He blinked at her a moment, then shrugged in a ripple of blue. "Never did appreciate it. All that foreign business. Can't understand a word they say."

"Then why attend?" Imogene asked, perplexed.

"Everyone attends the opera," he informed her as if that should have been obvious.

"Certainly everyone with taste," Imogene replied, unable to keep her voice from heating.

"Or imagination," Vaughn added.

Imogene sat up in her chair as he stepped past a frowning Jenkins and entered the box. "Ladies, my lord, I thought I should pay my respects."

Her mother turned with a smile. "Mr. Everard, welcome. I believe I saw your entire family just down the way."

Vaughn inclined his head. "My cousin Jerome has recently returned from the country with his new wife, Adele. And of course you know my cousin Captain Everard and his betrothed, Lady Claire Winthrop. They send their regards as well and hope for an opportunity to renew the acquaintance." He nodded to another footman who had accompanied him.

"How kind." She rose with a hush of amber velvet. "I haven't seen Claire in an age. I'll just go over for a moment. I'm sure Imogene can entertain you gentlemen."

Vaughn and Lord Wentworth bowed as she left with the Everard footman, then eyed each other. Imogene thought she'd never seen Jenkins stand so straight at the back of the box, as if hoping one of the gentlemen would do something to give offense and offer him the excuse to eject them both.

"You were saying it takes imagination to enjoy the opera, Mr. Everard," Imogene said, leaning back in her seat. "Do explain. I'm sure his lordship would appreciate the education, and so would I."

The minx. Vaughn could see the laughter dancing in Lady Imogene's green eyes. He could certainly understand the contrast he and the toad must make, fire and ice, reaction and regulation. Unfortunately, in his experience, regulation was far more likely to win approval.

Nevertheless, he sat in the chair next to hers, leaned back and crossed his legs as if intent on staying for a while. Lord Wentworth frowned at him.

"The opera, like poetry or a novel, joins with the audience in participation," Vaughn explained. "The words, the music, even the costumes evoke different memories in each of us. We enter into the story, as it were, empathize with the hero or heroine, feel what they feel. As their vision widens, so does ours. We become the story, if you will."

She was regarding him with a fascination that would likely have made him preen under other circumstances. The toad merely raised a brow. "Nonsense. No idea what's happening with the fellow on the stage. No interest in finding out."

Vaughn glanced up at him. "Then I suspect we have nothing in common, sir."

Wentworth nodded. "Right there. I don't lie."

Vaughn rose slowly, gaze fixed on the maw worm in front of him. "Are you implying that I do?"

His opponent raised his dimpled chin. "No need to imply. Statement of fact. Led me to believe you and the marquess are on good terms."

"My father and Mr. Everard spoke only this afternoon," Imogene informed him. "He was remarkably civil."

For once the toad did not back down. "Not what he told me. Surprised you'd show your face here, Everard. If the marquess was in residence, you wouldn't be welcomed."

Vaughn took a step forward, eyes narrowing. But

suddenly, a curvaceous bundle of outraged femininity stood between him and his accuser.

"How dare you!" Lady Imogene cried, head so high the curls at the back of her head teased Vaughn's nose. "This is my family box, sirrah, and the last time I checked, you were not a member of my family. You will apologize to Mr. Everard immediately or quit my presence, and if you choose the latter, it will be a long day before you are admitted again, I promise you."

The spitfire! Vaughn was caught between applauding her and hoping he'd never have to face her wrath.

The toad evidently had the same thought, for he washed white. "Beg pardon," he said with a bow. "Must have misunderstood your father. Swear he said Everard was to be avoided at all costs. Forgive me."

He'd addressed his entire speech to Imogene. Vaughn could not have cared less; he was more interested in the undertone of the words. He was fairly certain no one had seen the altercation in the park. If Lord Wentworth was suddenly aware that Imogene's father was angry with Vaughn, he had to have spoken to the marquess since then. How had the toad managed that when it seemed even the marquess's family didn't warrant a conversation? And if they had spoken, why did he not know the marquess had avoided the opera?

Imogene stuck her pert nose in the air. "I should be more inclined to believe your apology, my lord, if you had directed it to Mr. Everard as I requested."

The toad's square jaw clamped tight as if Vaughn didn't even deserve one of his short sentences. Lady Imogene raised a hand and pointed to the door. "Out, sirrah. Now."

The footman threw open the portal and glared down

at the recalcitrant fellow. Vaughn had to fight a smile
that the look wasn't directed at him for once.

The toad sagged. "Beg pardon," he said, head bowed
as if he spoke to the toes of Vaughn's evening pumps.
"Only have the lady's best interest at heart."

Imogene dropped her arm.

"There at least we can agree," Vaughn replied. "But
it seems you've had words with the marquess recently.
Any idea how Lady Imogene and I might do the same?"

She turned to beam at him, but Lord Wentworth
took a step back. "Saw him over dinner. Only a chat.
Thought to learn more tonight. Not sure when we'll
next meet." He bowed as Imogene faced him once more.
"Your servant." He straightened and hurried out. The
footman remained at the open door, his look at last
aimed at Vaughn.

Vaughn turned his back on the fellow.

Imogene shook her head. "I truly expected better of
Lord Wentworth. Are good manners too much to expect from someone who calls himself a gentleman?"

"Civilization has surely fallen," Vaughn replied. He
took her elbow and led her back to her seat. Mindful
of the footman glowering in the background, he lowered his voice.

"Forgive me for rushing you, but I expect your
mother to return any moment. Do you have any news
for me?"

Her face puckered. "I didn't manage to catch my
father, and I have no idea why he chose to eat dinner
with Lord Wentworth when Mother and I were waiting
at home. I'm so sorry."

Though he hadn't thought she'd be successful, he still
felt the drag of disappointment. "No need to apologize.
I appreciate all your help."

Dimples popped into view on either side of her peachy lips. "Delighted as always, Mr. Everard. And perhaps I could ask a favor of you?"

"Anything," Vaughn agreed, then immediately regretted it, as the fire kindled in those green eyes and she leaned even closer, until he could smell the lavender she must use on her hair.

"I believe the lady who met my father this afternoon is seated just a few boxes away," she whispered with a conspiratorial grin. "Be a dear and introduce me to her."

Chapter Nine

Of course he disagreed. He clearly didn't want to play a part in introducing her to a woman her father should not know. And he called himself a rake!

"You are merely delaying the inevitable," Imogene said when he'd given several persuasive arguments on propriety and safety and efficacy of time. "The curtain will rise any second. Let us be off."

He shook his head. "Does anyone ever refuse you anything?"

"Rarely," Imogene replied, lifting her skirts and heading for the door. "Now hurry."

Jenkins blocked their way. Though he said nothing, hand on the door, she could tell by the look in his eyes he thought she was making a grave mistake. Imogene merely smiled, head tilted back to meet his gaze. With a sigh he opened the door and let them out. Imogene pointed to the door to indicate he should remain behind. His jaw tightened, but he did as she bid.

If he had worried for her reputation, he had no cause for concern. She and Vaughn were hardly alone. Ladies and gentlemen strolled up and down the corridor, foot-men carried refreshments to their mistresses and masters and a young boy darted past, folded note in one hand. Imogene paused only long enough to be sure her mother wasn't in sight, then started out with Vaughn toward the other box. With each step of her satin-covered slippers, she thought she was walking toward answers.

A man responded to Vaughn's knock at the door. He was tall and wide, and a scar crossed his bulbous nose. His hard gray eyes narrowed. Imogene smiled at him. His expression didn't change.

"Ah, the Bull!" Vaughn declared, reaching out to clap the behemoth on a shoulder so wide it threatened the fabric of his coat. "That was an exceptional display last month, a veritable feast of power and might. I thought you had him at the end."

The man's face cleared, and he smiled ruefully, revealing a missing front tooth. "So did I, Mr. Everard. So did I."

"You will prevail next time," Vaughn assured him. "Just keep up your left, and don't let him inside your reach."

He nodded, head rolling forward and back on his thick neck. "Right you are, sir."

Vaughn tipped up his chin. "May we pay our respects to the lady?"

The man's gaze traveled back to Imogene. "She's not in a mood to be helping any chicks at present."

Imogene wasn't sure what he meant by that, but Vaughn stepped between her and the boxer.

"My companion is a lady. She has no need for Madame Toussel's protection. If I hear a word about this meeting, you can expect to meet me at Jackson's Boxing Emporium."

Imogene stared at him. His head was high, his shoulders stiff and arms poised. The brute in the doorway was clearly a pugilist, and he outweighed Vaughn by at least two stone. Yet the other man immediately took a step back and lowered his gaze.

"Beggin' your pardon, ma'am, sir. But the lady is out visiting, and I'm not sure when to expect her back."

Vaughn took Imogene's elbow. "In that case, I wish you well." He turned to go.

Imogene resisted. "Shouldn't we ask to wait?"

His grip was determined. "No. We count this as a missed opportunity, and we move on."

She allowed him to lead her back down the corridor, but her mind kept whirling, clicking through options, discarding that one as too daring, this one as too fanciful. As they reached the door of her box, she managed to draw her arm from his fingers.

"It was very kind of you to help me this evening, Mr. Everard," she said. "I do hope I'll have the pleasure of your company again soon."

He leaned closer, searched her gaze. "What are you up to?"

Imogene widened her eyes. "Why, Mr. Everard, whatever do you mean?"

He chuckled, straightening. "It won't work, you know. You're a hideous liar."

Imogene couldn't help her giggle. "Well, I haven't had much practice. And I truly didn't intend to start. But you clearly would prefer to give up the chase, so what I do from here is my own affair."

He raised a platinum brow. "Your mother might have something to say about that."

"You would carry tales?"

Her surprise must have been evident from her voice, for he threw back his head and laughed. "Far be it from me to report on anyone's misdeeds," he said when he'd sobered. "But if you are intent on intrigue, allow me to assist."

Imogene grinned. "I was hoping you might say that." She leaned closer. "I think we should find this Madame Toussel and see what she's up to."

He leaned closer as well, until she could smell the clean scent of him. "Are you certain you wish to travel that road? You may not like what you find at the end."

Possibly he was right. Something tugged at her, warned her this was folly, but she pushed the thought aside. That woman had some connection to her father. Imogene needed to understand it.

She linked her arm in his. "I'm certain. Where shall we start?"

"This way," he said.

She thought perhaps he'd take her to some secret part of the opera house, where wicked men did dark deeds. Instead, he led her out onto the balcony that ran across the back of the lobby. Each row of boxes debouched onto it, with stairs leading up and down on either side. From her vantage point, she could see the crowds strolling about the lobby, procuring refreshments and comparing opinions on the music and performers, all under the glow of a crystal chandelier mounted high in the frescoed ceiling.

"There," he said with a nod, and she sighted the lady, moving from group to group, pausing here, hurrying past there. Madame Toussel never actually stopped long enough to engage anyone in a lengthy conversation, and the men who were accompanying ladies were careful not to meet her gaze. But her head bowed close to theirs, lips moving, before she drifted on.

"She's passing secrets!" Imogene realized. She turned to Vaughn. "We have to intercept her."

Vaughn's mouth quirked, but whether he was fighting a smile or a refusal she didn't know. "There are any number of reasons for the lady to address those gentlemen. She likely knows each one. Madame Toussel hosts a well-respected salon. Gentlemen and ladies come to enjoy her wit, her hospitality and her connections."

Imogene frowned, gaze returning to the lady below. "If all is as innocent as you say, perhaps we could ask for an invitation."

Vaughn's hand touched her arm, a soft brush that seemed to travel straight to her heart. "That might not be wise."

Madame Toussel was moving closer to the stairs, apparently having completed her rounds, and Imogene could see her clearly. She had hair as dark as midnight, swept back from a patrician face. From her painted cheeks to her well-molded bosom, she was the picture of wealth and excess. As Imogene watched, the lady lifted her skirts and climbed the stairs.

Imogene elbowed Vaughn. "This is my chance to meet her."

She thought he grumbled something about obstinacy under his breath, but he moved to intercept the lady. Her cool blue eyes looked a bit curious as Vaughn bowed over her beringed fingers.

"Madame Toussel," he said, positioning himself to keep her from continuing down the corridor for her box. "Fortune smiles that I might find you here."

"Mr. Everard," she said, voice low and musical. "I have not been so fortunate this Season. I was beginning to think my salon had lost its charm."

So he, too, had spent time with this woman? Why hadn't Imogene ever heard of her?

"Your many admirers would surely convince you

otherwise," Vaughn replied. "I am doubly remiss, however, for I meant to thank you for the letter of condo-
lence on my uncle's passing."

She inclined her head. "London will never be the
same without him."

"There we quite agree. And, alas, I will never be the
same if I am denied your company another day. Can you
ever forgive me?" He took her hand and pressed it close.

Imogene was not surprised to see the lady's look
soften. "Charming rogue," Madame Toussel murmured.
"How can I refuse you?"

He bowed over her hand. "You are generosity itself.
I could not help noticing that you were issuing invitations just now. What must I do to earn one?"

What a clever fellow! Imogene waited for the lady
to spill her secrets, but Madame Toussel's face closed,
and she drew back her hand. "A private affair, sir. You
are not on the list."

Imogene took a step closer. "Is my father on the list?"

Madame Toussel frowned as if noticing her for the
first time.

"Allow me to introduce my companion," Vaughn said
reluctantly, Imogene thought. "Lady Imogene Devary,
Madame Eugenie Toussel."

Madame Toussel's head came up, and for a moment
Imogene thought she saw her diamond gaze cloud with
panic. "The Marquess of Widmore's daughter?"

"The same," Imogene said, trying for her most win-
ning smile. "And as I believe you know my father well,
I'm sure you wouldn't mind extending an invitation to
Mr. Everard and me."

Madame Toussel blinked, and a puzzled look came
over her face. She glanced at Vaughn, then back at
Imogene.

"I regret that I am not at liberty to discuss the matter. Your father was quite adamant on that point, and I would never advise you to cross him."

A bell chimed in the lobby, and the crowds began making their way toward the stairs. The second act was about to start.

Madame Toussel took a step away. "A pleasure to meet you, Lady Imogene, and to see you again, Mr. Everard. Perhaps I shall run across you both in Vauxhall tomorrow night." Neither Imogene nor Vaughn moved to stop her as she swept past them for the corridor to the boxes.

Vaughn frowned after their quarry then turned his gaze on the lady beside him. Eugenie Toussel could be a difficult lady, yet Imogene had stood her ground, clearheaded and confident. Now he could almost see the thoughts churning beneath her curls.

"What are you thinking?" he asked.

She shook her head. "I don't know. She made it sound as if Father was directing her, yet to what purpose? And what was that business about Vauxhall Pleasure Gardens?" She glanced at Vaughn. "You apparently know her. What do you think she was doing tonight, this afternoon?"

"I'm not entirely certain," he replied, choosing his words with more than his usual care. He knew what Jerome expected, but every moment in Imogene's company and he felt her being drawn deeper into the darkness.

As if she could see the struggle inside him, she put a hand on his arm. "Tell me."

Vaughn eyed her. Her chin was tilted up, lips trembling. Everything about her begged for the truth. Who was he to deny it?

"Very well," he said. "There have been rumors that she is a French spy."

He thought she might gasp, perhaps deny the possibility or the implication to her father's reputation. To his surprise, she grinned, the smile lighting her face. "Well, that explains everything!"

Vaughn raised his brows. "Then explain it to me, for I confess I do not see the picture so clearly."

"Don't you?" She shook her head in obvious wonder. "I'm amazed I never considered it before. We do have a war on, you know."

Vaughn quirked a smile. "Yes, so I understand. But what has that to do with your father's actions?"

She glanced at the people passing and motioned him closer. Her eyes positively sparkled in the shadows along the wall. "I think Madame Toussel *is* a French spy, and Father is trying to trap her, to learn what she knows. She may even be involved in your uncle's death." She sagged against the wall. "What an answer to a prayer! At last we know the truth."

Vaughn would have been only too glad to agree with her, if he had believed her assessment. Unfortunately, he thought there was another explanation for the marquess's involvement with the French émigré and her mysterious messages. The men Madame Toussel had approached had one thing in common: their ambitions overreached their abilities. Such men could be dangerous, but to France or England?

He couldn't burden Imogene with his suspicions, not until he had proof and then only to protect her. If her father was the man Vaughn feared, only heartache lay ahead for the marquess's family.

He took her arm and walked with her to the door to her box. "You have your answer, then. I'm glad it pleases you."

She stopped outside the box, cocking her head. "Why do I sense that it doesn't please you? My father is very clever, Vaughn. You needn't worry for him. He'll find the person who killed your uncle."

It was not her father's safety that concerned him but hers. He offered her a bow. "How could the sparrow assail the mighty oak? It seems I can leave everything in your father's capable hands. With that happy thought, I wish you a pleasant evening, Lady Imogene."

"Not so fast, sir," she said as he straightened. "While I am certain my father can deal with the French, I am less certain he can deal with the person attempting to darken his name."

Did she suspect his motives? He held himself still, watching her. "And who would dare sully the scion of the Marquess of Widmore?"

She puffed out a sigh of pure vexation. "That's what I cannot determine! I wrote to Monsieur Chevalier, and he was no help."

"A shame," Vaughn agreed, warring between pride at her ingenuity and dismay that his suggestion had put her in touch with the criminal.

"A great shame," she said. "I'm obviously still missing an important piece of this puzzle. I wish I were as good at this espionage business as you are!"

He smiled at a passing couple and stepped closer to Imogene. "I would not say that word so loudly in this climate."

"Oh." She flushed the most appealing color. He wanted to reach out and touch her cheeks, feel them warm against his skin. He held his hands at his sides.

"You're quite right," she said. "Forgive me. I merely meant that you see things I do not."

For good reason. She chose to see only the bright spots in the world. He'd seen enough of the darkness to appreciate the bright but too much to fully believe that the bright could overcome it for long. "Perhaps you'll believe me, then, when I say that the matter is best left to others."

She frowned. "Not at all! Who will speak for my father? The War Office? They are far too busy. The Admiralty? For all I know, one of their spies is behind it!"

"Did you not just tell me your father is capable of fighting his own battles?"

"When he sees them coming, certainly. But I suspect he's been too busy to realize someone is trying to blacken his name. We have to help him."

Vaughn was fairly certain that she would not like the answers she was seeking. But again, the truth would come out. Perhaps it would be easier for her if she discovered it for herself. "What would you have of me?"

Her thankful smile fed something inside him he'd all but forgotten. "I'm not certain as yet. Give me tonight to think on it. May I ask you to call on me tomorrow, say one?"

He ought to refuse, despite his orders from Jerome. The closer he grew to Imogene, the more painful their ultimate parting. For if he proved her father a villain, he plunged her into scandal and she'd end up hating him for it. And if her father was somehow innocent, as she hoped, then the moment the marquess became aware of an abiding friendship between his darling daughter and the ne'er-do-well nephew of his old friend he would surely put a stop to it.

Yet what was one more meeting, one more hour?

It would clearly please her, and it would surely do no harm, at least to Lady Imogene.

He bent over her hand and pressed a kiss against her knuckles, feeling oddly humbled. "Tomorrow, then. Every moment until then will seem an eternity."

Chapter Ten

When the knocker sounded on the front door at a quarter to one the next day, Imogene grinned. It seemed Vaughn was as eager to see her as she was to see him. She'd considered the matter of her father a great deal since returning from the opera last night, and she thought she could convince Vaughn to take her to visit Madame Toussel. He said the lady knew a great many people. With the right persuasion, the French émigré might confess who was blackening the marquess's name.

Of course, a trip to see Madame Toussel would also give Imogene time with Vaughn. She did not have to consider why that pleased her so much. She felt alive in his company, purposeful, capable. Perhaps, oh, perhaps, he was the gentleman God intended for her. She just had to clear away all this unpleasantness, and her father could be made to see reason.

But when Jenkins paused in the doorway of the music room a few minutes later, he had other news.

"You have callers, your ladyship," he announced. "Your mother asks you to join her in the withdrawing room."

Callers? Then it wasn't Vaughn. Imogene shook her head at herself as she rose and followed Jenkins from the music room. She should have expected a few visitors today. Elisa often dropped by in the afternoon, and Kitty had called earlier. The visitors waiting for her now could even be other gentlemen who had shown interest, perhaps with an apologetic Lord Gregory Wentworth in tow. She still didn't understand the connection between that fellow and her father. Surely the marquess would see through his pretensions immediately. Vaughn certainly had.

But at the sight of the two women in the elegant withdrawing room with her mother, Imogene froze in the doorway.

"There you are, dearest," her mother called. "Come make your curtsy to Lady Winthrop."

Gathering her wits, Imogene politely bobbed a curtsy, spreading her green sprigged muslin skirts to the lovely blonde seated next to her mother on the settee. "Your ladyship, how nice to see you."

"Lady Imogene, a pleasure," she returned with a smile that warmed her pale blue eyes. Now which dressmaker had designed that frothy concoction of muslin and lace the lady was wearing?

"I believe you know my friend Samantha, Lady Everard," she continued.

Imogene turned to the girl standing by the fireplace. Like her sponsor, Samantha Everard was all conciliatory smiles. Her golden curls were tamed back from her face to fall behind her in a contrived disarray Imogene's maid had never mastered, her muslin gown was embroidered all over with four-leaf clovers and a double row of the fine work adorned the high waist and hem.

Imogene forced a smile. "Lady Everard, welcome."

The girl returned her smile with far more warmth. "Thank you."

"I asked Lady Winthrop to call today," Imogene's mother explained. "Our brief visit last night at the opera intermission was entirely insufficient."

"Completely," Lady Winthrop agreed with a nod that didn't so much as ruffle her honey-colored curls.

"Oh, lovely," her protégé declared. "Then you won't mind if I spirit Lady Imogene away for a good coze, as well."

Imogene racked her brain for a way to refuse. She highly doubted Elisa and Kitty would appreciate her making a new friend of the beautiful Lady Everard. But to her surprise, Lady Winthrop looked nearly as determined to prevent the conversation.

"No need for you to leave," she assured the girl, reaching out to pat the seat of the chair nearest her in obvious invitation. "I'm certain Lady Widmore would be delighted to have you and Imogene join us."

Her mother's response dampened Imogene's hopes. "Surely there's no reason to bore these two young ladies with our stories. Imogene, why don't you show Lady Everard the song you composed?"

"Oh, how marvelous!" Lady Everard proclaimed, stepping forward.

Imogene was certain her mother was trying to help her and Lady Everard become better acquainted, but she was afraid the effort would be wasted. Unfortunately, she knew what was expected. She kept her smile in place. "Certainly, Mother. If you'd join me, Lady Everard."

The girl followed Imogene out the door. Imogene thought she'd start talking immediately. From the way she'd enthused about every statement in the withdrawing room, she could easily be one of those endlessly chatty girls who could not be content with companionable silence.

But Lady Everard said nothing as they descended the stair. In fact, Imogene caught her glancing about wide-eyed, as if the Devary household was not what she had imagined. Imogene supposed the pale blue walls, soaring ceilings, polished wood furnishings and dusky Oriental carpets were enough to impress. But surely an heiress and baroness in her own right was used to such finery.

Imogene led the girl into the music room, stopping to watch her gawk at the elegance of the Adam-style ceiling with its fanciful swirls, then headed for her piano in the corner.

Her companion put out a hand to stop her as Imogene reached for her sheet music.

"You needn't go to any trouble," she said. "I merely wished to speak to you in private about my cousin."

In private? Something must be wrong. Imogene felt as if a rock had dropped into her stomach. She let the music fall back onto the rack. "Has something happened to Vaughn?"

Samantha frowned, withdrawing her hand. "Vaughn, is it? That didn't take long."

"He gave me leave," Imogene said, face heating.

Her lips were tight. "After you threw yourself at him."

Imogene's head jerked up. "I did no such thing."

"You most certainly did," Samantha said. "I heard you at the ball. You asked *him* to dance."

Imogene swallowed. "Well, yes, but I had cause."

Samantha put her hands on her hips, fists crumpling the fine muslin. "Really? I have it on good authority you never met until that night. He didn't even know your name until Cousin Richard told him."

So Vaughn hadn't known who she was when she'd approached him. He'd chosen to dance with her merely because she intrigued him.

"You have no call to smile like that," Samantha scolded her. "This is serious."

Imogene sobered and nodded. "I can see you are concerned. But I promise you I would never do anything to harm your cousin."

Samantha shook her head. "I'm not sure I believe you. That's why I encouraged Lady Claire to accept your mother's invitation and bring me with her on this visit. I've heard the stories. What was it—four rejected last Season?"

The four proposals had been easy to refuse. They had come from men who would never meet her family's needs. She could still only hope Vaughn would meet those requirements. But she had no intention of explaining that to Lady Everard.

"A lady," Imogene replied with a lift of her chin, "does not discuss such matters."

Samantha broke away from her to pace about the room, skirts protesting her sharp movements. "Well, I haven't been a lady for long, but it seems to me that someone who encourages a gentleman only to drop him when his heart is engaged isn't entitled to the name lady either."

Imogene gripped the edge of her piano. "You presume a great deal for only having met me."

Samantha paused to glare at her. "And you presume a great deal if you think I would allow you to use my cousin. As it is, I must ask you to stop encouraging him. Vaughn has been through enough."

Enough? What had happened to him? Had he loved another and been rejected? She could not imagine any woman so heartless. And she was surprised to realize she may have misjudged Lady Everard, as well. The girl was clearly concerned about her cousin, and not, Imogene thought, because she wished another beau in her quiver.

"Please don't concern yourself," Imogene replied. "I have the utmost respect for your cousin. He is a talented poet. What lady wouldn't be thrilled by his attentions?"

Her brow cleared, and she steepled fingers against her lips. "Oh, dear. I'm so sorry. Have I gotten this backward, then? Is he pursuing you?" When Imogene refused to answer, she shook her head. "He flirts with every lady, you know. That's how he earned the reputation for being a rake. I know from experience that you mustn't think you are special to him."

Imogene flinched. No! His cousin was wrong; she had to be! Imogene hadn't realized how much she'd come to enjoy Vaughn's company until that moment. She liked when his gaze lit at the sight of her; she liked the way his husky voice murmured her name. She loved sharing confidences, working together to solve a greater problem, to make a difference. And she thought he felt a similar enjoyment when they were together.

She refused to believe he was only toying with her. Lady Everard had been wrong about Imogene's intentions. She must be wrong about Vaughn's, as well.

"My friendship with your cousin is between the two of us," she said stiffly to Samantha. "If you are finished, I'm sure your sponsor would be delighted to have you join her and Mother."

Samantha grinned, reminding Imogene suddenly of

Vaughn, as she returned to Imogene's side. "Leave just when we're becoming acquainted? How silly."

Imogene stared at her. "You are a strange girl."

"I'll take that as a compliment." She picked up Imogene's latest work and glanced over it. "Did you really compose this?"

My, but her ideas jumped from one to the next. Imogene didn't know whether she was expected to order her from the room or share her deepest feelings. "Yes, that's my work."

Samantha stuck out her lower lip. "It looks rather good. I'd love to hear it. Only don't ask me to attempt it. I can manage a song on the pianoforte, but I'm no genius like you obviously are."

Imogene frowned at her. "I don't understand. One moment you're warning me to leave your cousin alone, the next not to take him seriously, and now you praise me?"

Samantha set the music down. "I tend to speak my mind, a mortal failing in society, I'm learning. And I would be delighted to be your friend, but I'm concerned your father's dark deeds might come between us."

Realization struck, and Imogene gasped. "So you're the one spreading the rumors!"

Samantha frowned. "It's not a rumor. It's the truth. Your father challenged mine to a duel, and mine came away dead."

Imogene felt cold all over. "My father would never kill anyone."

Samantha's face was sad as she tidied the pages. "I said the same thing about mine when Vaughn first told me my father dueled. But that's what a duel means, you know. Two men fight until honor is satisfied, and sometimes honor is only satisfied when the other man is dead."

"I understand the meaning of a duel," Imogene told her. "But you're wrong. My father doesn't duel."

"It seems to be an aberration," she agreed, gaze remaining on the notes as if they somehow held answers. "As far as I can tell, he always had my father deal with anything he wanted settled in that way."

"That can't be true," Imogene argued. "You don't know my father."

She glanced up then with a frown. "Certainly I know your father. He visited Dallsten Manor where I live in Cumberland every summer. A shame he never brought you. I imagine we could have had some fun."

Imogene shook her head, not to deny the suggestion but to clear the thoughts that swirled around her like crows intent on carrion. "My father never spoke of Cumberland. And he certainly never spoke of some anger for your father that would have caused him to challenge him to a duel."

Her face scrunched. "I was certain I had all that right." She leaned closer. "They don't like to worry me, but I overhear my cousins talking, and I can put together the pieces."

"Well, you obviously put them together in the wrong order this time," Imogene said.

She straightened. "Did I? I'm fairly sure Vaughn sees the same. This issue has been his burning purpose for weeks—to learn your father's reasoning and expose him. He must have discussed this with you, considering you're friends and all."

Imogene felt behind her for the wall, braced her shaking limbs against it. Could this be true? Could that have been Vaughn's purpose all along? His questions, to her, to her father, must take on a whole new meaning if Lady Everard spoke the truth.

He had confessed he thought to use Imogene to reach her father, but she had assumed that was to learn the truth about his uncle's death, not to seek proof of his theory that her father was the cause!

"We've spoken about your father's death," Imogene told Samantha. "But I can't accept your word that my father is a killer. You can't understand him like I do."

Samantha sighed as if she pitied Imogene. "I didn't really know my father until after he died. Be thankful you still have an opportunity to help yours."

She was extremely thankful. Because they had to be wrong, all of them. And she'd prove it, if it was the last thing she did.

Vaughn had one goal that day before meeting with Imogene: to discover the marquess's whereabouts. After leaving Imogene at the opera, he'd attempted to intercept one of the men to whom Eugenie Toussel had spoken. As a man, they had left the opera after the intermission, in some cases abandoning their families. Even the French émigré's box was empty as the second act began, as if she had fled after Vaughn and Imogene had accosted her.

Whose summons had they received? Whose call did they hurry to answer? He feared it was the marquess's.

He also feared none of them would be willing to discuss the matter the next day. But he tried to locate a few of them, and his card was refused at every door. However, though the marquess and his minions might have gone to ground, the toad would find it more difficult to go missing, Vaughn thought, given the fellow's personality and presence in society. Vaughn located him easily at Tattersall's.

The Horse Repository was thronged with gentlemen, as it generally was the day before an auction. They came to look over the latest acquisitions, hoping to determine which riding horse, hunter or racer to bid on. The toad was standing under the arched portico, hands behind the back of his navy coat as if making sure he wouldn't touch the bay mare being paraded past by a helpful groom.

"Good morning, my lord," Vaughn drawled, strolling up to him. "Care to explain your remarks last night?"

The fellow shook his blond head, not even bothering to meet Vaughn's gaze as he dropped his hands to the sides of his chamois breeches. "Surprised you'd approach me without the lady to fight your battles."

Heat licked up him, but he held himself calm. "And here I thought you'd apologize for your churlish behavior, not compound it."

He snorted, and the horse shied. Dismissing the groom with a wave, he turned to Vaughn, blue eyes colder than the breeze blowing through the compound. "Did it only for the lady. Father's too important to my future."

"Indeed." Vaughn drew closer. "Promised to elevate you for services, is that it?"

The toad glanced in either direction as if to make sure all the men nearby were otherwise engaged, then leaned in. "Look, you insignificant insect," he said, glaring down at Vaughn from a few inches above him. "I've worked too hard to gain the marquess's trust. Won't jeopardize it for a puffed-up poet who can't remember to keep his blade in his sheath."

Vaughn raised a brow. "Why, my lord, you have hidden depths."

"More than you know." He took a step back. "Now, sir, conversation's done. Do not approach me again."

Vaughn watched him stalk off. No more stilted conversations? What a pity. But he still had one clue. For some reason, Eugenie Toussel had invited him and Imogene to Vauxhall tonight. He intended to be there and to make sure Imogene stayed away. If the marquess and his followers were massing, Vaughn wanted Imogene safely elsewhere.

Unfortunately, his search for answers had made him twenty minutes late for his appointment with Imogene. He could only hope she'd be forgiving. As he stood on the steps of the Devary home, he adjusted his top hat and brought the knocker down on the polished door.

The familiar footman opened the door, an unmistakable sparkle in his eyes.

"Mr. Vaughn Everard to see Lady Imogene," Vaughn told him.

"Mr. Everard," he said, triumph in every syllable, "is once more unwelcome in this house." And he slammed the door in Vaughn's face.

Vaughn frowned. Interesting. How had he become *persona non grata* again? He took a step back and eyed the house. It was possible that Lady Imogene had tired of his company. She may have realized he was not the hero she had imagined and wisely severed their connection. But given his suspicions about her father and the man's actions in the park the day before, it was equally possible she was in danger. He would not leave until he knew.

He considered again climbing to the withdrawing room, but he could not be sure of finding her there and he wasn't about to risk hanging for breaking a window. He could resort to the *Romeo and Juliet* gambit again but only if he could determine which room she occupied and whether she was alone.

He descended the stairs and crossed the front lawn, a tiny scrap of green against the white of the house. The windows facing him, he was fairly certain, belonged to a sitting room for receiving casual visitors. He no longer qualified even for that, it seemed.

He turned the corner and loped down the side yard, the gravel of the carriageway crunching beneath his boots. Someone must be preparing for dinner that evening, for the savory smell of roast beef wafted from the kitchen below the house.

From his previous visits, he thought the first window on this side was the music room. His guess was confirmed when the strains of a song fell on him like a soft summer rain. He paused to listen.

She was playing with her usual precision, and he could imagine her at the keys, face alight with joy, body poised as if to run a race. This song was different somehow, as if she was pouring a part of herself into it. He recognized the melody and was surprised as the words came to his lips.

"How can it be that I should gain an interest in the Savior's blood?"

He remembered where he'd heard it. His uncle had disappeared last Christmas Eve, and Vaughn had been hard-pressed to locate him. It wasn't the first time. Uncle had the habit of falling into a dark mood, a period when nothing seemed to soothe him. Vaughn would rise one morning and find him missing, with no note of explanation, no word of where he'd gone or when he'd return. Vaughn would generally run his uncle to ground somewhere in London within a few days to a week.

This time had been near St. Mary's Church in Marylebone, a few days after Christmas. Uncle had been walking along, humming the melody and occasionally breaking into song. Vaughn had been certain he was in his cups and had dragged him home to sleep it off.

But his uncle was never the same after that. He'd lost interest in his usual haunts, spent time with old friends trying to convince them to change, as well. It was as if something he'd seen, something he'd heard had affected him.

"Amazing what faith can do for a man," Uncle had said when Vaughn had finally questioned him about his altered outlook. "Come with me to services at St. George's next Sunday and see."

Vaughn had refused. This so-called faith was merely Uncle's latest whim, he was certain. Vaughn had chosen notoriety and infamy over propriety. Such choices could not be unmade, could they?

The final notes faded, and he felt something touch his cheek. He wiped at it and realized his glove was damp. A tear? Oh, but he was slipping. He hadn't cried since the day his father had given up on him and given him away.

But he couldn't lose his chance now. As another melody drifted from above, he bent, snatched up a handful of gravel and tossed it at the pane. The music stopped, and he waited.

No face appeared at the window.

He scooped up another handful and threw it.

Still nothing.

"I know you're there," he called.

The sash flew up, and Imogene glared down at him. Her curls were barely contained by a green ribbon the color of her eyes, and her cheeks were turning red. "Hush! Oh, hush! Do you want to have to take on the footmen again?"

Vaughn put one hand on his heart. "I would brave any danger for a moment with you."

Her eyes flashed like a sword in the morning light, and he felt the mortal wound. "Stop," she said. "I know what you want, and I won't let you hurt my father. Go away now before I set Jenkins on you."

Chapter Eleven

Vaughn felt as if someone had siphoned the air from his lungs. "Forgive me," he managed, "but what do you mean?"

Imogene glanced either way, then leaned farther out the window, until her face was only a few feet above his. Anger danced in her gaze, but he saw something else, too—pain and disappointment. Though he ought to be immune to the look after receiving it so many times from his father and grandfather, it cut into him as easily as a knife through butter.

"Your cousin was here," she hissed. "She told me what you suspect of my father. You're wrong, and I won't have any part in making you think you're right."

She could only mean Samantha. What was the girl thinking? They had no proof; any accusations were calculated to have just this effect. Small wonder Imogene suddenly loathed him.

"Let me in, please, Imogene," he said. "I can explain. I would never do anything to hurt you."

For a moment, he thought she would relent. Her face softened, her lips trembled as if holding back words with effort. Then she stiffened her shoulders, pulled back and braced both hands on the sash.

"I'm afraid we have nothing more to say to each other, sir. Don't bother calling again. And leave our rocks on the ground." The sash slid down with a bang that rattled the pane.

Anger poked at him, forced him back from the house. Condemned men were allowed to speak, sometimes from the very steps of the scaffold! But then, his thoughts, his words, had never held any value to his father and grandfather. Perhaps that's what had first driven him to put them down on paper. He'd been gratified when his poems proved popular. It was as if the world had finally acknowledged something of worth in him. He should not let one harsh word from Imogene, and a justified one at that, make him forget that now.

She clearly expected him to take himself off, perhaps lick his wounds. She persisted in seeing him as a gentleman who would react in a civilized fashion. He could prove otherwise. He could show her exactly how a rake and a scoundrel behaved.

But something inside him cringed at the thought as he walked away from the Devary house. Invisible hands pressed against his chest, weighing him down. He barked a laugh as he came to the corner of Park Lane, earning him a concerned frown from a passing gentleman.

It seemed that, once awakened, his conscience refused to be stilled. How ironic, and how inconvenient. His drive for revenge had led him toward honor instead. Unfortunately, the marquess must be stopped before someone else died. He would simply have to find a way to protect Imogene in the process.

Even if she refused to help him or let him help her.

His mood was dark enough that the footman scrambled aside as Vaughn entered Everard House. The fellow recovered sufficiently to point him toward the withdrawing room, where his cousin was entertaining a visitor. At least that was good news, he reflected as he climbed the stairs.

Even with Lady Claire as sponsor, some of the families of the *ton* hesitated to welcome Samantha into their midst. The fact that Uncle had kept her a secret, cloistered away in Cumberland until his death, made them doubt her legitimacy. And Uncle's own reputation made them doubt her respectability. The ladies were slowly coming round, as her invitation to the Mayweather ball indicated, but she still had much to do if she was to fulfill the requirements of her father's will and be welcomed in all the homes that had refused him entrance.

Of course, he supposed she could have a suitor. The gentlemen of London seemed more disposed to like her, and Vaughn didn't think her fortune was the only lure. From her beauty to her vivacious character, Samantha Everard was a rare handful.

But the man seated beside her on the sofa did not warrant her attentions.

"What are you doing here?" Vaughn demanded, stopping in the doorway.

At his question, Lady Claire glanced at him from her seat by the fire, and Samantha turned, wide-eyed, pulling her fingers from the grip of the toad. "Cousin Vaughn, what's wrong?"

Her visitor didn't rise or even look in Vaughn's direction. "Here to see Lady Everard. No business of yours."

Vaughn strode into the room. "Certainly it's my business if a worm has the temerity to crawl across my apple." He felt his hand going for the blade he had once worn at his side and closed his fist on air instead.

"Vaughn!" Samantha hopped to her feet, hands on her hips. "I am no one's apple!"

"That is quite enough," Lady Claire said, but Vaughn was surprised to find her look directed at Samantha instead of him. "My lord," she said smoothly with a smile to their guest, "please forgive our theatrics." She rose. "Mr. Everard, a word with you in private, if you please."

So once again he was to be silenced. Vaughn felt himself stand taller and met her look prepared to fight. Those cool blue eyes were remarkably heated, and he knew his Cousin Richard would not thank him for taking on his betrothed. She jerked her head toward the corridor. With a shake of his own head, Vaughn followed her.

"He's beneath her," he said as soon as they were outside, and he didn't much care that the fellow could likely hear him.

Lady Claire stepped right up to him. She was tall for a woman, so she didn't have to tip back her head to meet his gaze. "Of course he's beneath her," she said in a furious whisper. "Did you know he once encouraged Adele and then rejected her when her father's death robbed her of a dowry?"

Vaughn raised his brows. "No. I didn't realize there was a connection between the families except the proximity of their estates. But if he courted Adele, that only means he's too old for Samantha."

"There we agree, as well," Claire said. "Poor Adele cannot abide the sight of him, and I cannot find fault with her arguments. Unfortunately, Samantha will hear none of it. That's why I need your help."

"My help?" Vaughn cocked his head. "Shall it be swords at dawn or pistols at midnight?"

He thought she would take umbrage, but her crystal gaze merely narrowed. "Tempting. But that might provide the gossips with too much fodder." She tapped a long finger against her cheek. "Perhaps you could merely be uncivil, as you are so good at doing."

Vaughn chuckled. "You'd like me to goad him sufficiently to make him leave?" He bowed to her. "My dear, it would be a pleasure."

She smiled. "I could not, of course, allow a guest to be abused. But I do believe we are in need of refreshments, and I will probably have to speak to our cook, Mrs. Corday, directly to ensure they are appropriate for such an honored gentleman."

He'd always appreciated how that dulcet voice could turn iron with sarcasm. "No doubt."

She leaned closer. "You have five minutes. Do not disappoint me."

Vaughn grinned as she sashayed down the corridor. Then he strolled back into the withdrawing room.

"Lady Winthrop has gone to see about refreshments," he announced to the pair seated on the sofa. "I promised to serve as chaperone while she was out."

Neither of them looked overjoyed by the thought. The toad's back stiffened even further, if that was possible. And a thundercloud was building on Samantha's fair brow.

She turned to her companion. "Forgive me, my lord. I don't know what's gotten into my family of late." She offered him a smile that dripped with honeyed sweetness. "Being a man of the world, I'm sure you understand."

Of the world? As far as Vaughn knew the bumpkin shuttled between London and the family estate in Cumberland. It was his younger brother who traveled the globe in search of adventure. Considering what the brother had waiting for him at home, Vaughn could hardly blame him.

"Course," the toad said, leaning back. "Don't look down on you for your relatives."

Samantha's smile faded. "What's that supposed to mean?"

"Yes, my lord," Vaughn said, going to stand by the mantel where he could keep an eye on both of them. "Do you imply the name of Everard is somehow less than yours?"

Their guest raised a brow and glanced from Vaughn to Samantha as if surprised anyone would question the matter. "Earldom to barony. No comparison."

Samantha looked mollified by the answer, but Vaughn pressed his point. "So you value position more than character. Better a wicked earl than a noble baron?"

Now the fellow frowned. "What's character got to do with the matter?"

Samantha sat back. "Oh, my lord, everything!"

Vaughn smiled at her response. He was certain her sponsor and Imogene would agree.

The toad clearly had other ideas. "Goes without saying a gentleman is noble. No need to argue the point."

Vaughn straightened away from the fire. "Ah, but I love a good argument. Nothing like sharpening the wit to engage the senses. I contend that a man may be nobly born yet still live as a scoundrel."

Wentworth's upper lip curled. "You would know."

Samantha swallowed as she glanced at Vaughn, as if expecting him to make a scene.

Vaughn obligingly took a step forward. "Indeed I

would. I have the very evidence before me that a nobly born gentleman can contort himself into a craven cur who courts young ladies in a vain attempt to prove himself a man."

The toad rose, eyes narrowing, and Vaughn widened his stance, ready for the challenge. Samantha hopped to her feet and stood between the two of them, facing her guest. "What an interesting tale. He's a poet, you know. Such an imagination."

She turned her back on the fellow a moment to glare at Vaughn, but when she returned her look to the toad again, her voice had warmed. "But a gentleman of your renown surely has no time for tales." She took his arm and led him toward the door. "Or for prolonged visits. And I have much to do if I'm to be ready for our evening."

"Course," he said, his voice equally warm. "Until then." He bowed over Samantha's hand, laying a kiss against her knuckles. Straightening, he sauntered out the door.

"I can hear your teeth grinding," Samantha informed Vaughn as she turned.

Vaughn forced his jaw to relax. "Why would you encourage that cretin?"

She raised her chin. "I don't think he's stupid. He's handsome, wealthy and, as he pointed out, the heir to an earl. And he lives right next to us in Cumberland."

So that was the attraction. Samantha loved her home—the chance of a marriage that would return her so close to it would hold a definite appeal. "A gentleman needs more than geographic affinity to be a husband," Vaughn pointed out.

"Well," she returned, "I think he has potential."

"As a door stop." Vaughn shook his head. "You must know you were meant for better."

"Perhaps." She dropped her gaze, and even in his frustration he could hear her sigh as she returned to her seat.

Frowning, he went to sit beside her. "What's this? Did the belle of the ball lose her luster?"

She managed a smile. "Don't you find all this a bit… tedious? The balls, the routs, the musicales. They all seem to run together after a while."

Vaughn tweaked one of her golden curls. "Spoken like a true campaigner. I'd be more inclined to believe you, infant, if you'd been at this more than a few weeks."

Her smile widened. "Perhaps I overstated. But I am determined to meet the requirements of Father's will, and for that I must have one more eligible offer before the Season ends."

"You have another month or more," Vaughn said. "You needn't curry the attentions of that creature."

She made a face, hands rubbing at the muslin of her gown. "He isn't a creature. But I'll leave Adele at home tonight when we go to Vauxhall so she won't have to stomach his company."

Vaughn rose, unable to keep his seat. "Vauxhall? The toad is taking you to Vauxhall tonight?"

Samantha clapped her hand over her mouth as if to hold back laughter at his name for her suitor, but she nodded.

This could not be good. He had to dissuade her for her own safety. He crossed his arms over his chest.

"You intend to allow him to take you off to the pleasure garden in the dark? That's asking for trouble."

She dropped her hand, gaze turning mulish. "It's perfectly acceptable! Everyone goes to Vauxhall!"

Especially tonight of all nights, it seemed. "Too true," Vaughn admitted. "For the price of a few shillings, any man, woman or child, be they saint or hardened sinner, can have the pleasure of viewing the gardens."

Samantha raised her chin a notch. "I'll have you know the Devarys are going to be there. Lord Wentworth said so. Even Lady Imogene will attend!"

Something tightened inside him, and he turned for the fire. He'd have to protect both Samantha and Imogene, then. "Interesting," he drawled, putting a hand on the mantel to keep his fingers from clenching. "If Vauxhall is such a marvelous place, perhaps I should accompany you."

"Oh, no!" Samantha leaped to her feet and closed the distance between them. "I will not have you picking fights. You leave my suitor alone!"

"Delighted," Vaughn returned, straightening to meet her look for look. "So long as you do the same with Lady Imogene."

She stilled. "Oh. She told you I was by, is that it?"

The pain of their parting was still lodged inside him. "She refused to see me. Ever again, it seems. What exactly did you say to her?"

Samantha wrung her hands and began to pace the room. The long strides, so like her father's—and his, for that matter—snapped the muslin against her ankles. "I may have mentioned our suspicions about her father."

Vaughn shook his head. "Why? You'd only anger her, and if she takes the tale to her father, he may well gain the advantage over us."

She glanced up. "I never thought of that."

Vaughn threw up his hands. "At the moment you don't seem to be thinking at all! What possessed you to approach Lady Imogene to begin with?"

She stopped, dark eyes begging for his understanding. "Well, you were spending an inordinate amount of time with her."

"Because she is the surest way to her father."

Now her voice pleaded, as well. "Was that the only reason?"

How could he answer her? He scarcely knew his feelings for the fair Imogene. "If I had other reasons, they are no affair of yours."

Her voice was small and quiet. "Perhaps not. But I thought you should be spending more time with me."

Vaughn narrowed his eyes at her. "I see. So because I didn't dance attendance on your every whim, you decided to risk all our plans along with our chance to uncover the marquess's secrets and expose him to the world."

"I'm sorry!" Her face was puckered. "You offered for me! I thought, I hoped… Oh, never mind!" She pushed past him and ran from the room.

Vaughn did not follow her. This was one issue she'd have to work out herself. Samantha was a darling girl, but surely she knew he had not been serious in his offer of marriage. How could he offer that to anyone? Marriage required commitment and uncompromising devotion. He knew some couples who thought otherwise, but they made a mockery of the institution, just as his father and mother had made a mockery of their marriage. When he married, if he married, he intended it to last forever.

And there lay the rub. He was too like Uncle. Little held his interest for long. He craved challenges, new experiences. He'd never met a woman who could understand those needs, much less help him meet them.

Lady Imogene's face came to mind, but he pushed

the thought away. He was beginning to think she had the stamina and creativity to match him. But she deserved a better man, and they both knew it.

Still, attending Vauxhall could prove useful. He'd escort Samantha and keep an eye on the toad. But his true purpose in attending had little to do with either of them. He feared danger walked the moonlit paths of the pleasure garden. He would not allow it to harm his cousin or Imogene.

Imogene, however, had considered asking her mother to forego this trip to Vauxhall. Her heart was still bruised by the afternoon's events. Sending Vaughn away had been the hardest thing she'd ever done. As he'd gazed up at her, she'd thought for a moment that she'd wounded him, that her opinion meant more to him than she'd have thought possible. He'd looked so penitent, so concerned, she'd nearly relented. Perhaps if she'd let him explain she would learn his cousin was wrong.

But no! She had to be strong. It was abundantly clear that he meant to harm her father. By his own admission he was using her to that end. He cared nothing for her. And so she could not afford to care for him. By spending these past few days focused on him she had failed in pursuing her goal to help her family. She must marry a man who would uphold the family honor. Vaughn, it seemed, would never fit that role, so she needed to find other prospects.

Besides, something was going to happen here at Vauxhall. Hadn't Madame Toussel invited Imogene and Vaughn to attend tonight? French spies could be stalking the walkways. Unfortunately, she wasn't sure how she'd know.

Vauxhall was always crowded. Anyone with a few shillings could gain entrance, stroll along the lantern-lit paths and sway to the music of the orchestra. She and her family had season tickets, and her father loved attending the concerts and events there.

She found herself missing him again as she sat beside her mother behind the table in their private box on the ground floor of one of the rows of boxes. Jenkins and one of their under footmen stood at the entrance and rear of the box to protect and serve them, their black coats and powdered wigs as elegant as the romantic oil painting of a ruined castle that hung on the back wall.

To the left of the box, the two-story tower of the Rotunda was lit from top to bottom with more than a hundred lanterns. Under their glow on the open platform of the upper story musicians plied their bows across cellos and harps or ran their fingers up and down flutes and horns.

Dozens of people milled on the grass below, shiny satins mixing with soft cotton. She'd sighted Lady Everard on Lord Wentworth's arm, her lovely faced flushed with pleasure, and Imogene had forbid herself to think of Vaughn. Three gentlemen stopped by to pay their respects, and she'd regretted having to refuse their requests to promenade. She simply wasn't up to it.

Other people she knew well were thronging the supper boxes that curved around the Rotunda. More strolled up and down the Grand Walk, past groves of elm, lime and sycamore and statues of famous composers and mythical figures. As twilight progressed, thousands of lanterns would be lit, setting the space to sparkling.

Her father had loved the spectacle, particularly the fireworks that exploded each night. Tonight, as if to match her feelings, the sky above was cloudy, threatening rain, and there was a chill in the spring air that made her wish she had brought a shawl to cover her white satin gown.

From the chair beside her, her mother reached out to squeeze her gloved hand. "You've been in the dismals all afternoon, dearest," she murmured over the strains from the orchestra, the rise and fall of conversation around them. "What's wrong?"

Imogene couldn't prevent her sigh. "Mr. Everard was not the man I thought. I find that rather sad."

Her mother gave her hand another squeeze. "I'm very sorry to hear that. I was willing to give him time to prove himself."

"So was I," Imogene replied, but another sigh slipped out before she could stop it.

Her mother drew back. "Now, then, you made the right decision in coming tonight, even if your father had to cry off. Here at Vauxhall we have the lovely opportunity to observe the gentlemen on parade."

Despite her feelings, Imogene laughed. "Oh, Mother, that sounds as if we're going shopping!"

"And so we are," her mother said with a determined nod, "for the perfect gentleman for you. If we are successful, by the time Mr. Everard shows his face again, you will be entirely too busy with your other suitors to pay him any mind."

Imogene smiled, but she had a feeling it would take a great deal more than a marvelous Vauxhall evening to remove Vaughn Everard from her heart.

Chapter Twelve

As if Imogene's mother sensed her hesitation to start looking for another suitor at Vauxhall, she leaned closer and offered Imogene a conspiratorial wink. "Let's make a game of it. I'll go first." She straightened and raised her chin as she gazed out over the passing crowd. "There, by the statue of Mr. Handel, the gentleman with the bronze waistcoat."

Imogene glanced that way with a frown, but she easily spotted the man who had caught her mother's eye. "Lord Sidney Pallisher. He's gone through his entire inheritance, Elisa told me, and is looking for a wealthy bride."

Her mother immediately refocused. "The fellow in the green coat, then, escorting the young lady to better hear the music."

The man in question bent to whisper something in the girl's ear. She jerked to a stop, slapped his face and marched back the way she had come.

"No," Imogene and her mother chorused.

Imogene laughed again. "Not so easy, is it, Mother? Let me try." She glanced around once again, seeing gentlemen of every shape and size, smiling, frowning, speaking to great purpose, listening solemnly. One was moving toward her, each step as if intent on claiming her and her alone. His pale hair and white waistcoat contrasted with his tailored black coat and breeches. Like the Vauxhall sky, Vaughn Everard was equal parts darkness and light. His gazed locked on hers. Her breath caught.

"Unfortunately," she murmured, "I'd prefer a gentleman just like him."

As if he knew it, Vaughn bowed before their box. His voice was as warm as the light shining from the bandstand. "I came to view all the wonders of the moonlit garden," he said, "and here I find its two greatest treasures gathered in one spot."

She knew another pair of ladies would have giggled a response, invited him in. Her mother drew out her fan and opened it with a snap. "Dear me, Imogene, I do believe the breeze has come up. I hear nothing but wind."

Imogene bit her lip at the expression on Vaughn's face, half surprise and half affront.

"Sad what passes for conversation these days," she agreed with her mother, trying to keep the laughter from her voice.

He went down on both knees, white silk stockings pressed against the grass, and lifted clasped hands to them. "Fairest of the fair, I beseech you to have pity on me. I have clearly earned your wrath. Tell me how I may make amends."

Imogene's mother leaned closer to her and raised her fan to cover her conversation. "I do see why you favored him, dearest. Are you certain you cannot forgive him?"

Her mother could not know how greatly she was tempted. Those dark eyes implored her to forgive, to forget, not only his transgression but her goals. Yet even as she raised her head, telling herself to be strong, she saw another man making his way through the crowds. She gasped as she recognized him.

"Do get up, Everard," her father said, clapping Vaughn on the shoulder. "You look like a fool."

As Vaughn leaped nimbly to his feet, Jenkins stepped aside from the entrance of the box to admit her father. "Good evening, my dears," the marquess said, coming around behind the damask-draped table. "Sorry I was detained."

Her mother blushed as he bent and kissed her cheek. Imogene moved over a chair so her father could sit between them. Like Vaughn, his coat and breeches were black, but so were his waistcoat and cravat, as if he'd gone into deepest mourning. He offered Imogene a smile that faded as he glanced at Vaughn.

"Still here, Everard? A shame no one seems to care."

Imogene frowned at her father's cruel remark, but Vaughn took a step forward. "My uncle thought you cared, once. For his sake, walk with me. We must talk."

Did he mean to give her father an opportunity to explain, after all? Her father showed no inclination to accept the offer. He leaned back and stretched out his arms, one around her, one around her mother. "I have been talking all day. Tonight, I intend to spend the evening with my two ladies. Perhaps another time."

Vaughn's jaw was tight. "Gladly. Where and when?" Again he made it sound a challenge.

Her father didn't take it that way. "Tomorrow, ten, at my office in Whitehall," he replied. "Now be a good lad and go enjoy your evening, even as I plan to enjoy mine."

Vaughn bowed, but when he straightened he put both hands on the table in front of Imogene, his gaze on hers.

"Lady Imogene," he murmured, "I beg your pardon for anything my family said that might have disturbed you. I hope you know I wish you only the best." He released the table, stepped back and bowed once more, deeper, arm wide as if humbling himself. Then he straightened and strode away.

Her father pulled in his arms. "Singular gentleman. I hope you will understand, Imogene, when I say you are not to see him again."

Imogene, who had been following Vaughn's retreat with conflicted emotions, blinked. "Father?"

Her mother put a hand on her husband's. "Mr. Everard has proven himself a great admirer," she explained. "He seems to care for Imogene."

"No doubt," her father clipped. "She has a sizable dowry to commend her."

She refused to believe that the only reason a gentleman might court her. "Do you see him as a fortune hunter, then, Father?"

His eyes narrowed as he gazed in the direction Vaughn had gone. "I fear Mr. Everard thinks only of himself, a sin of all the Everards I have met."

"That was not my impression," her mother assured him.

"Enough!"

Imogene's mother recoiled at the outburst, and Imogene stiffened in her chair. Her father's face was florid; his hands gripped the arms of the wooden chair so tightly she thought he might rip them from the supports. "I am finished discussing Mr. Everard," he said through clenched teeth. "Imogene will have nothing further to do with him. I trust I have made myself clear."

"Yes, dear," her mother said, settling back in her seat and fluttering her fan before her scarlet face.

"Yes, Father," Imogene said, watching the rapid movement of the painted silk.

"Good," he said, and Imogene thought he was making an effort to calm himself. He took a deep breath and ran his hands back through his hair. As he lowered his arms, Imogene saw one hand was palsied. "Now," he said with a smile as if his outburst had never happened, "let us enjoy the evening."

Before Imogene or her mother could speak, he rose. "There goes Breckonridge. I must have a word with him. I'll only be a moment."

Now was her chance to talk to him without burdening her mother. Imogene scrambled to her feet. "Let me come with you, Father. I'd like your advice on a matter."

Her father put his hand on her shoulder as if to pat it, but she felt him pressing her down, forcing her back into her seat. "I'd be delighted to discuss it with you, Imogene, when I return." He smiled at her mother. "I'll be back shortly."

Imogene frowned as Jenkins stepped aside to let him out, and her father walked away. She could see the man he'd mentioned, the dark-haired Parliamentarian Malcolm Breckonridge, taking his seat in the supper box opposite them, yet her father had walked completely past the man. Instead, the marquess seemed to be heading deeper into the hedged walks.

"I don't understand," Imogene said. "Why promenade alone? He knows how much you enjoy the sights."

"He doesn't want our company."

Her mother's voice was so choked that Imogene immediately shifted closer again. In the shadows under the lip of the box, her mother's face looked white.

"Mother! What's wrong?"

Her mother bit her lips a moment before answering,

as if gathering her dignity. "I'm sorry, dearest. This is a matter between your father and me. I shouldn't trouble you with it."

"Oh, Mother, it's no trouble." Imogene gripped her hands. "Please, tell me what's bothering you."

Her mother's lips trembled as she lowered her voice. "These long hours, this time away from us. I begin to wonder—is there someone else?"

Like Madame Toussel? Could the French émigré have a claim on her father's affections? No, surely he had too much honor to forsake his marriage.

"No, Mother, that cannot be," Imogene said. "Father loves you!"

"Once," her mother agreed with a sniff. "But that was before Charles died and I was unable to bear another heir. Your father knows everything he's achieved, everything entrusted to him, will disappear on his death. I fear the knowledge presses on him. And he won't talk to me."

Imogene wanted to hug her, but she was afraid of attracting undue attention. The last thing her mother needed was an audience of gossips.

"I know, Mother," she said. "Charles's death changed everything. But I have a plan."

Her mother frowned. "What do you mean?"

"You know peerages can be recreated under certain circumstances," Imogene explained. "Our line might die out, but the crown could recreate the marquessate for someone else."

"Certainly," her mother replied, "but I don't see how that does us any good. When your father passes, I'll have my marriage portion, but the estates and house will revert to the crown."

"Not if I marry the right man," Imogene insisted. "If

I choose someone who's clever and popular and from a good family, Father might be able to persuade the king to make my husband the new Marquess of Widmore in the event of his death. The title won't have to fall into abeyance, and we won't have to scrimp to make ends meet."

"Is that why you're so careful in choosing a suitor?" Her mother shook her head. "Oh, Imogene, you mustn't marry for your father's sake or mine."

Imogene touched her mother's cheek, where tears were sparkling. "Now, then, I didn't mean to make you cry! I know this is the right thing to do, Mother. It will ease Father's concerns and ensure that you never lose your place in society. And if I find the right man, he'll be someone I can love, as well."

"Like your Mr. Everard?" her mother asked, watching her.

Once more the words felt like a blow. "Mr. Everard is charming and handsome, but we both know he's unlikely to appeal to the king or Parliament."

Her mother waved her handkerchief. "I would not be so sure. His family may be on the scandalous side, but he is noble. And you cannot deny his popularity."

Imogene's heart gave a lurch, as if in violent agreement. "I don't recall a poet being given more than a knighthood."

Her mother tucked away her handkerchief and faced front as if the matter was decided. "I would leave that to your father."

"Easier said than done," Imogene replied. "First we must convince him to let me see Mr. Everard at all!"

Her mother nodded. "We'll succeed. The matter is too important." She seemed to relax after that. Imogene faced forward, smiling at the people passing, but her mind would not be still. She'd thought she could go forward with her plan without Vaughn, but it seemed her heart was set on him. Convincing him that her father was innocent would be difficult. But she thought convincing her father to allow her to associate with Vaughn would be harder still.

For no matter what she'd said to her mother, she knew something was wrong with her father. His actions tonight reminded her of the days leading up to Charles's death. Then it had been as if he'd lost his heart. What troubled him now?

When friends stopped by to visit with her mother, she knew what she must do. She stood and approached Jenkins as he waited at the entrance to the box.

"I need your help," she murmured.

"Whatever you wish, your ladyship."

She glanced up his tall frame. His steely gaze was out over her head, his shoulders broad and powerful in his black coat. "I need to find my father."

His gaze lowered to hers, darkened. "Vauxhall can be a dangerous place for a lady alone."

Imogene swallowed. "That's why you're coming with me."

She thought he might argue or at least ask her mother's permission before moving. But Jenkins motioned, and their under footman, who had been waiting at the back of the box to help serve supper, took Jenkins's place at the entrance.

"I'll protect you, your ladyship," Jenkins promised. He retrieved the cloak she'd left in his care and draped it about her shoulders.

"You're a rather handy fellow to have around, Mr. Jenkins," she said.

He bowed her ahead of him. "It is my honor to serve, your ladyship. I believe he went that way."

Hoping Jenkins's presence would be enough to deter any ruffians, Imogene slipped out into the Vauxhall crowds.

A short while later Vaughn leaned against a tree and braced one foot back on the bark. This night was not turning out as he'd planned. He hadn't been able to spot Eugenie Toussel or any of the men from the opera in the crowds. Worse, he hadn't managed to convince Imogene of his regrets before the marquess had dismissed him. He intended to make that appointment tomorrow morning, but he could not believe his lordship would be so accommodating.

He'd tried keeping an eye on the three Devarys from a distance, only to see his lordship leave almost immediately. Odd to abandon his wife and daughter when his only stated goal for coming to Vauxhall was to enjoy their company. Vaughn had followed him, but he'd lost the marquess among the shadows, as if the man's evening black had been chosen for concealment.

Vaughn refused to return to his own box where the odious Lord Wentworth was casting sheep's eyes at Samantha. He wanted more to return to Imogene's side, beg her to speak to him, ease her concerns. And that kept him planted with the tree.

He could see the Devary box now, the lords and ladies laughing with the marchioness. While he'd been following her father, Lady Imogene had left. Very likely some savvy fellow had requested her hand in a promenade. Vaughn could picture her strolling through the moonlight, eyes laughing up at the gentleman, lips murmuring the secrets of her heart. If it had been him, he'd have found the perfect spot—a rose arbor perhaps, the perfume scenting the air, or a vantage point overlooking the Cascade, the waterfall that would shortly be lit in shining glory. He'd touch her silky cheek, draw her gaze to his, bend his head and caress those lips with his own.

But it wasn't to be him. He shook off the vision. Moonlit kisses were for rakes who didn't care the cost or besotted gentlemen ready to offer marriage. At the moment he was neither, and it remained to be seen what he would be.

Yet even as he debated going to look for Imogene, another familiar face stole past him: the toad, moving quickly and with surprising purpose. Vaughn frowned. The fellow was alone, and by the way he kept glancing around as if fearing to be noticed, he wanted it that way. Interesting. The toad generally preferred the attentions of his peers. Certainly he ought to be enjoying Samantha's attentions tonight. What forced him from her side? Was he off to meet the marquess?

Vaughn slipped deeper into the shadows and pursued.

He'd thought the rudesby knew where he was going, but the toad's path was a rambling one, taking this turn and that and always away from the most traveled areas. Twice the fellow missed his direction and had to double back, forcing Vaughn to leap into the shrubbery to avoid detection. He did not want to know the state of his cravat. He had just extricated himself from a particularly difficult boxwood when he heard voices.

"'Bout time you got here," a man growled. "Everyone's arrived but you."

"Had to be certain I wasn't followed," the toad declared.

"Well, you failed," another man sneered. "Everard

is right behind you, but never you fear. We'll take care of him."

Vaughn stiffened in the act of flicking leaves from his sleeve. Something else moved in the shadows, sneaking closer to him, and he didn't doubt for a minute that mischief was its intent. Oh, for his blade! But without means of defense, there was nothing for it. Though it went against everything he stood for, he'd have to run.

A man crashed through a shrub and lunged for him. Vaughn twisted out of his way. Another came barreling around the corner. Vaughn ducked under the fellow's swing, used the motion to trip the fellow and darted down a side path. He heard the rattle of their boots on the gravel as they pursued him.

Were these more followers of the marquess? They seemed a harder breed than the gentlemen from the opera. What were they doing in Vauxhall? It wasn't unknown for people to be accosted or robbed if they strayed too far from the beaten path, but these men had implied some sort of secret meeting was about to take place, one they intended to protect. He had to find his way back to the crowds, or he was in trouble.

He glanced behind him. The fitful moonlight showed three men stalking him. As he'd suspected, these were stocky brutes, very likely used to swinging their ham fists to make their points. They were not intending to give him a polite reprimand. They meant for the authorities to find his bloodied corpse.

He darted down another path, hoping to see brighter lights ahead. But someone had doused the lanterns, leaving only the restless light of a cloud-shrouded moon to pick out the hedges in silver. He stumbled along, feeling his way, throwing himself through the darkness.

But try as he might, he couldn't shake the hounds at

his heels. He could hear the shrubs protesting the men's passage, the grunt when a heavy body shoved through a hedge. They seemed to know the dark recesses better than he did. They were moving to cut off his retreat, forcing him away from any chance of help. He didn't have much time.

Lord, if You hear sinners, help me!

He didn't have much faith in his prayer or the kindness of the God who was supposed to hear it. He thought he might easily die this night, and he wondered whether anyone besides his family would mourn him. What was one less poet, after all, one less rake in the world?

Suddenly, a figure in white darted into his path with a flash of moonlight on satin. Even as he tried to pull up his headlong flight, she motioned to him.

"This way!" Imogene hissed, snagging his arm and drawing him into an alcove among the hedges. She wrapped her cloak about them both and held him tightly under the wool. He fancied he heard her heart beating in time with his, an erratic tattoo that thundered with the knowledge that death followed.

But not this night. His pursuers pounded past, and the sounds faded into the darkness until it was only him and Imogene in all the world.

He couldn't see her under the fabric; he could only feel her pressed against him. Thankfulness welled up inside him. It seemed the most natural thing in the world to lower his head and kiss her.

He had kissed any number of other ladies over the years when they'd offered their lips willingly. This was different. She trembled against him, threw her arms around his neck and hugged him closer. He felt as if everything he was and hoped to be was locked against her soft lips, begging for acceptance, for faith, for a moment to see the world as a place of possibilities again.

He'd been running to save his life, but it dawned on him that the greater danger lay here, in Imogene's arms, for here he might lose his very self.

Or find it.

Chapter Thirteen

Imogene melted. She'd never been kissed before, never allowed a gentleman close enough to want his kiss. The warmth of Vaughn's body against hers, the pressure of his lips, the emotions singing through her blood were like nothing she could have imagined. She couldn't think, couldn't move. She only knew she didn't want him to stop.

But stop he did, withdrawing slowly, as if he had relished the touch as much as she had. "Thank you."

A laugh bubbled up. "Do you always thank the ladies from whom you steal a kiss, Mr. Everard?"

"Only when I mean it." She could hear the humor in his voice, as well. He pulled the cloak away, and the cool night air rushed over her. She shivered as she bundled the wool closer.

It was hard to make him out in the shadows of the hedges on either side, but she heard him move to the opening. His silhouette was a darker shape against the night as he turned from side to side to gaze up and down the path.

"It seems they've gone," he reported. "Do you know the way back?"

"Yes," she said, moving to join him on legs that still felt a little shaky. "And I'll show you, after we talk."

He turned, and the moon broke free of the clouds to anoint the planes of his face. "Willing to talk to me now, are you?"

Imogene tapped him on the shoulder. "Yes, but don't you dare ascribe it to that kiss! Something's troubling my father, and I want you to tell me what you know about the matter."

She thought he might protest, but he took her hand and wrapped his fingers around hers, his grip strong, steady. "Let's get you safely back among the living first."

Though disappointment poked at her, she could see his point. She'd been lucky to find this hiding place, and who knew when those ruffians would circle back and discover it, as well. She'd heard about robbers stalking the unwary in Vauxhall, but who would have thought they'd dare to take on someone as formidable as Vaughn Everard? Yet what other explanation could there be for finding him this way?

Now she nodded and allowed him to lead her onto the path, then pointed him in one direction. *Please, Lord, get us back safely!*

She felt a certainty she knew didn't come from inside her. It hadn't been easy following her father into the trees, even with Jenkins' help. She and her footman had set off along the paths of Vauxhall, Jenkins's size and fierce scowl deterring more than casual interest. They'd spotted the marquess down toward the end of the Grand Walk, near the golden statue of Aurora, but even as she'd raised a hand to hail him he'd slipped into the trees behind the statue.

She thought surely Jenkins would balk at following

him, but her footman seemed to think his lordship was in danger as well, so he'd all but dragged Imogene in pursuit. Still, they'd lost her father several times. Only the fact that the taller Jenkins could peer ahead or step up on a stone bench to locate him again had allowed them to trace him so far.

Then they had come to the fork in the path, which she and Vaughn were now approaching. It was a small clearing among the trees, unlit save for the moonlight above, with branches leading in all four directions like points of a compass. Vaughn turned to her expectantly.

"This is where I lost Jenkins," she said. "And my father. I was looking for either of them when I spotted you and those men." She nodded to the path on the left. "That way leads back to the Grand Walk."

Vaughn obediently turned in that direction. Though he strolled along as if out for a constitutional, she could feel the tension in his arm, see it in the way his head was cocked as if listening for sounds of pursuit. Try as she might, all she could hear was the rustling of branches as if the trees were leaning forward to catch a glimpse of them as they passed.

"So you were following your father," Vaughn murmured. "Why would he be out here, so far from the celebrations?"

Imogene shook her head. "I have no idea. Why were you out here?"

He ducked under a low-hanging branch. "I was following your friend Lord Wentworth. It seems the darkness is all too popular this evening."

Lord Wentworth? She would never have suspected him for admiring nature, or art for that matter, especially not after the way he'd sneered at the opera. "Do you think he's in league with the French?"

His grip on her hand tightened, but his voice was light. "I do not believe the French have sunk so low."

Imogene held back a chuckle. The night was so still, she could hardly believe hundreds of people waited somewhere beyond the trees.

"Then I cannot think what my father is doing out here," she said. "And now I've lost him and Jenkins, too!"

His grip eased. "Very likely your footman will be the most annoyed by that fact."

"I know." Imogene sighed. "I'll make it up to him. I just had to find my father, and the only way to do it was to split up. Jenkins fought me on it, but in the end he had to obey. I, however, have a choice."

"What do you mean?" The frown was evident in his voice.

"My father ordered me to have nothing more to do with you."

"Indeed." She couldn't tell if he was amused or annoyed. Somewhere close by came a deep thud, and he froze, putting her behind him as if to protect her from it.

The sky above them brightened with a thousand sparkles that crackled in the air. She could see the glow reflected in Vaughn's hair.

"They've started the fireworks," Imogene realized. "We should hurry."

He picked up speed, feet skimming the gravel as lightly as a bird's. Imogene had to lift her skirts with her free hand and scurry to keep up. Ahead, she saw the lights surrounding the golden statue.

Vaughn pulled up at the edge of the trees. "Wait a moment."

The cannon boomed again, and the sky brightened in silver and white. She could see him peering out into the night, look intent, as if he could frighten off any other ruffians by his gaze alone. If she'd been his enemy, she'd have thought twice. As it was, she wanted to reach out, stroke the lines of worry from his eyes and bring back his smile.

The light faded, and he drew her out onto the walk. Other couples stood arm in arm, but they were far enough away and entirely too absorbed in each other or the spectacle in the sky to notice Vaughn and Imogene.

Still, he released her hand. "You shouldn't be seen with me here. It isn't safe."

She couldn't believe him. Holding his hand had felt far safer than standing here without that support. "What do you mean? Those men, why were they chasing you?"

His gaze kept roaming the area, as if he could find his assailants even now. "I stumbled across a secret meeting. They wanted their secret kept."

She felt colder even as another firework burst above to the murmurs of appreciation from the watching crowd. "They would have beaten you?"

"Very likely they would have killed me."

When she shuddered, he took a step closer. "Make no mistake, Imogene," he said. "You saved my life."

She forced her fears aside and gazed up at him. "Turnabout is fair play, Mr. Everard."

He inclined his head. "Then we are even. I'll walk behind you until we can see the supper boxes, then I'll watch you safety there."

Imogene stiffened. "What about our talk?"

He bent his head and as the night brightened once again, she could see the care lining his face. "Soon. I never lie, remember, Imogene? But do not ask me to risk your life, for I won't do it, not even to save my own."

How could she argue with that? Always he protested

he was no hero, yet always he acted the part. Still, she didn't think he'd appreciate it if she were to point that out.

"Very well," she agreed. "But name a time, a place."

He answered readily enough. "Tomorrow, three in the afternoon, Hyde Park, the path to Kensington. If your father can hide there, so can we."

After making sure Imogene had reached her family box safely, and cringing at the scold her mother delivered, Vaughn returned to the Everard supper box. He wasn't surprised to find Samantha and her sponsor sitting alone. Whatever business the toad had had in the dark recesses of Vauxhall, he knew Vaughn had intruded. Even his exalted consequence would balk at showing his face again tonight.

"We should go," he told Samantha from the grass below the second-story box.

She frowned from her seat. Her pale muslin glowed in the light of the lanterns affixed to the structure, and her hair gleamed more gold than the gilded arch on either side. "Why?" she demanded. "Lord Wentworth will wonder why we've left."

"Rather you should wonder why he abandoned you," Vaughn countered.

She raised her head in defiance, but Lady Claire put a hand on her arm. Vaughn rather thought she resembled the golden statue he'd just passed, all elegant lines and stern features. "What should we know about the gentleman, Mr. Everard?" she asked.

Vaughn felt as if a dozen eyes watched his every move, as people in the other supper boxes shifted seats, focused on the lone figure below. "Nothing I can tell you here," he replied. "I know you came in his coach.

Give me a moment, and I'll hunt up a hack. Then I'll escort you home."

Samantha's look darkened, but he didn't know if it was because of her suitor's actions or his own.

She pouted in the hired coach as they set off for the bridge that would return them to the north bank of the Thames. He knew she would have preferred the dark water crossing, with its hint of adventure, but he was in no mood for company.

Lady Claire seemed more savvy. She sat next to Samantha across from him, her gaze thoughtful in the light of the coach's lanterns. "I believe you were going to tell us a tale, Mr. Everard," she said as the coach bumped over the bridge and the lights of London brightened the interior further. "You know how we enjoy your literary license."

Vaughn smiled. "Very well. There was once a toad who fancied himself a man. He pursued everything fashionable. He had his coat cut by Weston, his boots by Hoby. He tamed his croak to resemble speech, though he tended to forget a word or two along the way."

Samantha giggled.

"He met with surprisingly good success," Vaughn continued, leaning back, "for the *ton* always welcomes the new and novel, and those who entertain are sure to please. His success, unfortunately, went to his feeble mind. He made two fatal mistakes. First, he dared to court the most beautiful girl in all of London…"

"In all the land," Samantha corrected him.

Lady Claire raised a honey-colored brow. "Might as well make it in all the world."

Vaughn inclined his head. "In all of creation, then. As you can imagine, her family took umbrage."

"And where did they take poor Mr. Umbrage?" Samantha asked, laughter in every word.

"To the Tower," Vaughn intoned. "But not, alas, for his impertinence in thinking himself worthy of courting the girl. No, you see his second mistake was more vile. He thought to align himself with powerful men, men interested in toppling the very crown of England."

"No!" Samantha cried, still laughing.

"Yes," Vaughn replied, making his voice hard and unforgiving. "Your suitor has aligned himself with our enemy. I fear whatever they have planned will burst upon us shortly, as clear as the fireworks over Vauxhall and just as explosive."

Samantha sobered, glancing between him and her sponsor. "Do you truly think they mean to attack the king?"

It was evident Lady Claire thought as much, for her look was leveled at Vaughn. "You must go to the authorities."

"And tell them what? That Wentworth seems to have secret business with the marquess? That the marquess is not seen frequently with his family? That he refused to discuss the matter with me? We have no proof."

"We have Monsieur Chevalier's testimony," Samantha put in.

"The word of a man who confessed to espionage and attempted murder—and a foreigner besides." Vaughn shook his head. "No one will take his word against the marquess's."

"What do you intend to do?" Lady Claire asked.

Vaughn shrugged. "He offered to meet me tomorrow."

Samantha stiffened. "Don't go! It's a trap!"

He smiled at her. "Have no fear, infant. The location

he suggested was his office in Whitehall. He won't dare show his hand there."

"If he won't show his hand," Lady Claire pointed out, "you'll likely get no answers either."

"Perhaps not," Vaughn agreed. "But for his friendship with Uncle and the fact that he is Lady Imogene's father, I owe him the opportunity for an explanation."

"Lady Imogene." Samantha said the name as if it soured her tongue. "I think you let her rule your emotions."

Once he would have hotly denied it. Now he wasn't so sure. "And if it was your favor I curried, I doubt you'd complain."

She grinned at him. "Of course not."

"But you won't go alone," Lady Claire said. "I'm sure Richard or his brother would be delighted to accompany you."

This time he did bristle. "I need no one's protection."

"Certainly not," she agreed. "I was thinking of the poor marquess. I would not want to be in his shoes should your suspicions prove true."

As it was, she needn't have worried. Vaughn presented himself at his lordship's office at precisely five minutes to the hour of ten the next morning. It was a narrow suite, with an antechamber at the front, and the paint was none too new. Perhaps the marquess's power was already waning. Or had his superiors suspected him of seeking positions beyond him and decided to keep him under lock and key?

Unfortunately, the secretary working at the desk in the antechamber shook his head.

"My apologies, Mr. Everard, but I haven't seen his lordship this morning and neither has the Prime Minister or the First Lord of the Admiralty. If you find him, please let him know his presence is urgently needed."

Vaughn thanked him and left. He hadn't truly believed the marquess would meet with him. But the fact that his superiors couldn't locate him was more concerning. Had they realized the danger he posed to England, or were the marquess's plans coming to fruition?

Vaughn made the rounds in case news was circulating: White's, Tattersall's, the Exchange, the Horse Guard's parade. Everywhere, life went on as usual. Ladies and gentlemen cheered the lovely May weather, complained about the rising cost of goods and worried that Napoleon would cross the Channel. Indeed, *The Times* reported that all naval ships had been ordered to sea because of rumors that the French squadrons had been seen crossing the Atlantic, perhaps to prey on British territory in the West Indies.

No one seemed aware that as great a danger might lurk in the very streets of London. And there was no sign of the marquess. Vaughn's only hope lay with Imogene.

He found himself in Hyde Park ridiculously early. The park was already crowded—it seemed everyone wanted to enjoy the balmy weather. Nurses walked while their charges scampered around them. Gentlemen rode by on prime bits of horse flesh and ladies strolled arm in arm, sharing confidences.

Yet despite the prosaic scene, he could feel the anticipation rising inside him. He caught himself brushing back his hair under his top hat and straightened his arms at his sides. Why was he always so intent on looking his best, acting his best, in front of Imogene? Despite his intentions, her good opinion had come to mean too much to him. When all this was over, he'd have to determine what to do about the matter.

He reached the path to Kensington and waited under the shade of a tree, fully expecting to see the Devary coach round the corner. Instead, a short time later, he sighted Imogene hurrying along the path, alone, satin ribbons bobbing under her velvet bonnet. Had she no care for her reputation, her safety?

He immediately shook his head at the thought. Had *he* no care? Very likely he was the one endangering both her reputation and her safety by his very presence. He came out from under the tree and went to meet her.

Her peach-colored muslin skirts swung to a stop as she paused. Her cheeks were bright from her walk, and he thought her hands trembled just the slightest as she let her arms fall. "Oh, but I'm glad to see you."

Another time the heartfelt words would have warmed him. Now he could only think of protecting her. "Why did you come alone?" he asked. "Where's your footman?"

She grimaced. "At home. Last night, Jenkins heard Father forbid me to see you, so I doubt he would have been delighted to accompany me today. And he's still put out about me losing him in the garden. He's afraid he'll be discharged. Besides, things are at sixes and sevens at home."

She took a breath as if to steady herself and looked him right in the eye. "My father has disappeared. Tell me you had nothing to do with it."

Chapter Fourteen

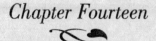

Imogene stood on the grass of Hyde Park, watching Vaughn's face. She was certain she'd see the truth written on it. He wore his emotions so openly, and she believed his claim that he never lied. Still, she lifted a prayer to know the truth.

"I had no part in this," he said, dark gaze on hers. "I promise."

Imogene nodded, feeling as if she could take a deep breath. She'd been fairly confident that she would need more than Vaughn to solve this mystery, and it seemed she'd been right. "Thank you."

"Tell me what happened."

She nodded again, setting off along the path. She had to do something, even if it was only to keep moving! He fell into step, a steadying presence beside her.

"Father never returned to the box last night in Vauxhall," she told him, the breeze darting past her bonnet to touch her heated cheeks. "Mother became sufficiently worried that she sent Jenkins to find him, again, but our footman came back alone and no wiser. Since we'd arrived on our own, we left without him. But Father never came home last night, and he sent no word."

Outside the edge of her bonnet she could see his black-booted legs, matching her stride. His tone was more thoughtful than concerned. "Has he ever behaved this way before?"

"Once." Imogene shuddered, remembering.

He stopped, and she turned to face him, tilting back her head to look up at him. His face was sad, as if he felt her pain. "What happened?" he murmured.

"It was when my younger brother died," Imogene explained. She found her hand gathering up the soft folds of her muslin skirt and forced her fingers to open. "When the physician pronounced my brother dead, Father walked out of the room with no word to Mother and me. He didn't return until the next day. Mother said he needed time to think."

"He would leave you alone at such a time?"

Others—the physician, the vicar—had reacted in a similar manner. Oh, they would never speak against the mighty Marquess of Widmore, but their pitying looks to her mother and their tight-lipped responses about the situation told Imogene they thought her father had been lax in his duty. He was the head of the family. He should be there to console and be consoled. When she had come to realize that each person grieved in a unique way, she'd understood that what her father needed was to escape his duty.

"Mother and I managed," she said. "I think that's when I first appreciated that I had someone else to lean on when I was troubled."

"Your mother," he guessed.

She smiled. "No, my Father, my Heavenly Father." When he frowned, she hurried on. "I know some people don't like to admit that. But it was true for me. Prayer, comfort, they merged into one, and I'll always thank Him for that."

"How old were you?"

Now her fingers were tangled in the ribbons of her bonnet. She dropped them back to her sides before they untied the satin. "Fourteen. Young enough to be impressionable, I suppose. But old enough to suspect why Father left us. He wasn't just mourning Charles. My brother was his last hope for a legacy."

He shifted on his feet as if the idea had never occurred to him. "There are no heirs? No cousins, cadet branches?"

Imogene swallowed the lump that was rising in her throat. "None. Father had the College of Heralds make a thorough search. Unless I do something, my father will likely be the last Marquess of Widmore."

He cocked his head, gaze narrowing. "Unless *you* do something? Why does the lot fall to you?"

She bowed her head, unwilling to see his reaction to her plan. "I'm all that's left. And titles can be recreated. My husband could be the new Marquess of Widmore."

"And what a splendid gentleman he'll have to be."

She winced at the bitterness in his tone. It seemed he could not see himself in the role, and that made it harder for her to envision it.

"He will be," she said defiantly, raising her head once more. "I have every expectation of marrying well."

He was silent a moment, gaze going out over the grass to where the park abutted St. George's Row and a line of houses. A lock of platinum hair teased his cheek. "I imagine you will marry very well indeed. What man wouldn't wish to court someone so talented, kind and beautiful?"

Oh, but her cheeks were heating again. She should

probably thank him for his praise, but the words seemed to stick to the roof of her mouth. Did he know that she'd hoped he might be that man? *Father, I can't confess that. I just can't!*

As if he knew her discomfort, he dropped his gaze to hers. "So we return to your father and his sudden disappearance. Has something happened now? Anything that would drive him to despair?"

"Nothing!" Her cry must have conveyed her fears, for he reached out and drew her into his embrace.

"Easy," he murmured against her bonnet. "I know how worried you must be. I searched every inch of London, it seemed, when Uncle disappeared."

Imogene's throat constricted. "But Vaughn, you found him dead!"

He rubbed his hand along her arm. "I'm certain your father is very much alive. I have a feeling he's been planning this for a long time."

Imogene frowned. "Planning what? To work so hard for his king that he must resort to disappearing for a moment alone?"

"No." He pulled away, though both hands remained on her arms. "I never wanted to burden you with this, Imogene. Believe me, I fought the picture that has been painted of your father. But as each part was sketched, the outline became clearer."

Imogene knew she was trembling. He was so sure of himself, so careful in the way he leaned forward to gaze inside her bonnet, as if weighing whether she could take the confession. He didn't want to tell her. But she had to know. *Help me be strong, Lord!*

"Tell me," she said.

He nodded and dropped his arms to his sides, straightening as if she'd lifted a weight from his shoulders. She could almost see it hanging poised between them, ready to descend on hers.

"It is highly likely," Vaughn said, "that your father is colluding with the French to help Napoleon invade England."

Imogene started to shake her head in denial, but he held up a hand.

"Hear me out. Several things support the theory. For one, it appears he has held secret meetings with a group of men over the past few years."

Imogene made a face. "Those could be efforts for the War Office."

"Possibly," Vaughn allowed, "but doubtful, as my uncle was involved. No one in Whitehall would have trusted him with a secret, and for good reason. He liked stories too well."

"Then why would my father trust him with these so-called secret meetings?" Imogene demanded.

"Because your father thought he could control him. I'm not sure he succeeded. My uncle tended to dash after every whim."

Imogene put her hands on her hips. "Another way you take after him, it seems."

His jaw tightened. "I knew you wouldn't like hearing this. But you did ask."

"And if these meetings were so secret," she challenged, "how do you know about them?"

"I didn't," he replied, "until Uncle died and I first met my cousin Samantha."

Imogene's hands fell. "You never met her until your uncle died?"

"I didn't know she existed until the solicitor told us about Uncle's will. We were all taken by surprise." He shook his head as if the fact still amazed him. "She was raised in Cumberland in an old manor house. That's where your father held his secret meetings and just might be the reason Uncle never told anyone about her."

Imogene rolled her eyes. "So now you'd have my father colluding with your uncle, as well!"

"Oh, they were partners. I have no doubt of that. I was fourteen when they set about rescuing the French from the guillotine." He eyed her. "Do you remember that?"

Imogene shook her head with a frown. "Father helped French aristocrats during the Revolution?"

He nodded. "He and Uncle were quite a pair, into every scrape at times. You would have been six or seven then, so I'm not surprised you didn't know. Most people didn't know. Uncle swore me to secrecy."

"But if they were heroes, why do you think my father is the enemy now?" she begged, finding it all too easy to imagine her father braving death to rescue his friends in France. "If he helped the French aristocrats, why support Napoleon? He isn't exactly a friend to the nobility."

"And neither, I fear, is your father." He started walking again, and she paced him, muslin brushing her ankles with each step. "We do have a scrap of evidence," he explained. "My cousin Richard found a piece of paper remaining from a meeting. It was burned around the edges as if it had drifted from the fire. The men who met in Dallsten Manor in Cumberland wanted to hasten revolution."

Imogene sidestepped a tuft of grass. "But you just said Father tried to help those affected by the French Revolution."

"Not the French Revolution," he corrected her. "These men want revolution in England."

Imogene jerked to a stop. "How could any English-man countenance revolution!"

He stopped as well, hands clasped behind him as if to prevent himself from touching her. "I asked myself that, especially because Uncle seemed to be helping them. I think he saw only the glory of the fight, the idea that all men would be equal. He never particularly liked being a baron."

Did her father like being a marquess? Most of the time it seemed the role came easily to him. But she could remember when he seemed troubled by his duties. "If we were meant to rule," she'd heard him tell her mother once, "then it falls on us to rule well." Surely he would never support the overthrow of the crown!

"My uncle must have disagreed with the effort in the end," Vaughn continued, "for it seems he tried to convince your father to change and was killed for his trouble."

Imogene took a step back from him. "This is the same nonsense your cousin told me," she said, face hot inside her bonnet. "But that's all it is—nonsense."

"I wanted it to be," Vaughn assured her. "But there's more. The physician who returned my uncle's body said there was one witness to my uncle's duel, his valet, Repton. The valet disappeared that night. I tried to find him and failed. It was only after my cousin Richard went to see your father about the matter that we located the man."

"You see?" Imogene cried. "Father helped you!"

He leaned closer again, and the look in his eyes held pity. "Repton was found dead, floating in the Thames."

Imogene recoiled. "So you claim my father killed not once but twice?"

"Three times," he said, as if determined to drive

a blade through her heart. "A footman named Todd showed up at Dallsten Manor after Uncle died. He claimed Uncle had hired him, and his reference said he'd worked for your father. Todd attempted to murder my cousin Jerome and threatened his wife, all so he could steal a porcelain box from us. When we asked a Bow Street Runner to look into the matter, he discovered that Todd had been killed here in London, in the St. Giles area."

Imogene couldn't stand to look at him. She set off up the path for Kensington, feeling as if each step was an attempt to outrun the stories. "So naturally you'd suspect my father," she shot at him as he joined her. "Wealthy marquesses usually stroll through the worst part of London, hoping to stumble upon servants to murder."

Out of the corners of her eyes she saw him spread his hands before his green coat. "He won't meet with me, and he risked your life to avoid my questions. Does that sound like an innocent man?"

"No, it sounds like a hunted man, a man desperate for a moment of peace." She hadn't realized she was walking so fast until her foot caught on a rock and she tripped. His hand was immediately at her elbow, steadying her. She pushed him away.

"You claim you had nothing to do with his disappearance," she said, glaring up at him, "but I begin to think you drove him to it with your accusations!"

His face was pale, his eyes haunted. "I have made none—I have only asked for answers. Why do you think I never spoke of this until now? I have no useful proof to give you or the authorities. I want to be wrong! I would like nothing better than for your father to offer an explanation. But when he runs to avoid facing me, what am I to think?"

"That you have dishonored an innocent man," Imogene insisted. "I know my father. He would never take a life, never work against the king. He's spent his whole life protecting the innocent! You just told me yourself about the lives he saved."

"Lives of the French," Vaughn corrected her. "Those who share his heritage."

Imogene stiffened. "So you see him as tainted, too, simply because his mother was born in the enemy land? For shame, Mr. Everard. You of all people should know that a man should not be judged by the blood that flows through his veins."

He went still, as if she'd slapped him, and immediately she hurt for him. She reached out a hand, but it fell short of touching his silver-shot waistcoat.

"I'm so sorry," she said. "I didn't mean to cast aspersions on your mother."

He puffed out a breath, head bowed so that the brim of his top hat shaded his eyes. "Why not? I certainly cast a number on your father."

Imogene managed a smile. "We really are a pair, aren't we?"

He took her hand and brought it to his lips. The touch only reminded her of the kiss they'd shared the night before. That moment had been full of promise. Now she feared what the future might hold.

His gaze met hers, begged for understanding. "Forgive me for troubling you. I am honored you allow me to breathe the same air, Lady Imogene."

She clung to his fingers as he lowered her hand. "But what are we to do, Vaughn? I cannot believe my father is guilty of the crimes you suspect, and you cannot believe him innocent."

"I am doomed to frustration unless I have proof," he replied, cradling her hand in his.

"Yet who else wonders about his behavior?" Imogene insisted. "His friends, his colleagues at the War Office or the Admiralty?"

"They were urgently seeking him when I stopped by this morning," Vaughn offered.

Imogene shook her head. "Something's wrong. Perhaps there's someone else involved, manipulating things to make it appear my father is to blame."

Vaughn frowned, fingers kneading hers as if he too longed for action. "But who? I know only two gentlemen besides my uncle who might be linked to this. One was Lord Winthrop, Lady Claire's husband, and he is dead."

"And the other?" Imogene pressed.

One side of his mouth turned up. "Lord Gregory Wentworth."

"Oh, surely not," Imogene said, then laughed at the grin on his face.

"Agreed." He sighed and released her. "This is maddening! Someone put that bullet through Uncle's heart, drowned Repton and shot Todd. Three men are dead! That is a fact."

Just then a carriage turned off the main drive and headed in their direction. Imogene threaded her arm through Vaughn's and set them walking toward the palace in the distance.

"Perhaps the three deaths aren't connected," she suggested, amazed she could even discuss such a matter without flinching. "Perhaps we should be looking for three culprits."

"Again you say 'we,'" he replied, tone light.

Imogene squeezed his arm. "You brought these matters to my attention, sir. You cannot expect me to dismiss them."

"Why not? Sometimes it seems everyone else has."

The carriage, a high-perch phaeton drawn by a team of dappled gray horses, was quickly overtaking them. Imogene stepped off the path, and Vaughn joined her.

"The matter concerns you, and therefore it concerns me," she assured him.

"And the fact that I suspect your father is the villain in the piece has nothing to do with your interest."

Imogene waved a hand. "Certainly not. That suspicion doesn't bear additional discussion."

Vaughn frowned and pulled her farther from the path. Imogene glanced at the phaeton in time to see it veer accordingly. Vaughn whipped the hat from his head and waved it wildly. "Ho! There are pedestrians here!"

The horses thundered on. Imogene could see the foam flying from their bits.

"Run," Vaughn ordered. "Now!"

Vaughn seized Imogene's hand and tugged her to the left, back the way they had come. All he had to do was get them beyond the horses' path, and they would be safe. She stumbled on her gown, and he caught her up against him, turning her away from the vehicle. The phaeton rumbled past, the wind whipping her skirts tight to her legs. She clamped her free hand to her bonnet.

Vaughn steadied her, then glanced after the carriage. What had the driver been thinking? Even as he watched, the fellow was slowing the horses, then turning them. He might be coming back to apologize, but Vaughn intended to take no chances.

"Into the trees," he said to Imogene. "Hurry."

She didn't argue. She lifted her skirts and darted across the grass as the carriage picked up speed again.

Vaughn pulled her under the branches of a sycamore and pressed her back against the bark. "Stay here."

"While you are flattened? Never!"

Her gaze was bright, her pointed chin raised like a weapon. The fire in her never ceased to amaze him or to appeal to his heart. "And here I was congratulating myself on your obedient nature," he teased.

She snorted, a decidedly unladylike sound he could grow to love.

Vaughn bent his head to peer inside her bonnet. "Stay here, so I needn't fear for your safety. Please."

Her look remained defiant, but she snapped a nod.

Vaughn ventured out from under the tree. The carriage had passed, rolling back to the more populated areas of Hyde Park. The driver glanced back and for a moment met Vaughn's gaze.

Vaughn's eyes narrowed as Lord Wentworth whipped up his horses and disappeared around the bend. It seemed Vaughn and Imogene had both been wrong. The toad had the capacity to kill. The question was, who was he after: Vaughn or Imogene?

Chapter Fifteen

As soon as he was certain the carriage had gone, Vaughn called Imogene out from under the tree.

"Are you all right?" he asked as she joined him in the sunlight.

She was glancing around the grass with a frown. "Fine. What of our murderous coachman?"

"Fled to plead his conscience, it seems," Vaughn replied. "But I'll feel more comfortable when I know you're safely at home."

"You think this has something to do with my father, don't you?" she challenged, her gaze returning to his.

Vaughn shrugged. "Very likely, I fear."

"Then why," she asked, "would I be safer at home?"

Vaughn raised his brows. "Surely your mother or your servants would prevent him from hurting you."

As if to prove it, she set off toward Mayfair, her skirts whipping, and he could only fall in beside her. "If he's capable of toppling the crown," she said, head bowed as if she watched her path, "he's certainly capable of doing away with his own daughter. But why, sir?"

Before Vaughn could answer, she shook her head. "No. I refuse to see my father's hand in this. I'll return home because Mother may need me, but first I want you to tell me what you intend to do next."

He hesitated. Warned as she was about her father's possible treachery, she might keep Vaughn's plans secret. On the other hand, believing her father innocent, what was to stop her from confessing all?

She glanced his way. Once more her intentions shouted from every inch of her body. Her face was pinched, her shoulders tight, her steps determined. "I won't give you away. You can trust me."

How easily she made the promise; how easily she trusted him. Should he not extend the same courtesy?

"My best chance of learning more at the moment is that driver," Vaughn said, taking her elbow to help her around a bump in the path. "I intend to find him and make him tell me what he knows."

She was looking ahead, so her bonnet hid her face, but he could hear the smile in her voice. "I would almost like to see that. Do remember, however, that Lord Wentworth has some pretensions toward being a gentleman. You cannot clap him in the stocks because it amuses you."

So she also had recognized their would-be assailant. "A shame to be sure," Vaughn drawled.

She glanced his way again, green eyes crinkled up. "You will report on your success, I hope."

"If I learn anything of import," Vaughn promised, "you will be the first to know."

She nodded as if satisfied, and they trudged along in silence a moment. How brave she was, how enthusiastic in her disposition. He could imagine many a young lady would have reacted differently to his suspicions, the galloping horses, the brush with danger: screaming, fainting and crying and wringing her hands. Imogene merely advised him to take care how he pursued his investigation.

They reached the fork in the path, with one side leading to the Oxford Street corner and the other toward the powder magazine.

"I should probably go alone from here so no one sees us together," she said, pausing. "Until we sort this out, I would prefer not to burden my father with the knowledge I had visited with you."

"So you intend to defy him."

She made a face. "I will discuss the matter with him at the first opportunity, I assure you. Until then, being with you is necessary to find him and assure his safety."

"Nobly said," he replied with a smile.

"Stop that," she scolded. "I'm not trying to go behind my father's back. I'm trying to protect all of us. The less my family knows of our involvement, the easier that protection will be."

He could not argue with her on that score. "Of course," he said. "There is one small problem, however."

"Oh?" She glanced up with a frown, and he leaned closer and tugged out the cluster of leaves that had lodged in her bonnet.

"There. All better."

She gazed at him, lips tilted in a smile, cheeks still flushed from their adventures. Her eyes were greener than the spring leaves and just as alive with promise. How could any man resist? He bent and brushed his lips against hers.

Desire and delight poured through him in equal measure. Why was it her and her alone that raised such feelings? Once again he found himself humbled.

She pulled back with a sigh. "Really, Mr. Everard, I begin to think your cook is deficient in her skills and you must be starving. I shall have to come armed with pudding to protect myself if you insist on tasting me every time we meet."

Vaughn laughed as he straightened. "No confection can possibly compare to your sweet lips, my dear."

Her face was even redder. "Go on, now, and be careful. Send me word when we are to meet again."

He took her hand and bowed over it. "Your most devoted servant, Lady Imogene."

Releasing her and straightening again, he watched her walk away. But he wasn't surprised to feel as if she'd taken a piece of him with her.

Despite Imogene's brave words, Vaughn refused to let her out of his sight. He followed at a distance until he saw her reach her home, then set off in search of his quarry. The toad had to be acting under orders from the marquess, but Vaughn knew the fellow wasn't as adept at hiding. He'd been driving a phaeton, very likely his own from the quality of his team. He'd have to return home with it eventually.

Unfortunately, when Vaughn checked at his lordship's town house, he found that the fellow had already returned and left again. Making the rounds of gentlemanly haunts took a while, and the toad had apparently been ensconced in White's for an hour before Vaughn found someone willing to bring him in as a guest. He stalked through the comfortable rooms, searching. Gentlemen at cards glanced up and pulled their coins closer. Gentlemen reading the papers near the fire held the sheets higher, and more than one page trembled around the edges.

His quarry took one look at Vaughn approaching his

wingback chair and washed white. "Afternoon, Ever-ard," he said, though he stuttered on the name.

"How glad I am to see you, my lord," Vaughn said, pulling him to his feet. "I believe we have unfinished business you began in the park this afternoon."

The toad yanked free his arm. "No idea what you're referring to."

"Surely you remember," Vaughn said, aware of more than one gaze now turned their way. "It had to do with a phaeton and pair."

"Not interested," he said, stepping back, booted feet firm on the carpet. "Peddle your wares elsewhere."

Vaughn grit his teeth. Closing the distance, he lowered his voice. "I saw you, you maw worm. I know you were driving that carriage. Why did you try to run us down?"

Panic danced in the toad's eyes. "You're mad."

"You're the one who's mad if you think I'll stand by and watch a lady be hurt."

The panic disappeared like a candle snuffed out, leaving a cunning behind that chilled Vaughn. "The lady means nothing. My future depends on keeping you occupied. If she is hurt along the way, no one but you will weep."

Vaughn's hand moved of its own volition, twisting up into the creature's cravat and lifting the taller man right off his feet. "You will leave the lady alone."

The toad's eyes bulged. "Unhand me!" he rasped.

"I say, that just isn't done," someone murmured close by, and Vaughn heard chairs scrape and fabric protest as bodies moved.

He refused to let the man escape. "What are you planning? Tell me!"

"Never!" He kicked out, and Vaughn dropped him. Staggering, he gasped in a breath.

"I think, sir," said a portly older gentleman who had come up on Vaughn's right, "that you should leave."

"No." The toad held up a hand as he wheezed. "My right. Demand satisfaction."

Gasps echoed around him. Vaughn smiled. "A shame. You refused to answer my questions and give *me* satisfaction. Why should I gratify you?"

His eyes glittered. "Because unless you do, the lady in question will never be safe."

Something tightened inside him. If the toad could attempt to run Vaughn and Imogene down, would he stop at hurting Imogene in the future? Unlikely, given the way he was demanding a fight now. The marquess might have ordered the toad to keep Vaughn distracted, but surely even he would quail at the violence and recklessness of the toad's methods.

Vaughn knew he had to be stopped, yet he hesitated. Once the thought of a duel would have fired his blood. Once he'd have been the one demanding it. Now the thought of wounding a man, even the toad's sad excuse for manhood, seemed a sacrilege somehow.

"What's this?" Lord Eustace, the man who had let Vaughn in, pushed his way to the front of the growing crowd. A sandy-haired fellow in his early thirties, he was a great favorite with the ladies and gentlemen alike for his usually affable ways and skill at whist. "That's no way to talk, Wentworth," he said. "I suggest you apologize like a good fellow."

"A gentleman," the toad said, each word a nail in his own coffin, "has no need to apologize to the lesser orders."

The murmur turned against him now. "A gentleman

doesn't give cause to apologize," Lord Eustace countered.

Vaughn saw the toad grimace, tugging at his ruined cravat. Still, even though he had once craved Society's good opinion, something drove him harder now. "Well?" he challenged Vaughn. "What's it to be? The lady's safety or your own?"

"I'll second you, Everard," Lord Eustace said, blue eyes narrowing. "I don't much fancy a fellow who threatens a lady."

"Here, here," someone else put in.

"Hardly a lady," Wentworth sneered. "The tart in question has gone into the shrubbery with Everard a few too many times."

Ice water flowed through Vaughn's veins. "Take that back."

"Why? Afraid someone will question your heir if you marry her?"

More gasps echoed, and Vaughn heard someone mutter about Wentworth's odds of losing. He had little doubt he could teach the toad a lesson, but still something held him back. That new conscience of his was entirely too demanding.

"Rather question your intelligence for making such a statement," he countered, turning away in disgust.

He felt the toad's hand on his shoulder. "Don't you dare walk away from me, you coward!"

Vaughn looked back at him, and the toad dropped his hand. "Do you honestly think I care what you think of me?"

"You may not care for your own honor, but you care about hers. Shall I say her name aloud? Shall I let all these fine gentlemen know who to seek for their next mistress?"

The thought of any man approaching Imogene with such a degrading request made him ill. Half the men around him looked equally sickened. The other half looked far too eager.

"Primrose Hill, tomorrow at dawn," Vaughn said.

Wentworth's smile was triumphant. "Pistols, then."

"I believe," said Lord Eustace, stepping between the two of them, "that Mr. Everard is the aggrieved in this case. He shall have choice of weapon."

Choice? That had been taken from him. But perhaps this duel could serve one purpose. "The blade," Vaughn said. "And know this, Wentworth—when I win, I expect answers."

Imogene's afternoon was nearly as difficult. It had started nicely enough. She'd caught sight of Vaughn once as she'd walked home, and knowing he was watching over her made the trip somehow easier.

Still, she'd shied when she'd crossed the street and a carriage had turned the corner. The coachman had acknowledged her with a tip of his cap. She'd smiled with a shaky breath before continuing on.

Small wonder she was skittish! What had Lord Wentworth been thinking to come at them that way? She understood enough about horses to know they would balk at running down a person, but even a glancing blow from the carriage would have injured her or Vaughn greatly, and God forbid they should fall under one of the iron-clad wheels. What could have goaded his lordship to take such action?

Not an order from her father, she was sure. She refused to believe Vaughn's suspicions about the marquess. She could understand how he'd reached those conclusions, given the stories he'd told her. But there had to be another explanation. It was up to her to find it.

Her mother, unfortunately, was in no condition to help, even if Imogene had felt comfortable confiding the terrible tales to her. In the wake of her husband's disappearance, Lady Widmore had retired to her room with a headache that had required a dose of laudanum to nurse. She would not likely rise before dinner. The servants were equally unhelpful, tiptoeing around, faces drawn. With her father unaccounted for, they feared the worst.

She'd prayed for his safety twice already, but if she'd truly thought him in danger, she would have gone to the magistrates. As it was, she could not like hounding him any further. She only wished she knew how to help. Surely the best approach lay in clearing his name. But how?

Left to her own devices, she went to the music room, but her compositions failed to engage her. The notes blurred before her, and her fingers stilled on the keys. *You did not create me to live in fear, Father. Your Word says as much. You intended me for a purpose, and surely it was helping my family. Show me what to do now.*

Thoughts and concerns tumbled over each other in her mind. Vaughn wanted proof of her father's guilt. She wanted proof of his innocence. Would her father have left any evidence of his plans, whatever they were, in the house? She closed the keyboard and went to check his library.

The room was quiet and far too clean. A quick look in the desk showed that it hadn't been used for work in some time. Blank parchment stood ready for her father's hand, and his signet seal sat waiting near the wax. The only thing she had proved was that her father was well prepared.

She knew of one other place he might leave a clue as to his whereabouts. Imogene climbed the stairs to the chamber story and stood outside the closed door of her father's room. She had never entered his bedchamber before. There had been no need. Her father had always come to her, always supported her. Shouldn't she help him now, even if that meant trespassing on his privacy?

She turned the handle and entered. She wasn't surprised by the rich trappings of the room, the black marble fireplace, the brocaded draperies on the window, the velvet hangings on the bed. She was more surprised by the darkness. The walls were painted a deep purple above the gray wainscoting, the materials all a rich crimson. Her feet sank into the thick pile of the carpet as she crossed the floor.

There was little sign of the father she knew. His valet would keep his clothes neatly tucked away, and the maids had cleaned the room so thoroughly that not even the scent of his cologne lingered. A silver-backed brush lay on his dressing table next to a royal-blue porcelain box.

Odd. They had a number of pieces of porcelain lying about the house: vases, candlesticks, even a candy box shaped like a woman's slipper. She couldn't recall seeing this box before. It couldn't hold jewelry. Her father wore relatively little, and he'd have the valet lock up the priceless pieces when he wasn't using them. She reached for the lid.

From downstairs came the sound of the knocker. Imogene started and pulled back her hand. Feeling as if she had somehow violated her father's trust, she hurried from the room and shut the door, leaning against it a moment as she caught her breath.

She heard the murmur of voices below—Jenkins's welcome and a woman's response. It wasn't Vaughn then. Trying not to sag in disappointment, she ventured to the landing in time to see Jenkins apologize for sending Elisa Mayweather away.

"It's all right, Jenkins," Imogene called, causing them both to look up at her. "I'd be glad for a friend right now."

The footman accepted Elisa's bonnet, and her friend started up the stairs. Something of what Imogene had been feeling must have shown in her look, for Elisa's face puckered. "Oh, you've already heard, then."

Imogene laughed as she met her at the top of the stairs. "Most likely not," she said, linking arms with Elisa and leading her toward the withdrawing room. "But your company is very welcome either way."

Elisa blushed as they entered the room. "You may think otherwise when you hear my news."

"Nonsense," Imogene said, taking a seat on the sofa and motioning her friend down beside her. "Today has been beyond astonishing already. Any gossip you have cannot compare."

"Even if it has to do with Mr. Vaughn Everard?" Elisa asked, dark head cocked so that one curl rested along her neck.

Imogene stiffened, feeling as if the cherubs above her were about to come sweeping down around her head. "What's happened?"

"Lord Wentworth challenged him to a duel," Elisa said breathlessly. "My brother had it from Lord Eustace's cousin, who was in White's when it happened."

Imogene shook his head. "Well, he's clearly mistaken. His lordship would never be so bold as to challenge Vaughn Everard to a duel in public."

"Everyone thinks it's suicide," Elisa agreed, hands rubbing at her muslin skirts. "But challenge him he did. And there's sufficient confusion over the reason. Apparently Mr. Everard took umbrage about his lordship's remarks concerning a lady."

A lady? It couldn't have been her. Even Lord Wentworth had finally understood how little she admired him, for it had been clear last night that he had switched his allegiance to...

Imogene gasped, and Elisa clutched her arm. "You know who she is, don't you?"

"I'm not certain," Imogene said, the words like ash in her mouth, "but it may be his cousin, Lady Everard."

Elisa released her with a nod. "So the wagers are going at White's, my brother said. I'm terribly sorry, Imogene. I know you set your cap at Mr. Everard."

She had. She knew it, too. She wanted him to be the man to take over her father's legacy. She wanted him to be a man she could believe in. She wanted him to be the man God had intended for her.

He'd kissed her twice. Was that because he was the rake he claimed or because he'd come to care for her? How was she to know the truth? *Give me strength, Father. Show me what's right!*

"I'll be fine," she said to Elisa. "I'm glad you came to tell me." She scooted closer. "Now, what did your brother say about time and location?"

Elisa's brown eyes were wide. "Oh, Imogene, you cannot think to go!"

Imogene raised her chin. "I certainly can."

"But your reputation!"

"You leave that to me," Imogene insisted. "Now, spill. I have much to do if I'm to be ready."

Chapter Sixteen

Vaughn also had much to do to prepare for the duel. He conferred with Lord Eustace, who promised to make all the arrangements—a neutral fellow to stand as judge, a physician to attend the injured and a set of new dueling swords so neither party would have the advantage.

"Thank you for your help," Vaughn said as they parted in front of White's.

Eustace grinned, lighting his long face. "Lord Wentworth has needed a comeuppance for some time. It's a shame it required such drastic action, but I won't be sorry to see him humbled. Perhaps he'll even come away from this a better man."

"In my experience," Vaughn replied, "men don't change because of duels. What they were going in, they'll be coming out. I'll simply be happy with some answers."

Eustace cocked his head, threatening his top hat. "And what answers would those be?"

"A private matter," Vaughn assured him. "I'll see you in the morning."

He turned before the man could press him further.

Unfortunately, he feared he would not be able to es-

cape such questions at home. Jerome or Richard might
try to stop him, or offer their services as his second. He
wasn't sure how to handle either response. Uncle had
always been Vaughn's second, except for his first duel
at Eton. He still remembered that day. Life at school had
never been easy. He simply couldn't sit so still, take in
the lessons that seemed to drone on forever. His masters
had complained of his inattention and punished him for
what they saw as insubordination. In their minds, activities were regulated, disciplined pursuits to improve
the mind or strengthen the body. They had no appreciation for imagination, for enthusiasm about a subject.

Their frustration over his poor showing had infected
his fellow students. He'd ignored the taunts impugning
his intelligence, his dedication. Then one day a boy
named Freddie Ingram had stepped forward after dinner.

"A shame you're so buffleheaded, Everard," he'd
sneered, his friends flanking him as they stood in the
common area. "Must be a family failing. I heard your
mother couldn't memorize her lines at the theater either.
My father said she was much better behind the curtain
than in front of it."

Vaughn had pushed up from his chair, and the room
had fallen silent. Even Freddie had known he'd gone too
far, for he'd taken a step back, crowding his friends.

"Midnight," Vaughn had snapped. "The rear yard.
Bring your sword—and your courage if you can find it."

Freddie had brought neither. Instead, he'd gone sniv-
eling to the Don, who had ordered Vaughn expelled. He
didn't know what he'd do if his cousins Jerome and
Richard had a similar reaction now.

So he waited to return to Everard House until he was
certain they'd all gone out. Samantha seldom lacked for

invitations each night, and his cousins and their lady loves generally accompanied her. As it was, Vaughn slipped into the house to find it all but deserted.

For once the quiet suited him. He had enough noise thrumming through his mind. A few days ago he would never have doubted the outcome of the duel. Now given the toad's attempt on their lives earlier, he had to assume the fellow would be a determined opponent, perhaps even violating the rules to secure an advantage. It was even possible that Vaughn could lose.

He shook his head as he paced about his bedchamber. Uncle had always condemned such thoughts. "Focus on your skills, lad," he'd say, sitting back with his feet propped up on a hassock by the fire. "Don't let the fellow climb inside you."

Yet the night before his fatal duel, what had Uncle done? Had he lost his focus? Was that why he'd died? Or was more involved? Why hadn't he brought Vaughn along? Had he lost faith in Vaughn? Or found faith in something greater?

Facing possible death, perhaps he, too, should seek a higher power. He seemed to remember that a fellow should pray to align his life with God's will, but he couldn't claim to know the Almighty's purpose in all this. Did God want Vaughn to triumph or to be punished on earth for his sins?

He glanced at the ceiling, trying to imagine someone beyond the green and white who actually cared about him. "Tell You what. You do as You see fit. And so will I."

He frowned as he lowered his gaze. That didn't sound remarkably pious. Rather pitiful, actually, as final words went. He held himself still and closed his eyes.

Lord, I don't know what tomorrow will bring. But

*then, if we humans were truthful, none of us know. We
go about our lives making plans, thinking we'll be alive
to achieve them, when You have something else in mind
all along. So I ask nothing for myself. You know what
I am. I ask only that You protect Imogene. And I thank
You for listening to someone like me.*

As he opened his eyes he had to own he felt a bit better. In fact, the poem that had been teasing him all day
strolled to the front of his mind, beckoning.

He went to the desk and pulled out the folio of his latest work. He could not know how it would be received.
One day he'd be certain everything was the most glo-
rious contribution to literature since the Bard, and the
next he'd consider tossing it all away as rubbish. Yet
if he were to die tomorrow, how would he want to be
remembered?

He dragged out the chair, sat at the desk, studied the
blank page remaining. Why not? What harm could it
do? If he died, Imogene would know that he had given
his all. If he lived, he could always pull the book back
from the publisher. He seized a quill, uncorked the ink
and set about writing. He'd finish the book tonight and
have it delivered to the publisher in the morning. The
poor fellow had been begging for weeks, relaying the
wishes of his many subscribers, promising to get the
poems out in a remarkably short time.

He imagined if it were billed as the last words of
Vaughn Everard, the publisher would make a fortune.
He could only hope to keep the fellow impoverished
for a while longer.

Dawn was still a dream beyond the horizon when
the hired carriage rolled to a stop at the foot of Prim-

rose Hill. The grassy slope was no more than a darker smudge rising toward a leaden sky.

"Good place for a highwayman," Jenkins said, peering out the window.

Imogene gave him what she hoped passed for a brave smile, though her hands were icy inside her gloves. "There hasn't been a report of robbery out this way for months."

Her footman did not appear mollified. His elegant black coat and breeches were covered in a dark wool cloak, and he'd pulled the hood up over his powdered wig until all she could see was the tip of his sharp nose.

"This is still no place for you, your ladyship," he grumbled. "And I won't beg your pardon for saying so."

Imogene bit back a sigh. They'd been arguing over the matter since she'd first approached him late last night. Her head footman thought she was being foolish for coming here, and he'd threatened to tell her mother and father. But as her mother was still asleep and her father still missing, he had only the butler Mr. Prentice to appeal to, and Imogene knew Jenkins feared the august butler would discover the other ways the footman had aided her recently.

"With you beside me," Imogene said, "I feel perfectly safe. Now, how are we to find this duel?"

"It will be near the top," Jenkins said with obvious reluctance, "where the ground is flatter. From here, we walk."

He opened the door and jumped out to hand Imogene down onto the grass. She could smell the moisture in the air and could see the faintest glow on the far horizon. The trill of insects and chirp of birds chasing them stilled as she and Jenkins moved through the grass. She'd donned her cloak as well, but her wool skirts swirled past the opening as she walked. In seconds, the material was damp with dew, hanging heavily against her boots.

"Hush, now," Jenkins said as if she'd been playing a battle hymn instead of climbing in silence. "They should be just ahead." He bent low and skirted the edge of the hill. Imogene tried to copy him. With her head down, she could just make out the grass seeds spotting her cloak and decorating her boots.

Then she heard the murmur of voices, and her heart started beating faster. Ahead the grass had been stomped down in a square about twelve feet across, and someone had dug a line in the dirt at the back of each side, as if trying to hem the space. On opposite edges of the square stood a group of men, huddled together and casting glances at their opponents. The closest group included Lord Wentworth.

Imogene's head must have inched up in her attempt to get a better look because Jenkins grabbed her hand and tugged her back down. "Careful! You mustn't be seen!"

"But I must see!" she hissed back.

He glanced around, then pointed to a rise at the left of the tableau near the very crown of the hill. "Up there. Quickly."

Imogene scrambled after him.

Lying flat on her stomach, the grass tickling her nose, she watched the men below. She could see Vaughn now, partnered by a man she recognized as Lord Eustace. Where were his cousins Jerome and Captain Richard Everard? Didn't they know about the duel? Did they disapprove?

He looked so alone, a spot of light in the darkness with his pale hair and white muslin shirt. He'd removed his coat and waistcoat and was rolling his shoulders and squatting on the ground only to spring back up again.

"Warming up his muscles," Jenkins said as if he knew she was wondering. "A gentleman wants to be in top shape to meet his opponent."

Imogene tore her gaze away from Vaughn to glance at Lord Wentworth. He wasn't warming anything. He stood, stiff and tall, chin up as if disdaining preparation. His coat was off, too, and Imogene was surprised to find that he seemed taller than Vaughn.

"What happens next?" she whispered to Jenkins.

He shifted on the grass as if trying to get comfortable in the morning chill. "They'll meet in the middle. One of the gentlemen will have a few words for the occasion, then they'll set to."

Imogene swallowed. "But Mr. Everard doesn't have to kill him, does he?"

"No, your ladyship," Jenkins murmured. "And I hear tell he doesn't kill when he duels. Mind you, some of the duels happened outside London, so it's none too sure. His first duel was at Eton, when he was only fourteen."

"Truly?" Imogene asked, but Jenkins's gaze had returned to the field and widened, and she realized the men had walked to the center of the square, where another man from Lord Wentworth's camp held out his hand. "Mr. Everard shall call it."

"Tails," Vaughn said, voice sharp.

The man nodded, then opened his hand to toss a coin in the air. The metal glinted in the rising sun. The fellow and his lordship bent to see how it landed. Vaughn merely waited.

"Heads," the man proclaimed, straightening. "Lord Wentworth?"

"My back to the east," he said, shifting in that direction.

"Too bad," Jenkins murmured. "Mr. Everard will have the sun in his eyes."

Imogene frowned, but Lord Eustace had now entered the square. He held two slim blades on a roll of velvet.

"I have inspected these and so has your second, Lord Wentworth, and we find no fault in them. Do you accept them, gentlemen?"

Vaughn wrapped his fingers around the hilt and drew the blade in a dizzying arc. "It seems a suitable weapon for dispatching a dastard."

His opponent lifted his blade as well and sighted down the length. "It will do," he said, lowering it.

"Then take your positions," Lord Eustace said.

Imogene felt her body tighten, as if she were the one having to face that length of metal. Vaughn settled himself a few feet from the center, the blade held lightly in his grip. His gaze remained on his opponent, watchful. She thought Lord Wentworth looked remarkably cool as he took up the spot opposite him.

"You can save yourself a great deal of trouble," Vaughn said, "if you simply apologize now and tell me the truth about your dealings."

"Nothing to tell," Lord Wentworth replied. "Just doing my duty to support the Marquess of Widmore. Save your breath."

Imogene caught hers. So he claimed to support her father. Had the marquess put him up to this to keep Vaughn from her? Surely her father didn't need someone like Lord Wentworth to do his work for him.

Below her, Vaughn brought the blade up before his face in salute. Lord Wentworth held his sword down.

"Heaping insult after insult," Jenkins murmured.

Imogene's hands clenched in the grass.

Lord Eustace glanced at each man, and they lifted their swords to cross them in the center. Lord Eustace reached up to hold them in place.

"Won't he be cut?" Imogene whispered.

"Dueling swords are only sharp on the point," Jenkins replied. "I had to clean a set for the marquess once. They're heavier than they look. I'd not want to have to fight for my life with one."

She hadn't time to do more than wonder why her father would need dueling swords before Lord Eustace spoke again.

"Remember, it is only to first blood," he instructed. He glanced at Lord Wentworth. "Ready?"

"Get on with it," he answered.

She thought Lord Eustace stiffened, but he turned to Vaughn. "Ready, Mr. Everard?"

"At your disposal, my lord."

Lord Eustace nodded. "Then may honor be satisfied. Lay on!"

He released the swords and backed away. So did Vaughn. But Lord Wentworth raised his blade and rushed forward. Imogene gasped, but Vaughn crouched and fended him off easily.

"Careful, now," Jenkins said, and Imogene realized he spoke as if he was advising Vaughn. "His lordship has the longer reach."

Her hands knotted in the grass as the men began circling each other. Lord Wentworth was more cautious now, tapping at Vaughn's blade as if trying to find its weakness. He seemed to have calmed, steadied, until he very much appeared to be Vaughn's match.

But as she watched, she could see the differences between them. His lordship's movements were wide and strong, like an ax attempting to cut down a tree. Vaughn's were light and precise, the scalpel lancing through disease. The point of his sword never went beyond the sides of his body, and the movement seemed more guided by his wrist than his arm. The determination on his face, the hint of a smile that said he was enjoying this, chilled her more than the morning air.

"How long can this go on?" she whispered to Jenkins, wincing as Lord Wentworth's blade flashed past Vaughn's cheek.

"Two minutes," he returned. "Then they take a break before starting again."

Again? Her heart would never stand it! Already it demanded that she race down the slope, put herself between the two men and force them to stop.

Vaughn seemed to be losing patience, as well. "Swear to me that you'll leave the lady alone and we can end this now," he said, parrying a thrust that nearly reached his shoulder.

The lady? She swallowed, thinking of his golden-haired cousin.

"If even her father cannot care about her safety, why should I?" Wentworth countered, thrusting again.

Her father? Lady Everard's father was dead. Then this duel could not be about Samantha. What other woman could have come between the two men?

Heat flushed up her and just as quickly fled. Vaughn was fighting for her. He might lose his life because of her.

She rose. "I have to get down there."

Jenkins pulled her back down. "Are you mad? You may have to sack me, for I won't let you do it!"

Imogene shrugged him off and glanced down at the fight.

"Her father's actions have no part in this fight," Vaughn was saying. "You know what is right."

"Right?" Lord Wentworth swerved around Vaughn's thrust. "What would an Everard understand of right?"

"Enough," Vaughn said, "to know it when I see it."

He leaned to the left, and his lordship shoved his blade forward. Up under his guard, Vaughn drove his point home.

Imogene cried out, feeling as if her own heart had been run through. Vaughn's head jerked up even as he pulled back, the tip of his blade red. She could not move, could not breathe. As if Jenkins knew it, he grabbed her and dragged her down the hill, away from where Lord Wentworth's body was falling onto the trampled ground, away from where all her hopes had been shattered.

For Vaughn Everard could not be the man she'd thought him. Lord Eustace had said the fight was to be first blood. All Vaughn had had to do was nick his opponent, scratch his arm, his finger. Instead, Vaughn had chosen to injure him, perhaps fatally. Even if he thought he was protecting her, his actions were dishonorable.

She pressed her fist against her mouth as she stumbled along beside Jenkins, trying to keep from crying out again. She was a fool! Vaughn had told her himself that he was a rake, and she'd refused to believe him. Her mother had had doubts about his constancy, and Imogene had argued for him. Elisa had implied he was a scoundrel, and she'd waved her friend away. She could no longer hide from the fact that he was not a gentleman.

But neither was Lord Wentworth. She'd considered him a fool as well, but he had a darker motive, just as likely to kill, given his threat with the carriage yesterday. She'd misjudged him and nearly lost her life in the process.

Had she been wrong about her father, as well? Did he care nothing for her and her mother? Lord Wentworth's words seemed to imply as much, yet how could she believe him?

Were there no good men left in the world?

She wasn't sure how she made it back to the waiting carriage. She only came to her senses when Jenkins touched her elbow and helped her inside. As he sat across from her, he thumped on the roof to tell the driver to take them home. From somewhere nearby she thought she heard her name shouted. She closed her eyes, burrowed deeper into her sodden cloak, misery clinging to her just as thoroughly.

Father, forgive me. I thought I knew better. I thought if I believed hard enough, everything would work out. Vaughn would be a gentleman. My father would still love me. I could make life easier for my mother. Now I realize I know nothing!

The comfort she craved seemed to slip further away every second. The momentum of the horses as they set out pressed her back against the seat, but it was nothing to the weight on her heart. Was there no one worth believing in? No one she could count on?

Never will I leave you; never will I forsake you.

A tear rolled down her cheek at the remembered verse, and she reached out with all she had. *Please, Father, help me! I don't know what to do. I don't know who to trust. Show me Your will in this.*

Something landed on the roof, setting the carriage to rocking. Imogene's eyes popped open. Hood thrown back, Jenkins glared at the ceiling, clutching the bench to stay in his seat.

With a splinter of wood, the door was wrenched open, and Vaughn swung himself inside to land on the floor in a crouch.

"Forgive the dramatic entrance," he said, eying Imogene. "But we must talk."

Chapter Seventeen

The footman recovered first. "Mr. Everard," Jenkins said, "I will ask you to leave this coach now."

With the carriage still bumping along the uneven ground at the base of the hill, Vaughn wondered where the fellow thought he could go. It had been hard enough climbing aboard as the carriage was starting to leave. If he hadn't had a little height coming down the hill, he would likely have missed.

Unfortunately, Jenkins's look brooked no nonsense. Vaughn knew the fellow was taller than he was and probably stronger. Strength and height were why footmen were chosen, after all. And he certainly owed Vaughn no favors. But the tension of the duel was still singing through Vaughn's veins, and he thought he could topple monarchies singlehandedly if he chose.

Imogene did not look at Vaughn as she laid a hand on her man's arm. "Stop the carriage, Jenkins."

So she wanted Vaughn out, too. When her cry had pierced the morning, he'd looked up to see her staring down at him. Her anguished face had struck him more deeply than his opponent's blade ever could. She had to understand, he had to make her understand, that he had a reason for his actions.

So he'd bent over Lord Wentworth where the toad lay on the ground, fingers pressed to his wounded chest. Already the physician moved forward to help. Vaughn held up a hand to stop him.

"What is Widmore planning?" he asked the toad. "You owe me that for sparing your life."

The fellow's face was white. "Can't stop him. Too much at stake. New order of things." His eyes narrowed. "You'll pay then." He slumped in a faint.

"Mr. Everard, please," Lord Wentworth's second had insisted, and Vaughn had stepped aside to allow the physician to do his work. It had been clear he would get no more from the toad in any event, and Vaughn had to reach Imogene.

Now the footman called up to the coachman, and the hired hack slowed to a stop.

"Jenkins," Imogene said, voice as chilly as the morning, "Mr. Everard and I will take a walk. You are to watch from beside the carriage steps. If you see anything that disturbs you, you are to come to me at once."

"Your ladyship," he started, but she held up her hand.

"No arguments. I count on your discretion and your valor."

He did not look appeased, but he nodded. Then he opened the door and helped Imogene down.

Vaughn followed. He wanted nothing more than to take her in his arms and promise all would be well, but he was afraid to touch her. She looked fragile standing beside the coach in the early-morning light, as if she were made of fine porcelain and would crack at the least blow. She glanced around as if unsure of her way.

The coach had stopped near a copse of trees, the

leaves chattering in the breeze. The light from the rising sun gilded the branches with gold. "This way," she said, and Vaughn joined her along the path that led away from the coach.

She said nothing, huddled in her cloak, head bowed as if she watched each step around the trees.

"I know what you saw must have upset you," Vaughn said. "I can explain."

"I'm listening."

But not with an open mind. Her face, usually so eager and warm, was shut tight, pinched as if in pain. She'd already judged him and found him guilty. Was there no one who had faith in him?

Before I formed thee in the womb, I knew thee; and before thou camest forth out of the womb, I set thee apart.

A Bible verse again? *Are You trying to reach me, Lord? Forgive me, but it is both poor timing and a poor choice of words. If You know me so well, why make me different, why set me apart?*

She stopped at the base of a spreading oak and turned to meet his gaze. "I said I'm listening, Mr. Everard. Have you nothing to say for yourself, after all?"

Vaughn took a deep breath. The energy of the fight was fading, leaving his limbs heavy, his mind fatigued. "I had to fight him."

"So it appears. I suppose I should thank you for protecting my honor."

Relief was immediate. "Then you understand."

"Oh, no. How could I?" She peered up at him. "Did you have to kill him?"

Vaughn stiffened. "I didn't kill him. His wound is serious, but the physician is already tending to it."

She frowned. "You know I can verify the truth of that easily enough."

"Certainly, but you have no need. I never lie, remember?"

Her laugh was hard. "No, only maim it seems. You'll pardon me if I find both equally dishonorable."

Once he would have laughed to be called dishonorable; now the appellation stung, particularly from her. "Perhaps we have different definitions of *honor,* then," he said, trying to keep his tone light. "I won't allow anyone to threaten those I care for."

Something flickered across her face. Was she pleased he cared about her? "Some would call that commendable," she said, though the tension in her voice nearly belied the statement.

Vaughn shrugged, feeling muscles beginning to tighten. "But you don't."

"It's the way you protect me I find abhorrent," she protested. "I thought you wanted answers. You'd be hard pressed to question a corpse!"

Or an insensible man, as he'd just proved. "He told me enough. Lord Wentworth is working for your father."

She threw up her hands. "So of course you take the word of a dastard over mine."

Vaughn shook his head. "You are not involved in your father's plans. He is."

"So he apparently claims, but I have seen no proof of it." She lowered her hands to rub them along the wool of her cloak as if fighting off a chill. "In fact, I have precious little proof of anything save your ability to cause trouble. You warned me you were not a gentleman, Mr. Everard. Perhaps I should have listened sooner."

All at once, he was tired—tired of his quest, tired of trying to live up to the expectations of others, tired of justifying his choices. He spread his arms wide, and she fetched up against the tree as if she thought he meant to strike her.

"This," he said, "is who I am. A man sworn to love and protect those he cares for. A man who lives in the moment, never knowing what life might bring. A man with blood on his blade, but never life's blood or the blood of innocents. I cannot be content to follow. I must do what I believe is right, no matter the consequences. If that makes me less than a gentleman, then so be it. I care nothing for what others think."

"And here," she murmured, gaze on his, "you claim not to lie."

He pulled in his arms, but she strode forward and poked a finger in his chest before he could speak.

"You care entirely too much what others think," she accused. "Oh, you hide it behind a wall of bravado and beautiful prose, but you want to be appreciated, to be admired. That is evident by your actions, by the look that comes over your face when someone wrongs you. What did you write? 'A man is the sum of his dreams less the darkness of his deeds.'"

He felt as if she had pulled out his heart. "Do not confuse the man with his poetry."

"Do not make the mistake of thinking you can divorce them." She put her hands on her hips. "What am I do to with you, Vaughn Everard? I see so much that is bright and good in you, yet I cannot reconcile that with the shadows."

He fought a smile. "Someone once said that God shines the light, and we cast the shadows."

"Yes," she said, dropping her hands. "The famous poet Vaughn Everard. Perhaps you've heard of him."

Vaughn waved a hand. "Entirely overrated. Hackneyed phrases, misplaced meter, jumbled imagery."

"And completely compelling, much like the man himself."

He cocked his head. "So what would you have of me?"

Her look challenged him. "What would you offer?"

In that moment, he wanted to offer her everything: his world, his life, his heart. He could fall on one knee, beg her hand in marriage, confess he would never be whole without her. If he could make a good marriage with any woman, it would be with Imogene. But surely she deserved better.

So he bowed, deeply, arm spread like a courtier of old. "My utmost devotion, your ladyship."

"I suppose," she said, as he straightened, "that will have to do."

He eyed her. The pallor had left her face, and he thought he saw a hint of the usual sparkle in her green eyes. "Then I am forgiven?"

"Does one forgive a wooden chair for being hard? A knife for being sharp? You are who you are. It seems I must accept that."

If she accepted that, she would be the only one save his uncle. Small wonder he felt his heart stir in her presence. "Then accept this as well—Lord Wentworth has been taught a lesson, one I hope he will not soon forget."

"And implicated my father in the process."

He inclined his head. "I'm sorry, but yes."

She made a face, her pert nose wrinkling. "I cannot accept that, you know. I want to prove to you that my father is innocent. What would make you doubt this theory of yours?"

She could not know how often he had doubted, that

she was one of the few people who could make him abandon his quest entirely. "I'm no longer sure," he confessed. "Once I would have settled for your father's word, but he's done too much to confirm my suspicions."

"There must be something," she pressed, gaze imploring. "Shall I bring his sword so you can see it carries no stain from your uncle's blood?"

Vaughn smiled at her. "A good swordsman knows to clean his blade. And my uncle was shot."

"His dueling pistols, then, to show they haven't been fired."

"No doubt he has more than one gun at his disposal."

She frowned. "Well, not knowing where he is, I can hardly have him sign a statement protesting his innocence. Have you no other ideas?"

Vaughn shrugged again. "The only evidence we ever had was a box, royal-blue Sèvres porcelain, and it was stolen from us."

She paled and took a step back from him, eyes widening. "About this big?" she asked, hands held six inches apart and trembling.

"So I understand," Vaughn replied with a frown. "Do you have a similar piece?"

She nodded as she lowered her hands. "It appears we do. I saw it yesterday, in a place of honor on my father's dressing table."

Imogene felt as if she'd been pulled into a windstorm, her emotions tossed about like fallen leaves. She'd only just decided to trust Vaughn, trust her feelings for him, when she realized she knew where to find the evidence that could well prove her father's guilt.

He must have realized it as well, for he grabbed both of her arms and held her tight. "Take me to it now."

A movement caught her attention. Jenkins had evidently seen Vaughn's touch as an attack, for he was striding toward them, face set. She ought to run to him, run away from the knowledge that had burst upon her. How could she bear to learn her father was a fraud?

Yet what proved guilt could as easily prove innocence.

"I'll bring it to you," she told Vaughn, slipping from his grip. "And we'll open it together. Meet me at Mr. Town's shop on Bond Street at eleven."

He nodded and pulled back to raise his hands in surrender. "I have no claim on your lady, Jenkins."

"Glad I am to hear that, sir," the footman replied, moving between them. "I should hate to have to oppose you."

"It's all right, Jenkins," Imogene said. "We can go now. Good-day, Mr. Everard."

He bowed. "Your servant as always, Lady Imogene."

They were words any gentleman might say, yet she thought she heard so much more beneath the common phrase. It spoke of devotion, of willingness to lay down his life for her. She had to force herself to turn her back and walk away. Perhaps that was why her feet moved faster with each step.

"Are you all right, your ladyship?" Jenkins murmured beside her as they approached the waiting carriage.

"Yes, thank you," Imogene replied, but she knew it wasn't completely true. She was considerably better then when she'd seen Lord Wentworth fall, but she feared what she'd find when she returned home.

The carriage ride back to Mayfair at least gave her a

little time to get her thoughts in order. For the moment, she would take Vaughn at his word that Lord Wentworth was only wounded. What was more difficult were her feelings for Vaughn. He was right—she had tried to force him into an image she had crafted. She'd wanted a hero, a dashing fellow who embodied the poetry she'd read. The real man was far more complex.

He claimed to prefer his world chaotic, full of variety, surprises, adventure. She had been raised to routine, discipline. Admittedly, she'd already grown weary of attending the same balls, dancing to the same music, facing the same partners who knew her no better than the day they had first been introduced. He brought a sweetness of spontaneity to her life, like rich custard after roast beef.

A shame one could not live on custard. And a man of such varying interests wasn't likely to excel in one sufficiently to please the gentlemen in Parliament. In short, it was unlikely that she could have her father's title recreated for him.

He was not the man she had planned for, and she'd been following that plan since Charles's death. Giving up Vaughn Everard should have been easy. But the very thought raised such anguish, such fierce refusal! Her heart fought with her mind, and she was fairly certain which would win.

Lord, what should I do? You say honor your father and your mother. How can I help either of them if I marry the wrong man?

Therefore shall a man leave his father and mother and shall cleave unto his wife and they shall be one flesh.

She'd heard that verse before, during a wedding of a friend last Season. But though it talked of a man, the same could be said for the woman. She'd been thinking about what it would mean to bring her husband into her family. Perhaps God meant her to think about starting her own family.

She wasn't certain about the answer any more than she was certain about her choices now. She'd left her father's room yesterday with the feeling that she had somehow betrayed him. That fear returned even stronger when she approached his room again later that morning.

Her mother had been eating breakfast when Imogene arrived home, but Imogene had hurried upstairs to change before her mother could wonder at the state of her clothes. As it was, her maid Bryson tsked as she took away the damp cloak and gown, and Imogene was certain the tale would reach her mother only too soon.

Dressed in a lavender wool gown that felt surprisingly good for the spring day, she hurried to the door of her father's room. Nothing had changed since she'd visited the previous day, but then why would it? Her father was still missing. Even so, she felt as if he was watching her every move as she went to the dressing table and lifted the box.

It was cool in her grip and light. What could it hold? She'd promised Vaughn they'd open it together, but she was highly tempted to take a peek now.

"Imogene?"

At the sound of her mother's voice, Imogene spun, box clasped behind her.

Her mother was standing in the doorway. Perhaps it was the dark colors of the room, but she seemed paler, her muslin gown a splash of white. She moved into the room as if her limbs were too heavy for her. "What are you doing in here, dearest?"

"Looking for something that would tell me where Father has gone," Imogene said, knowing that for the truth.

Her mother smiled sadly. "Aren't we all?"

Her depression clung to Imogene like a damp petticoat. "I only want to help, Mother. I hate that you must worry so."

"I will survive," her mother promised. "Forgive me for leaving you to your own devices yesterday. I trust you were able to keep busy?"

Imogene's grip tightened on the box, which suddenly weighed heavier. "Yes, thank you."

Her mother cocked her head. "And this morning? Bryson tells me you and Jenkins were out at dawn. A bit early for a constitutional."

"Oh, there were more people about then you might expect," Imogene hedged.

"And Mr. Everard is well?" her mother asked.

"Tolerably," Imogene replied, thinking of the duel that morning.

"Odd. I thought your father was very clear when he told you to have nothing more to do with the fellow. Neither of us has had the opportunity to convince him otherwise."

Imogene flushed. "You're right, Mother. Forgive me. But I'm not sure I know my own mind when it comes to Mr. Everard."

Her mother straightened with a sigh. "And I'm not certain your father knows his. Can you think of any reason he should have taken the young man in such dislike?"

A good question. Vaughn saw her father's antipathy as a sign of guilt. Perhaps her father had guessed at Vaughn's suspicions and refused to dignify them with a response. Either way, telling her mother about those suspicions was a sure way to hurt her.

"They disagree about his uncle's death," Imogene replied. "Father believes it was merely a duel. Mr. Everard fears it was murder."

"Oh, how horrid!" Her mother pressed her fingers to her lips a moment before lowering them. "If his family has a tendency to violence, Imogene, I could not countenance an alliance."

"I know," Imogene murmured, dropping her gaze to the thick carpet. "But there is so much good in him, Mother!"

Her mother closed the distance between them. "That good could just as easily be swallowed by evil. It only takes one stain to ruin an entire dress."

"But stains can be cleaned," Imogene protested, raising her gaze, "and gowns refurbished. A man can repent and find redemption."

"All that takes determination, Imogene, a will to change. I am not under the impression that your Mr. Everard wishes to find redemption."

"I think you're wrong, Mother," Imogene said. "Something tells me he wishes it devoutly. And I intend to do all I can to help him."

Chapter Eighteen

Vaughn took longer to return to Mayfair than Imogene. He had to make his way back up Primrose Hill to where his chariot and groom were waiting. The toad had been taken home, and all that was left was for Vaughn to pay the physician for his services, don his waistcoat and crimson coat and thank his second.

"You're a fierce fellow, Everard," Lord Eustace said, shaking his hand. "I'd much rather have you as a friend than an enemy." He pulled back and tugged the sleeves of his navy coat into place. "By the way, I plan to host a house party in Devonshire after the Season ends. I hope you'll accept my invitation to join us."

Vaughn frowned. "You're inviting me to your estate?"

Eustace grinned. "Why does that astonish you? If you weren't so prickly you might see that a good number of us are in awe of you. I'm just the first brave enough to chance an acquaintance."

Vaughn shook his head as he drove back to Everard House. He could not believe he'd brought this ostracism on himself, or that if he opened his eyes he'd find the rest of the *ton* welcoming him.

He'd tried to fit in as a child, craving his grandfather's approval. But something always seemed to go wrong. One Christmas, Grandfather had brought an artist in to paint a portrait of Jerome, Richard and Vaughn. Jerome and Richard had been at Eton then, with Vaughn set to start in a few terms, and they and their parents had been staying with Grandfather over the holidays.

Though Jerome had his usual charming smile in place, he kept lowering his head to consult his new pocket watch, as if he knew he had better ways to spend his time. Richard openly fidgeted in his fine clothes. Vaughn had stood still and composed, determined to prove himself. But as minutes turned to hours, his gaze had been drawn to the window. From a frozen sky came soft white flakes, drifting down. He could go sledding this afternoon!

"Mr. Everard!" the artist had cried, and Vaughn had turned to find himself at the window while his two cousins shook their heads and grinned at him and Grandfather scowled.

He found it difficult to look before he leaped, to think before he spoke. Over the years, he'd worked hard to keep his composure, to fight his urges. Only with Uncle had he felt free to be himself. Could it be there were others willing to accept him for who he was?

If thou dost well, shalt thou not be accepted?

Was that another Bible verse? He seemed determined to delve into the spiritual of late. His thoughts last night he put down to anticipation of the duel. What prompted him this morning to remember verses he hadn't heard for years? After all this time silent, did God suddenly wish his company?

I love them that love me, and those who seek me shall find me.

Something stirred inside him. It was also a day for revelations, it seemed. He remembered making the choice to forgo attending services, to stop the staid repetition of words he had never felt. Now something seemed to whisper that he had mistaken his way. That he had been the one to walk away from God. That there was more for him, if only he would seek it. He did not have to earn his place in God's affections but accept Him as a gift.

"Very well, then," he said aloud. "You have my attention. What do you want of me?"

"Beg pardon, sir?" his groom called from his place at the back of the chariot.

Vaughn laughed, feeling foolish. "Nothing, Babcock. Merely talking to my horses." Who were just as likely to answer him as God was.

He managed to return the carriage and horses to the stable behind Everard House and slip away without any of his cousins noticing. He wasn't ready for the recriminations, the demands that he wait for the authorities to act. The authorities had washed their hands of him and his uncle years ago. And Jerome and Richard should know by now that he was never one to wait.

Bond Street was already busy as he strolled down it just before eleven. In the most fashionable shopping district in London, merchants prided themselves on their fine wares and their unstinting service. Displays in the windows beckoned the elite with bright satins, polished wood furnishings and sumptuous pastries. Ladies passed him, followed by overburdened footmen carrying their packages home.

He found Mr. Town's shop at the upper end of the street. According to the sign over the gleaming front window, the place specialized in glassware, porcelain and fine antiquities. He pushed through the door, a brass bell overhead signaling his entrance with a merry chime.

Inside, wooden shelves lined the walls, and several wooden cases with glass tops and sides ran down the center of the room. He spotted fierce-faced dogs from China, a grinning bronze mask from Greece and something that looked suspiciously like an Egyptian sarcophagus leaning in one corner. A clerk, tall, ascetic and as elegant as the wares, came from the back of the shop.

"Good morning, sir," he said with a bow so deep it lifted the blond hair from his head. "How may I help you?"

"I'm not entirely sure," Vaughn admitted. "I was told to meet a friend here about a porcelain box."

To his surprise the clerk straightened and leaned closer. "They've gone ahead," he murmured as if he suspected the fellow in the sarcophagus might overhear. "The fires won't be lit tonight."

"Excellent," Vaughn said, mind whirling. What had he stumbled into? Who did this man think Vaughn was? "How can I help?"

He grimaced. "You're too late to reach the coast in time. Stay in London, and await further orders."

"I've a fast horse," Vaughn countered, trying to draw the fellow out. "Is there a spot along the coast that needs reinforcements? I might be able to make it."

The clerk's face was clouding as he straightened. "What task were you given?"

Vaughn waved a hand. "Never one with enough action for me. Where's your master? Perhaps I can appeal to him."

The other man took a step back, hand reaching into his black coat, and Vaughn braced himself to repel a knife or pistol. The bell tinkled as the door opened, and Imogene hurried in, a bundle under the arm of her green quilted-satin pelisse. The clerk dropped his hand.

"Oh, good, you're here," she said to Vaughn with a smile that cried relief. She glanced at the clerk. "Mr. Hennessy, isn't it? You've served my mother, Lady Widmore."

His face was white, his smile sickly, but he bowed just the same. "Your ladyship, an honor to be sure. How might I be of service today?"

Vaughn didn't think the man would dare harm Imogene, but he put himself in a position to intercept if needed.

"I'd like to know more about this," she said, oblivious to the tension curling through the shop. She unwrapped the shawl covering her bundle to reveal a fine porcelain box of a brilliant shade of blue. Vaughn recognized it easily from Jerome's description. He found himself leaning closer, fingers itching to touch it, to learn its secrets.

The clerk didn't flinch. "A fine example of Sèvres porcelain, from perhaps five years ago by the color of the blue. A few pieces were commissioned by the First Consul when he was given the office."

"Napoleon?" Imogene's hands must have been trembling, for Vaughn could see the box shaking. "Then how would we know? Surely such pieces are not sent to England."

"Very few," the clerk acknowledged. "I believe the former Ambassador to France has a set, and Lord Fox was sent one as a token of appreciation after the late hostilities."

Imogene cast Vaughn a look from under the brim of the feathered green velvet hat that perched on her chestnut curls. "Then an Englishman could come by it honestly."

"Possibly," the clerk agreed. "Though, mind you, some pieces have also been smuggled in. Not that this shop would ever deal in smuggled goods."

"Certainly not," Imogene said with a nod.

"Then you sold this piece to the Marquess of Widmore?" Vaughn interrupted, watching him.

The clerk adjusted his cravat. "I do not recall."

Imogene frowned. "But you must keep a record of all sales. Could you check to see if my father purchased this?"

Vaughn could see him swallow, but he suddenly brightened. "Certainly, only there's no need. I've just remembered. Your father purchased that as a gift for your mother, your ladyship. Of course, he swore us to secrecy, but I'm sure that promise did not extend to you."

Imogene nodded, but her frown did not ease. "Thank you, Mr. Hennessy. I'll be sure to mention you to my mother."

He bowed. "Your servant as always, your ladyship."

"Mr. Everard," Imogene said, turning to Vaughn, "I have some words for you. Would you be so kind as to escort me?"

"Everard?" The clerk jerked upright, hand diving into his coat.

Vaughn shoved Imogene away from the danger and launched himself at the clerk. They hit the floor with a crash that shook the cases, and Imogene cried out. Vaughn pinned the man to the floor and held him tight. The clerk glared up at him.

"Are you mad!" Imogene cried, hurrying closer.

"Stay back!" Vaughn warned. Angling one arm to cover both shoulders and the fellow's throat, he used his free hand to reach inside the clerk's coat. His fingers closed on something hard. He yanked out a knife and tossed it at Imogene's feet.

"Who is your master?" Vaughn demanded. "What's happening on the coast tonight?"

"I have no idea what you're talking about," the clerk said. He glanced at Imogene. "I swear, your ladyship, I only carry that knife to open shipments. I've done nothing to warrant such treatment."

Vaughn pressed on his windpipe. "A fine story, but you know it for a lie. Tell me who you work for!"

"Mr. Town," he wheezed. "I'm just a clerk!"

"Vaughn, please," Imogene murmured, stepping closer again. "This isn't necessary."

"It is absolutely necessary. Before you arrived, he was spinning tales of fires on the coastline and dark deeds tonight." He pressed down harder. "Tell me what you know."

"Nothing," he rasped out, eyes bulging. "Lady Imogene, have mercy! He's lying."

Beside him, Imogene stiffened, and Vaughn thought he would have to fight her, as well.

"I'm afraid you're mistaken, Mr. Hennessy," she said. "Mr. Everard never lies. But I suspect that you do. I didn't wish to say so in your presence, but I know this box was never given to my mother, and I'm not sure that was ever its purpose. I suggest you cooperate with Mr. Everard, or I very much fear your life may be in danger."

Vaughn grinned. "She knows me so well."

Panic flickered across the clerk's face. "All right. Let me up, and I'll show you the plans."

Vaughn eased up on the pressure, then allowed the clerk to rise. Hennessy rubbed his throat gingerly and grimaced. "They're at the back of the shop. If you'll just follow—"

He jerked away from Vaughn and ran.

Vaughn gave chase.

The back of the shop was a cluttered mess of packing crates, some closed, some spilling straw onto the wooden floor. Hennessy zigzagged through the chaos, pulling down boxes and shattering glass. By the time Vaughn clambered over the obstacles, the clerk was out the rear door and disappearing into the alleys of London.

Vaughn stopped and sagged against the door frame. Yet another clue gone. If the clerk spoke the truth, a group of men plotted to damage the signal fires along the coastline tonight. Should Napoleon's ships outwit the Navy, those fires were all that stood between England and invasion. Vaughn knew he ought to go to Whitehall and demand to see Lord Admiral Barham. But who would believe the word of a porcelain clerk or the wild Vaughn Everard?

He turned to find Imogene standing in the doorway from the display room, shawl slung over her shoulder.

"I take it he escaped," she said.

There was no blame in her voice, but he felt the guilt nonetheless. "Yes. And with him went my last hope."

"Not necessarily," she said. She pulled the box from behind her and gave it a shake. "Why don't we open it and see what's inside?"

Why did that smile never fail to warm her? She was quite tempted to throw herself into his arms as he pushed through the fallen crates to her side. For a moment, in the shop, faced once again with brutality, her choice had been clear. She could shy away from the darkness in him, pretend she was somehow better and force him from her life. Or she could accept that he was as imperfect as she was and help him become the man God intended him to be. Guided by the longing of her heart, the decision was easy.

She led him back into the display room and handed him the box. "Will you do the honors?"

"With pleasure." He positioned the box on the fingers of one hand and worked the clasp with the other. The lid swung back. Imogene peered inside, holding her breath.

The box was empty.

She exhaled, leaning back. "Well, piffle!"

"Not the word I would have chosen," Vaughn replied. Though he had to be as frustrated as she was, he angled the box this way and that, looking at it from every side, the bottom, the top. Imogene watched him, fascinated.

"It's too small to have a false bottom," she told him. "And I can't see how you could conceal a secret compartment under that velvet lining."

He shot her a smile. "Inventive, aren't you?"

She laughed. "A few too many gothic novels, I suspect."

He held the box out at arm's length as if distance would improve his view. "Then I must have read the same ones, for I see no sign of encrypted words or symbols. We have only one choice." He opened his hands and let the box fall.

Imogene gasped as it hit the floor and cracked into dozens of pieces. "What have you done!"

Vaughn crouched and flicked the larger pieces aside with one finger. "Destroyed what was before us to unearth its secret." He extracted a folded slip of paper that must have been hidden by the velvet lining and rose to offer the piece to Imogene. "Would you like to see what it says?"

Imogene stared at the note. This was it, the truth about her father; she knew it. How could she bear it if Vaughn was right? How could she ignore the note if it proved him wrong? She snatched the parchment from his grip and carefully unfolded it.

"It's to my father, and it's in French," she said, voice seeming to echo in the room and inside her.

"Can you read French?" he asked.

She nodded. "Father insisted upon it. French blood ran in our veins, he said. We should honor it as well as our English ancestry." She cleared her throat and made herself focus on the words.

"'You have my solemn promise,'" she translated, "'that you will be well rewarded when you help me defeat England.'" The signature was tall and the letters and the slash below them thick as if pressure had been put upon them to show the author's devotion. Still she recognized the name: Napoleon.

Imogene swallowed, unable to look at Vaughn, unable to see beyond the paper. The words blurred as tears scalded her eyes.

"You were right," she murmured. "He's a traitor. He's a traitor!"

She flung the note away, feeling as if it had infected her with some disease. She ought to see a dark spot on her hand, find lines crawling up her skin. The father she'd known—the loving, caring, loyal man—was a fiction. She wanted to be sick.

Lord, how can this have happened? What shall I do?

She felt Vaughn's arms come around her.

"Don't," she started. "I can't…"

"You need do nothing right now," he said. "Only

know that I'm sorry. I wanted to learn the truth, but I never wanted to hurt you."

She allowed herself the comfort of leaning against him, of resting her head on his chest. The world was falling around her, her tears were coming faster and her breath held a sob. He said nothing, merely rubbed her back with gentle strokes. For some reason, she felt as if he was hurting along with her.

"It's not your fault," she managed. "He made this decision, and he carried it out. If it weren't for your determination, no one would have known until it was too late."

Suddenly, the full impact of her father's deeds burst upon her. He meant to overthrow the crown, to allow the French to overrun England. Perhaps her brother's death had changed him, perhaps he'd hidden this dream behind a fair face his whole life. She could not know his mind, but she knew what she must do.

She wrenched herself out of Vaughn's embrace and stared up into his face.

"Oh, Vaughn," she cried, "are we too late? Will Napoleon's forces invade tonight?"

"It seems possible, given what we know now," he said, but so cautiously she thought he feared for her mind.

Imogene shook her head. "Then we must find my father."

He reached out a hand and lay it on her shoulder as if to keep her in place. "You cannot shield him, Imogene. This is proof of his villainy."

She swallowed. "I know that. I can see that. I'm not pleading for him."

He cocked his head. "Then what?"

"Don't you see?" she cried. "We must stop him!"

Chapter Nineteen

Vaughn gazed at Imogene, standing there equal parts grief and righteous determination. If he had ever doubted he was in love with this woman, he was a fool. But now was no time to declare his undying devotion. She was right. They had an invasion to stop.

He bent, retrieved the note and tucked it into his waistcoat pocket for safekeeping. "Before you arrived, Hennessy said the fires along the coast would be dark tonight. He seemed to think I was part of the plan. His words could have been code, or he could have meant that England is in danger."

She snapped a nod. "Then we must alert Whitehall."

"Agreed." He took a step closer, needing to touch her, to hold her, but he settled for a hand on her shoulder. "Are you certain you wish to help me? Your father will be considered suspect and very likely tried for treason. If he's convicted, his title will be attainted and his lands confiscated and he'll be sentenced to death."

She was so pale he thought she might fall over. "My mother and I will be outcasts, I know. But Vaughn, think of all the people who will die if Napoleon's army reaches the shore. Think what will happen if Britain falls!"

He pulled her into his arms again and cradled her close. "We will not let that happen. We will not bow to a tyrant."

She clung to him a moment more, and he closed his eyes and considered a future he had never dreamed possible. She and her mother would need someone to protect them. He wanted to be that person, to hold her when the worst happened, to help her find joy again.

Lord? You keep trying to talk to me. Perhaps You'll allow me to talk to You. I don't know if I can be the man she needs, but I will give my last breath trying. Still, I have a feeling only You can change me. Help me.

Imogene raised her head, offering him a tremulous smile. "Let's go tell the authorities."

Vaughn gave her a squeeze before releasing her. "I am your humble servant." Together, they moved for the door.

But just outside a crowd had gathered, at the head of which stood an older man and a wiry fellow in a red waistcoat. Vaughn felt his muscles tense, but Imogene brightened.

"Oh, a Bow Street Runner!" She hurried up to the man. "Sir, we have important news."

"In a moment, miss," he said, shoving her protectively behind him and standing taller. "Mr. Vaughn Everard, we have orders to return you to the Magistrate's Office on suspicion of murder. Will you come along peaceably?"

Murder? What was this? He could argue, but he doubted the Runner would listen. Vaughn glanced around, weighing his options. He could back into the shop and bar the door, but if the Bow Street Runner was worth his salt, reinforcements were likely standing ready at the rear door, as well. He might be able to fight his way through using the clerk's knife, but good men would be hurt in the process.

A month ago, he might not have cared. Now he looked at the faces of the men before him—some tight with apprehension, others bright with determination—and wondered how many were fathers whose children would cry over their loss, how many had sweethearts who would grieve.

He held up his hands. "You have nothing to fear from me. This is all a mistake. I've killed no one."

"Tell that to Lord Kendrick," someone called, "who's missing an heir."

Kendrick? Lord Wentworth's father? Had Vaughn's strike proved lethal, after all? He stood numb as the Bow Street Runner trotted forward and tugged Vaughn's hands behind him. He felt the heavy iron manacles clamp over his wrists and heard the ugly murmurs of the crowd. But all he saw was Imogene's face, staring at him as if she stood alone.

"I'm innocent!" he cried. "Imogene, I swear to you he was alive when I left him."

"Sing away," the Bow Street Runner advised, grabbing Vaughn's arm and leading him forward. "You're only calling for the noose."

Vaughn wrenched himself from the man's grip and darted to Imogene. "The note, my pocket—take it." Nothing was more important right now than saving England, but he couldn't let the Runner see the note. There was too much risk that the fellow would think Vaughn was hiding evidence. To cover his act, Vaughn bent and kissed her.

He felt her lips respond, the caress full of promise, full of faith. Her fingers ticked his stomach as she sought his waistcoat pocket.

He heard the crack of the truncheon against his skull even as pain exploded. With a gasp, he sank to his knees. Imogene reached for him, but others seized her arms and held her back.

"On your feet now," the Bow Street Runner ordered. "And no more nonsense."

Vaughn raised his head, every movement painful. They expected him to struggle, perhaps to curse. That was not the man Imogene deserved, the man he wanted to be, the man God expected of him. He knew that now. He bunched his muscles under him and leapt to his feet. They scattered back as if he held a weapon.

"Don't do anything rash," he said to Imogene before turning to the officer. "Lay on, MacDuff."

"The name's Dervish, not MacDuff," he said, oblivious to the Shakespearean reference from *Macbeth*. "And I'll only lay on if you misbehave again. Now, move."

Vaughn set out, feeling the warm wet of blood against his ear and hearing the jeers. But Imogene held a precious scrap of paper in her hand, and as he passed her she lifted it to her lips. Then she melted into the crowd and was gone. All his hope went with her.

Imogene hurried away from Bond Street, the note marking her father a traitor tight in her grip. The image of Vaughn, pale hair streaked with blood, dark eyes strangely at peace in the midst of chaos, refused to leave her. He couldn't have killed Lord Wentworth. He promised! She had to believe him, she had to believe in him.

Her breath caught, and a stitch poked her side. She stopped at the corner of Little Brook Street and forced air into her lungs. She should follow him to Bow Street and defend him to the magistrates, yet the note seemed to burn her fingers.

She held it up and frowned at it. She didn't want it to be true either. She wanted back the father who'd loved her, taught her, guided her. She hadn't realized how that man had slipped away, been eroded away, by his ambitions and his grief.

And had he never thought of the consequences? The lives that would be lost, the families torn apart? She'd heard the stories of Revolutionary France, the ravenous maw of Madame Guillotine. Did he truly want such a fate for England?

And what of his own family? Everything she'd worked to help him maintain, gone; everything she'd wished for her mother, ripped away; her own future, her chances of making a good marriage, destroyed.

Her stomach was roiling, and she swallowed to keep the bile from rising. She could not afford to grieve, not now. She had to stop him. But were her word and this note enough to turn the tide?

Don't do anything rash, Vaughn had said. And this from a man who acted in the blink of an eye! Yet suddenly she thought she understood why. Her family and her country were in danger, and the knowledge was like a stick in her back, shoving her forward. She was walking again before she remembered moving her foot. He'd been carrying his suspicions for weeks. How could he have waited patiently for others to act?

And how could she? Though it cost her everything, she had to see this through. But she would not lose Vaughn in the process. She was not in this alone. She knew just the person who could help.

* * *

The footman who answered her knock on the Everard House door quickly led her into a downstairs sitting room. Imogene barely had a moment to glance about at the blue-striped settee and chairs in front of a white marble fireplace before Samantha Everard, her sponsor and the dark-haired beauty who had married her oldest cousin hurried in, the rustle of their muslin gowns proclaiming their agitation.

"Lady Imogene," Lady Winthrop cried, rushing up to her. "Are you injured?"

Imogene frowned, then noticed they were all staring at her hat. Pulling out a pin and removing it, she saw that the feather was a sad loss, and a line of rusty red marred the green velvet.

"I'm unharmed," she assured them. "That's merely Vaughn's blood."

"What!" Samantha shouted, leaping at her.

Imogene took a step back, but Lady Winthrop caught the girl and held her. "I suggest you explain. Quickly."

"Forgive me," Imogene told them all. "I'm just a little rattled what with the duel, the note about my father being a traitor and Vaughn's arrest."

"I shall kill her," Samantha promised.

The dark-haired lady took Imogene's arm and led her to the sofa. "I don't believe we've met. I'm Mrs. Jerome Everard. Sit down and tell me exactly what happened, from the beginning, if you please."

Her brisk, no-nonsense manner calmed Imogene's nerves, and she found herself explaining their discovery in Bond Street to a rapt audience. Samantha Everard kept exclaiming through the tale, but Lady Winthrop maintained a tight hand on her arm as if to hold her in place beside her on the settee.

"And now," Imogene concluded, "I'm left with a note declaring my father a traitor, an invasion to prevent and Vaughn stuck at the magistrate's office over some mistake."

"Quite a day," Mrs. Everard said.

"Quite a tale," Samantha countered. "I don't believe a word of it. Cousin Vaughn is far too clever to allow himself to be caught like this. I think you're trying to keep us all busy so your father can escape."

Imogene bristled, but Lady Winthrop merely rose. "Easy enough to confirm the truth." She went to ring the bell, and a footman appeared in the doorway. "Orson, send someone to the Bow Street Magistrate's office and see if we can locate Mr. Vaughn Everard. Have our man bring back any news immediately. And ask Mr. Marshall to meet me in the entryway, if you please."

"Right away, your ladyship."

Lady Winthrop returned to Imogene's side. "Our butler, Mr. Marshall has the utmost discretion. I'd like him to take that note of yours to Whitehall." She held out her hand.

Imogene sat straighter. This was it. Her last chance to save her father and her last chance to save England. Samantha Everard was watching her as if expecting her to refuse to put her father before Vaughn.

Imogene laid the note in Lady Winthrop's hand, and the woman smiled at her, pale blue eyes lighting. "Well done. We'll have this settled soon, I promise."

She turned once more and headed for the door.

Mrs. Everard smiled at Imogene, as well. "While we wait, would you care for something to eat, perhaps some tea?"

Imogene started to decline, but her stomach protested, reminding her that she'd eaten nothing since rising before dawn. As if the woman beside her saw the answer to her question in Imogene's face, Mrs. Everard patted her hand and rose. "I'll just have Mrs. Corday, our cook, pull together a quick repast." Her look to Lady Everard was pointed.

Samantha shifted in her seat as Mrs. Everard left the room. "Do not ask me about the weather, for I couldn't care less."

"That makes two of us," Imogene replied. "And I fail to see why you must be so prickly. Surely you can see I'm on your side. I thought you would want to help your cousin Vaughn. And it isn't your father who'll be sentenced to death."

Samantha grimaced. "Is that what they'll do? I'm very sorry. I know what it's like to lose a father." She sighed. "Only pray that yours doesn't have some will that requires you to make a fool of yourself."

Imogene frowned. "A will? What are you talking about?"

She plucked at the embroidery running down the front of her gown. "My father was afraid I wouldn't be accepted among the *ton,* even by my cousins. So he set up his will to require them to help me complete three tasks to earn their inheritances." She ticked them off on her fingers. "I must be presented to the queen— done. I must be accepted in all the houses that refused my father entrance."

"Done," Imogene said. "You were welcomed in ours."

She smiled. "And others. It's amazing what declaring yourself an heiress will accomplish."

"And the third?"

Her smile faded. "I must receive three eligible offers

of marriage for my hand. My friend Toby was the first. Vaughn was the second."

The world was tilting again, and Imogene's hands clutched at the seat of her chair to keep herself steady. "I suppose I must wish you happy then."

She shook her head, golden curls dancing. "I refused him. Don't get me wrong. I'm inordinately fond of Vaughn. I suspect that's why I was so horrid to you when we visited at your house." She offered Imogene a smile of apology. "But I've come to realize that he doesn't love me, and I'm not content to settle for crumbs. I want a husband so much in love with me that he'll want to be with me no matter what issues and dangers come between us."

Imogene swallowed the longing that rose up inside her. She'd never thought of love that way, but she knew she, too, would settle for nothing less—and no one else but Vaughn.

Yet how could he bear to look at her knowing her father had killed his uncle and endangered England?

Lord, please help me make this right!

Mrs. Everard returned just then and led Imogene and Samantha to the dining room where meats, cheeses and bread had been laid on the sideboard. Lady Winthrop joined them as well, explaining that the note had been sent. The fact left a rock in Imogene's stomach.

The two women managed to keep the conversation flowing, though afterward Imogene wasn't entirely sure what they had discussed. She was merely surprised to find that she'd eaten everything on her plate.

They were just finishing when the footman returned.

"Mr. Everard was questioned by the magistrate for the murder of Lord Gregory Wentworth," he reported.

Samantha cried out, fork clattering to her plate. "Lord Wentworth is truly dead?"

The footman nodded. "Yes, your ladyship. Rumor has it that his valet found him in his bedchamber this morning with a great many wounds upon his body."

"I think that's quite enough description, Orson," Mrs. Everard said. Samantha looked so stricken Imogene thought she might be ill.

"He didn't die in the duel, then," Imogene told them. "That resulted in a single wound to his chest. I won't believe Mr. Everard struck the other blows."

"None of us will," Mrs. Everard assured her. "Did they detain him, then, Orson?"

"No, ma'am," the footman replied. "It seems the magistrate thought it equally unlikely he'd need to strike behind the fellow's back when he could have killed him easily at the duel."

Imogene relaxed in her seat. *Thank You, Lord, for vindicating him!*

"Then where is he?" Samantha asked.

"One of the officers told me he received a note at the office and left right away," the footman answered.

The ladies exchanged glances. "Who would write to him there?" Mrs. Everard mused.

"The same person as wrote him here, I suspect," the footman said, offering a piece of parchment. "This arrived a few minutes ago, addressed to Mr. Everard."

Lady Winthrop held out her hand. "I'll take that, Orson."

As soon as he'd given it to her, she opened it and frowned. "It appears to be from you, Lady Imogene."

Imogene rose and came around the table to her side. "That's impossible. Let me see it."

Lady Winthrop handed it to her even as the others gathered next to them.

"Mr. Everard," it read. "I am in dire need of your assistance. Please meet me at the Northumberland Building, Whitehall, as soon as you receive this. I count on your discretion." It was signed Lady Imogene Devary.

"We must go at once," Samantha said.

Mrs. Everard shook her head. "It's clearly a trap."

"And we have yet to hear how things went at Whitehall," Lady Winthrop reminded them.

Imogene's mind was whirling as madly as a clock about to strike. Of course it was a trap, and one most likely set by her father. The clerk from the Bond Street shop must have warned him that Vaughn was closing in. And now her father sought to use Imogene as the bait, no doubt sending the same note to several places in hopes of intercepting Vaughn. How easily her father dragged her into this mess, blackening her name along with his.

She would not allow him to harm Vaughn! She had imagination, drive and right on her side. *Lord, You promised to be with those who honor You. Be with us now! Help me save Vaughn and defeat my father!*

An idea popped into her head, perfect in its simplicity. Imogene smiled and sent up a prayer of thanks.

"I believe," she said, "that I know what to do. If I can count on all of you, we may be able to save Vaughn and England, too."

She glanced around at the three other women. Samantha Everard's gaze was stormy, but Imogene knew she would do anything to save her cousin. Lady Winthrop's honey-colored hair framed a frowning face, and Mrs. Everard had her dark head cocked as if giving the matter her full consideration.

She was the first to stick out her fist. "I will stand with you, Lady Imogene."

"As will I," Lady Winthrop said, aligning her fist next to her friend's.

"Of course," Samantha said, putting in her fist, as well.

Imogene had never seen the gesture before, but she thought she knew the proper response. She raised her hand and completed the square. "Agreed, then. Now, with the help of Mr. Jerome Everard and Captain Everard, let me tell you how we can prevail."

Chapter Twenty

Vaughn pounded on the door of the Devary house, every muscle tensed. He could still see the face of the street urchin who had handed him the note as Vaughn had left the magistrate's office. The boy had slipped away before Vaughn could question him, but the sick feeling that had swept over him as he read the note remained with him even now.

Lord, You owe me nothing, but I know You must love her if someone like me can love her. Please, keep her safe!

He'd wanted to rush to her aid, but he knew that he'd have to think this through if he hoped to bring them both safely out of it.

The door flew open, and Jenkins scowled at him. "Lady Imogene is not at home to visitors," the footman said, this time eyeing Vaughn with steely determination. "I suggest you go soak your head."

Vaughn almost bristled at the rude remark, then he realized Jenkins must be referring to the dried blood stuck to Vaughn's hair. He shoved his shoulder in the door to keep it from closing. "In good time. But is she home? Just tell me that. I had word she was in danger."

The pressure on the door eased. "Word?" Jenkins asked, head cocked suspiciously. "From whom? I spoke to Bow Street well over two hours ago when they came asking after you, and they should have gone right to her."

So that's how the Runner had tracked him down. "I heard from the lady herself more recently," Vaughn assured him. Taking a chance, he reached in his pocket and drew out the note signed with her name.

Jenkins glanced over it, the door swinging open beside him. "I recognize the hand."

Vaughn stiffened. "Then it is from her."

"No, sir." The footman's gaze was troubled. "That's the master's hand. I'd know his lordship's writing anywhere."

That same fear gripped him again, commanded him to move, to save. He forced himself to stand still. "Then tell me if Lady Imogene is home."

"She's out," the footman replied, returning the note to him. "Left before eleven and hasn't come home. The under footman who accompanied her tells me she dismissed him." He narrowed his eyes. "You wouldn't know anything about that, would you?"

"Far too much," Vaughn said. "But I'll bring her back, Jenkins. I promise."

"Then do it quickly, sir," Jenkins said, hand once more on the door. "I don't know how much longer I can fend off Mr. Prentice or her ladyship's questions."

"Answer one for me, then," Vaughn put in before the portal closed. "What do you know of the Northumberland Building?"

"Never heard of it, sir. Sorry." He'd shut the door then, and Vaughn had hailed a hack, knowing he had no other choice but to follow the instructions on the note.

A short time later he alighted from a hired coach in front of the Northumberland Building, just north of Whitehall. Running as the building did up against the Thames, it had apparently escaped the Great Fire of London, for it still wore the black and white half timbering of an earlier century. He had never visited government offices here, but the building might still serve an official purpose. With the uneasy alliances among the nations the past few years, some previously private buildings around Whitehall had been given over to government use.

He moved cautiously as he approached the recessed center doorway. He was most likely walking into a trap set by the marquess, who would be one of the few to know Vaughn would never refuse a request from Imogene.

As he opened the door, he stepped into the entryway. A long corridor stretched before him, leading deeper into the building. With the low ceiling, he felt as if he'd entered a mine. Only a grimy window at the end issued enough light for him to pick his way along. Unlike the other offices in Whitehall, where clerks scurried from room to room and lords and military men met in determined discussions, the Northumberland Building was quiet. He heard no murmur of voices, no shuffle of paper. Even the air smelled stale.

They had to know he was coming.

His boot heels echoed on the wooden floor as he started down the corridor. Each office he passed was dark. Those he peered into were empty, even of furniture. Dust accumulated in corners, and a rat scampered away from him.

A noise ahead of him made him glance up. A man stood framed in the dim light, but Vaughn thought he saw the white hair and lean frame of his enemy. The voice that spoke confirmed it.

"Ah, Everard," the marquess said as if he'd just stumbled across something he'd thought lost. "Good of you to join us. This way." He turned and went into the last room near the back of the building.

Vaughn followed, only to pull up in the doorway. Inside, a dozen men ringed the marquess, their coats dark and faces hard. Scars and misshapen noses spoke of violence, and reddened eyes and cheeks told of hard drinking. Height and breadth promised power behind their fists, even if half of them hadn't been holding knives or cudgels.

"I fear Lady Imogene hasn't arrived yet," the marquess continued in his pleasant tone. "Let us converse like gentlemen while we wait." He spun a wooden chair beside him on one leg until the seat faced Vaughn. "Make yourself comfortable."

Vaughn widened his stance. "I prefer to stand."

"Ah, but I prefer that you sit." He nodded to the men closest to Vaughn, who moved forward.

The fight was short and swift. Though Vaughn struck and ducked under the blows, his assailants were too many. He didn't reach the corridor before being hauled back like a sack of meal and flung into the chair. Ropes bound his hands behind him before the marquess's men returned to work on the far side of the room. As near as Vaughn could tell with one eye swelling, they seemed to be shifting dark powder into flasks. Making incendiaries, perhaps? Where did they intend to use the explosives?

In front of him, the marquess smiled as if he and Vaughn were meeting over tea at White's. His white hair remained unruffled, and only the dust sprinkling the sleeves of his navy coat said he had ventured near the gunpowder.

"There, you see?" he murmured. "Even you can behave civilly when compelled. Now, I have a few questions, and it will go easier for you if you answer them straight away."

Vaughn spit blood from his mouth, spotting the marquess's boot. "Why should I help you?"

The marquess glanced down with a frown, then pulled out a handkerchief and bent to wipe off the pink-tinged spittle. He wrinkled his nose in distaste as he straightened and tossed the offensive piece of fabric away.

"What do you know of my plans?" he asked as if Vaughn had never spoken.

"Remarkably little," Vaughn replied, "given the effort I've expended."

The marquess looked pleased, his gray eyes lighting. "Excellent. You were surprisingly determined. I hadn't realized the depth of your devotion to your uncle."

Vaughn held his body still, fingers working at his bonds. "He was equally devoted to you."

"Once," the marquess agreed sadly. "But he found faith, he said, in a higher power. As if there were any higher than me." He laughed, and his men's laughter followed like an echo from across the room.

"So you killed him?" Vaughn challenged, straining against his bonds. "Is that how you reward those who serve you?"

The laughter snuffed out. The marquess's eyes narrowed. "Death is not a reward, Mr. Everard. It is the consequence of failure. Your uncle knew that, yet he defied me. He thought a duel would bring me to my senses. Instead, he lost his, permanently."

So Vaughn had been right about his uncle's death. The fact brought him little comfort now. Why had he thought revenge would satisfy him? Nothing would bring Uncle back.

"And Repton and Todd?" Vaughn demanded, feeling the strands begin to give. "Did you kill them, too?"

The marquess frowned as if the question confused him. "Of course. I told you—that is the consequence of failure."

"What of Lord Wentworth?" he asked, carefully straining the rope against one of the rungs on the back of the chair. "Was he one of your followers?"

The marquess made a face. "A very disappointing one, I assure you. I had high hopes for the fellow— good stock, decent cunning, grand ambitions. But he proved singularly unreliable in completing his tasks. I had Eugenie invite him to attend our recent meeting in Vauxhall, and he nearly led you right to it. I asked him to court your cousin to keep you busy, and he came to care for the girl. He couldn't even kill you in a duel. I had to dispose of him." He tsked as if the fellow had been a ruined cravat. "Now, stick to the topic, if you please. Who else have you told about your suspicions?"

Vaughn was tempted to lie and name any number of people who knew the truth, but he feared he'd only put innocent people in danger. Besides, he'd trusted precious few with his plans. Part of his silence had been pride—he'd wanted to find Uncle's killer and seek the vengeance Jerome and Richard cautioned against.

"Regrettably, no one," Vaughn said, "or I wouldn't be here alone now."

The marquess tapped a finger against his chin. "Perhaps. But you Everards are a close bunch. I would imagine your older cousins know too much, as well. And there's the matter of the girl."

Vaughn needed no more impetus. His muscles bunched as he tore at the ropes. "Samantha is no danger to you. She knows nothing."

He dropped his hand. "My, but you are behind the times. She knows we met at her home. She held the box I asked her father to keep safe for me, though she didn't know its significance. I imagine even your dunce of a solicitor has reasoned out that I paid your uncle to keep the house quiet. She has only to tell the wrong story to the right person, and inquiries will be made. Why do you think I convinced your uncle to keep her a secret?"

"That was your doing?" Vaughn shook his head to cover the movement of his shoulders. "We were afraid Uncle didn't want to live up to his responsibilities."

His smile was sad. "Which would have been very like him, I fear. I counseled him against marrying that Cumberland girl. But he insisted. And he grew quite fond of his daughter, as did I, so much so that I tried to stop her from coming to London. I only needed a little more time without any interferences, but you Everards simply would not listen."

Before Vaughn could respond, he waved his hand again, exposing the lace at his wrist. "No matter. Today is critical. I'll send someone to her and the others to ensure their silence."

Vaughn felt chilled inside. He had to keep the fellow talking. Only a few strands of rope remained intact around his wrists. If he could break even one or two more, he ought to be able to free himself. "So you can darken the signal fires?" he pressed. "Help the French land?"

The marquess blinked. "Why no, Mr. Everard. So I

will be First Consul of England and every man will be free from these insufferable rules of inheritance. Then everyone who refused to give me the honor I am due will meet the headsman's ax, even your dear cousins, should they survive the day."

Vaughn felt as if the fellow had landed another blow. "You're mad!"

"Am I?" He smiled, and the sight sickened Vaughn. "Perhaps. But by this time next week, all England shall be mine."

"Not while I live," Vaughn declared. He snapped the last piece of rope and leaped from the chair.

The room exploded. He shoved and kicked and punched and dodged, using the chair to fend off his attackers. But always the marquess remained out of reach, giving way to his followers, who came hurrying from their deadly work. Indeed, the glimpses Vaughn caught of him as Vaughn fought showed a man singularly unconcerned with the action around him.

Suddenly the room was more crowded, and Vaughn realized others had arrived. The new group was more heavily armed and even more determined by the grim looks on their faces. He braced himself for an onslaught.

"Couldn't let you have all the fun," his cousin Jerome teased, forcing off a behemoth with his blade as he dashed past.

"Here!" Richard called to Vaughn and tossed him a sword.

Vaughn caught it easily, feeling as if he'd found a piece of himself. "Stop them from reaching the gunpowder!"

"I'm your man!" Richard shouted, rushing across the room.

From then on it was short work. A few of the marquess's men fought to the end, trying in vain to reach the explosives, but most dropped their weapons or fists and surrendered. The marquess himself stood aside and watched the fight with a smile as if he sat in his box at the theater and quite approved of the play. As silence fell, Vaughn could hear him humming to himself, following an orchestra only he could hear.

Jerome approached the man, sword held ready. "I fear I must arrest you in the name of the king."

"Pity," the marquess said pleasantly, "but right will prevail."

"It already has," Richard told him. "We have your explosives, and our friends in Whitehall told us that riders are on their way to the coast with word to protect the fires and to expect an invasion. The French won't land."

"We shall see," he answered patiently. "And the king holds no power over me. I call the tune in England." He raised both hands as if offering a benediction. "A shame my men must die for their failures, but we will overcome in the end."

His men shuffled their feet and hung their heads.

Jerome glanced at Vaughn with a frown. "Has he been like this long?"

"It seems to have crept up on us all," Vaughn assured him.

Jerome took the marquess's arm. "If you'd be so kind as to join me, my lord, we have much to discuss." Aside to Vaughn, he said, "I'll deal with this. In the meantime, I suggest you go out to the street. There's someone waiting to see you, and you owe her a debt of gratitude for saving your sorry hide."

"Your plan worked," Samantha reported, nose to the window of the coach. "Cousin Richard and his crew must have overcome the ruffians, for here comes Cousin Vaughn."

Imogene, seated across from her and trying to comport herself as a lady for once, felt her stomach jump. *Thank You, Lord, for protecting him!*

Samantha winced. "Oh, he got the worst of it, though."

That did it. Imogene pushed herself up against the glass, as well. His hair was unbound and flowing to his shoulders in a tangled curtain streaked with red. His crimson coat was torn, his boots speckled with things she didn't want to name, and he seemed to be limping. But he'd never looked more dear to her.

A moment later he opened the door and climbed inside.

"Are you all right?" she begged as he seated himself next to his cousin.

"It's nothing serious," he assured her, though now she could see that his cheek was turning purple and one eye was swollen. She longed to touch him, to hold him close. But another fear held her back.

"And…" she could hardly bear to ask "…Father?"

He glanced at Samantha, then at her, and she braced herself for the worst. "Jerome has him in hand. He wasn't hurt."

Imogene exhaled. "Thank you."

His smile was kind, but it spoke of regret.

"And did he have no explanation for his deeds?" Samantha demanded. "Did you learn the truth?"

"I did." He sighed, suddenly looking weary. "And it is not nearly as satisfying as I'd hoped. He admitted responsibility for Uncle's death as well as those of Repton, Todd and Lord Wentworth."

Samantha paled. "Oh, I see."

Imogene felt nearly as faint. "And the invasion?"

"That, too. He seemed to think he'd end up ruling England for Napoleon."

His eyes begged her to understand, but she couldn't. Had it all been about power, then? Had her father been so arrogant he thought himself better than anyone else, even the rulers God had appointed? Had he never considered that he was taking a life—four lives—for his own gain? How could he have so lost himself?

"I'm sorry," Vaughn said.

Imogene nodded, unable to speak.

Samantha glanced between the two of them, then gathered her skirts. "Jerome and Richard came in another carriage," she murmured. "I'll just ride home with them." She opened the door and gave her hand to the groom to slip out.

Vaughn was across the coach in a moment, gathering Imogene in his arms. The sobs came easily—tears of joy that he was safe, tears of thanks that England would carry on, tears of sorrow her father was lost.

"Why?" she asked Vaughn, pulling back at last. "Did he tell you that at least? Why did he do all this?"

Vaughn touched her cheek. "I'm not sure he knows. I fear he's gone mad, Imogene."

She shuddered and cuddled closer once more, taking strength from the arms around her, solace from his sorrow.

"You told me he lost control before, when your brother died," Vaughn murmured against her hair. "Perhaps his grief unhinged him."

Imogene choked. "To the point where he sought to make himself God? Oh, it is too monstrous!"

"He may well have started all this with good intentions," Vaughn insisted. "He may have wanted revolution, a changing of the regime."

"A way for all men to be equal," Imogene said, thinking back on things her father had said. "But still he wanted to be better than any of them. It makes no sense."

"Only in his mind, it seems. But he must have cast a compelling vision for men to follow him, for my uncle to believe in him. Somewhere along the way that vision grew tarnished. Instead of founding a better England, he fostered treason."

She clung to him. "What happens next?"

"Jerome will take your father to the authorities. His followers will be rounded up and tried." He pulled back to eye her. "I'm more concerned about you, Imogene. What will *you* do now?"

She swallowed. Her fingers were worrying in her skirt again, but she didn't try to stop them. She had to do something, anything, to make it through all this.

"I don't suppose there's much I can do," she admitted, and the panic inside her spiked. She forced it down. "I believe Mother has a little money from her family that won't be returned to the crown. We may be able to live on that."

Please, Lord, let us be able to live on that!

He took her hands. "It need not come to that. You could marry me."

Chapter Twenty-One

Imogene caught her breath and searched his gaze. But instead of the love she'd hoped for, she saw only worry.

"You are too kind, Mr. Everard," she said, "but you needn't feel obliged to sacrifice yourself for me."

He stiffened, releasing her. "Forgive me. I did that badly, a consequence of my battered state, I fear. Give me a moment, and I will offer you the kind of proposal you deserve."

He would launch into something grand, and Imogene couldn't bear it, not here, not now. She caught up Vaughn's hands, held them tight.

"Listen to me," she said, gaze on his. "Father's treachery changes everything. My mother and I will lose our place in society. I don't even know if I'll have a dowry."

His pale brows gathered in a frown. "Why would any of that matter?"

"Oh, my dear sweet rake." Imogene tried for a smile. "My family's scandal may not matter to you, but think of our children. The *ton* has a fearfully long memory at times. They will understand the gravity of my father's deeds and talk of them years after the fact. Our children will have to carry that legacy. Do you want them isolated or scorned?"

She saw the doubt darken his gaze. From what he'd said, he'd felt the sting of Society's disdain. He knew the pain of having a family member derided. She could not put him under that whip again.

She released him. "Now you understand why I cannot marry you."

"But I don't understand," he murmured. "Do you see position and perfection as mattering more than character and love?"

Imogene felt as if the whip had turned on her. "No! Of course not!"

He cocked his head. "Then think, Imogene. It was not position and reputation that kept me apart from Society but the flaws in my character."

"That's not true!" she protested. "You have an admirable character—loyal, determined, strong."

"And pigheaded, hot-tempered and arrogant," he countered. His smile tipped up at one corner. "But that's part of being an Everard."

Imogene shook her head. "You persist in seeing the worst in yourself."

"And you persist in seeing the best. And because you believed in me, I began to see my better qualities, as well."

He took up her hands again and held them cradled against him. "I never knew the love of family until Uncle took me under his wing. I never understood the love of God until your example set me seeking. And I never knew the power of love until I met you."

The tears were coming again. She couldn't seem to stop them. "I wish I could believe love is enough on which to base a marriage."

"Do you want more?" He smiled at her. "I am accounted a poet, and people say that poetry is the language of love. But if you prefer a more pedantic proposal, I can manage it." As if to prove it, he released her and took a moment to straighten his cravat with such puffed up self-importance that a laugh tried to force its way out through Imogene's tears.

"Once my uncle's will is settled," he said, nose decidedly in the air, "I can lay claim to five thousand pounds a year as well as the income from my literary efforts. The *ton* seems to find me increasingly respectable, so I am confident I can soon reclaim the title of gentleman, and I am a cousin to a baroness. In short, madam, I offer you sufficient income, prestige and connections to make me an eligible bachelor. And I assure you that fact amazes even me."

Imogene's laugh came out as a hiccough. "I consider you highly eligible, Mr. Everard. But you must see that I cannot offer you nearly as much."

His look turned serious. "No, only beauty, intelligence, talent, character, faith and love. What are those compared to a hefty dowry and an honorary title?"

Imogene's lips trembled. "I do love you, you know."

In a flash, he pulled her into his arms, and his lips reached hers. The touch stole her breath, fired her blood, made her dream of a future together, where love truly could triumph over all they had lived through the past few days.

When Imogene finally pulled away, she offered Vaughn a smile, then had to laugh at the smug look on his face.

"Do not think you can sway me so easily, sir," she warned with a shake of her finger. "We must deal with these concerns."

His smile widened. "Quite likely. But so long as I know you love me, they matter very little."

Imogene threw up her hands. "How can you say that? And let me remind you, sir, that I have not accepted your proposal."

"You will," he predicted, leaning back as if well satisfied with himself. "You've just spent a quarter hour in a closed coach with a rake. Marriage is the only option."

Imogene shook her head. "At the moment, my reputation is the least of my worries."

He reached for the door as if the matter was already settled. "I need to see that everything is resolved," he said. "Do you wish me to escort you home and help you explain the situation to your mother?"

Part of her would have felt safer in his arms, but she shook her head again. "No, thank you. I think I should speak to Mother alone."

He nodded, then reared up and pressed a kiss against her lips. A moment later and the door was closing behind him. He must have instructed the coachman where to go, for she felt the carriage start forward. She pressed her nose to the glass and watched as he raised a hand in farewell. Their gazes did not part until the coach turned the corner and hid Vaughn from her view.

As the hired coach turned the corner, Vaughn dropped his hand. He could feel exhaustion nibbling around the corners of his resolve, but exhilaration pushed it back. Imogene loved him! He could scale mountains, topple empires on that knowledge alone.

Yet her concerns remained on his mind as he made his way over to where the last of her father's followers were shuffling into a wagon to be taken to the magistrate's office. He knew too well the stigma of having a parent the *ton* could not accept. The Marquess of Widmore's fall from grace would be fodder for the gossips for years to come. If only he could find a way to spare Imogene that.

A tall man, his lean frame stiff with authority, stood watching the proceedings. As Vaughn approached, he doffed his hat in respect, and the breeze from the river ruffled his dark blond hair.

"Mr. Everard," he said, offering his hand, "I don't believe we've met. I'm Joshua Manning."

Vaughn shook his hand. Manning had hard blue eyes, assessing, but the lines around his eyes and mouth told Vaughn that he had a tendency to smile under other circumstances. "And which branch of the military do you support, Mr. Manning?" he asked.

Manning frowned as the doors of the wagon were shoved into place. "Any and none, Mr. Everard. That was good work today, by the way. We've had our eye on the marquess for some time but were never able to prove anything."

Vaughn glanced at the faces of the men through the grates on the otherwise closed wagon. Some were resigned, others bewildered, and a few frightened. Of the marquess there was no sign. Vaughn felt his muscles stiffen.

"What have you done with him?"

"He'll be taken care of, never fear," Manning said, and the determination in his voice did nothing to still his concerns.

"Did you see him?" Vaughn pressed, stepping closer. "The man is mad. Surely that should count for something."

Manning cocked his head. "Interesting. I had heard you were not one for compassion, Mr. Everard. I was also under the impression you'd made the marquess the single target of your vendetta the past few weeks."

Apparently everyone had noticed. "I've had a change of heart."

"And perhaps of faith?"

Vaughn blinked. Normally he would never have discussed such matters with a stranger, but something about this man told him the answer was important. "Yes, that, too."

Manning nodded, then leaned closer and lowered his voice as his men hustled past to mount their waiting horses and escort the wagon to the jail. "I promise you your request for compassion will be considered. I'm a member of the Carpenter's Club. We're just off St. George's Street. After today I can safely say you will always be welcomed there. Excuse me." With a nod, he doffed his hat and hurried away.

The wagon and its determined escort moved on. The street was deserted. The Northumberland Building stood as quiet as it had when Vaughn had arrived. But his tasks, Vaughn thought as he strode away to find a hack, were only beginning. Imogene had a longing for perfection. Perhaps he could give it to her, at least in one area of her life.

Imogene was not thinking about perfection. Trying not to lose herself in reliving that kiss with Vaughn, she'd leaned back against the squabs as the coach trundled toward Charing Cross. So it was done—her father in custody, his evil plans foiled. England was safe, and her life was in ruins. But perhaps not ruined.

Could she marry Vaughn? Could they make something good from all this?

And we know that all things work together for good

to them that love God, to them who are called according to His purpose.

She closed her eyes and clung to the verse. She'd missed His calling for weeks, thinking that she had to find the perfect man. Vaughn had been right in his assessment. To her sorrow, she'd counted prestige, position and perfection more important than character.

But the Lord knew better. He had brought Vaughn into her life for a purpose, and she thought it went beyond uncovering her father's misdeeds. *Oh, Lord, I want to believe Your promises. Thank You for helping me make a difference in Vaughn's life. I just don't want to see him hurt because of my family's mistakes.*

She didn't want to hurt her mother either by explaining what had happened, but she knew Lady Widmore deserved to hear the truth before it was reported in the papers or the authorities showed up at their door with questions. She steeled herself, saying a prayer for wisdom. She still wasn't ready as the coach swung off Park Lane. But apparently someone else was ready for her. The coachman had barely pulled up at the door of the Devary home before Jenkins ran down the steps to help Imogene alight.

"Did Mr. Everard find you?" he asked as she shook out her skirts.

"Yes, Jenkins," she assured him. "I wouldn't be here if not for his aid."

She thought a weight dropped from his broad shoulders. He ushered Imogene into the house.

"Is everything all right, your ladyship?" he murmured as he took her pelisse.

"No," she told him. "Where is my mother?"

"In the library," he said, but she could see the troubled look on his face as she set off.

Her mother was seated on the sofa by the fire, book open in the lap of her muslin gown. By her stillness, Imogene somehow thought the written words held no meaning for her. She must have made a noise, because her mother looked up and closed the book.

"Imogene! Where have you been? You gave me such a scare!"

Imogene went to sit beside her. "Forgive me, Mother. I have news about Father."

Her mother paled. "He's dead."

Imogene started. "No! At least, he was alive a few moments ago. But you must be brave." She went on to tell her mother what Imogene and Vaughn had learned and the consequences of her father's actions. They ended up in each other's arms, tears flowing.

Her mother drew back first. "There's nothing for us here, then. We'll have to retire from Society, perhaps find a place in the country where no one knows us."

The words tore at Imogene, but she knew her mother was right. "I've heard the Lake District is sufficiently remote," she offered, trying to find something good about their limited choices. "I've always wanted to see it."

Her mother managed a smile. "You were swayed by a certain poet, I think."

Imogene blushed, then realized her mother wasn't talking about Vaughn and Lady Everard's home in Cumberland. "Mr. Wordsworth does make it sound lovely in his poetry."

Her mother cocked her head. "And what of our other favorite poet, Mr. Everard?"

Imogene knit her fingers together, body trembling as she remembered their conversation. "He asked me to marry him."

"Before or after this business with your father?" her mother asked, face still.

"After," Imogene confessed, then hurried on as her mother brightened. "I fear he's only being noble. He knows the part he played in Father's downfall, and he hopes to make things right by taking care of me."

Her mother frowned. "Do you truly know him so little?"

Imogene blinked. "I thought I knew him rather well."

"So did I until I read this." Her mother pulled a piece of paper from the book in her lap. "The publisher, Mr. Murray, hopes to have a new tome out from Mr. Everard in the next month. He provided his subscribers with one of the poems this afternoon to whet their appetite. Read those stanzas."

Imogene took the paper and read the words.

Faith finds what mind and will deny
And lights the heart that wanders lost.
Love fills each void and heals the cry
Of one who could not count the cost;
Who spent a lifetime wondering why
And squandered time as so much dross.

Now hope flies close on gilded wing
And love can blossom in a kiss;
The dark dethroned like aged kings
That now will nevermore be missed.
And I who scoffed at many things
Believe again, and rise to bliss.

"Oh, Mother," Imogene murmured.

"You see," her mother said. "He has changed. He

loves you, Imogene. I am certain of it. I know you care
for him."

Imogene hugged the paper close. "I do. I love him."

"Then accept his offer. Find happiness."

"But what of you?" Imogene begged. "I can't leave
you alone."

"I've been alone for some time, dearest," her mother
reminded her, face once more sad. "Your father has
been distancing himself ever since Charles died. At
least now I know why." She patted Imogene's knee and
raised her head. "No, I shall be fine. A quiet house, a
rose garden, will suit me well."

Imogene wanted to believe that. But before they
could speak further, their butler came with news of
government men at the door, and Imogene knew she
had a duty to perform.

The next few hours flew by. Imogene helped her
mother meet with the men from the War Office. They
were kind and cordial, and no one implied the least
criticism, or seemed to think her mother or Imogene
had been involved in the marquess's plans. The last, a
tall gentleman of military bearing, Mr. Manning, even
went so far as to ask if there was anything he could do
for them.

"Tell us what's happening with Father," Imogene
begged.

He glanced between her and her mother, and she
thought his smile held compassion. "I regret I cannot.
And I must ask you to keep this matter quiet."

"We would be the last people to trumpet it," her
mother assured him. "And I am grateful for the government's circumspection."

"It has little to do with the government," Manning
said, rising to take his leave. "Though I understand ev-

eryone has agreed to be civil. And none of us wishes to be called to account by Mr. Vaughn Everard should we distress his lady."

His lady. Imogene sat in wonder as the gentleman left. Is that how the *ton* saw her? Had the rest of Society realized Imogene and Vaughn were in love before she did? Certainly they must know that he was capable of affection. Look at his devotion to his uncle, his cousin; look at the poem he'd penned. Where Vaughn loved, he gave his all.

Could she do any less? He had risked censure to offer for her. She should brave it to agree.

By the time she went to bed, she was exhausted. But her mother came to tuck her in as she had when Imogene was a child. Somehow she thought the gesture comforted her mother as much as it did her.

"We'll make it through, Mother," she promised.

"I know, dearest." Her mother slipped a lock of Imogene's hair behind her ear. "We just received a note. I thought you should know."

Imogene tensed. "About Father?"

"No. It was from Mr. Everard." She held out the page to Imogene with a tremulous smile. "Perhaps it is good news."

Hope blossomed, and her fingers shook as she broke the seal.

My love, it read, and went a long way to calming her overwrought nerves, *I regret that I have not been able to see you this afternoon. Tomorrow, alas, will likely be no better. I ask that you and your mother be ready for a drive the day after. We have much to discuss. Know that I remain your most devoted servant, Vaughn Everard.*

"He asks us to drive with him the day after tomorrow," Imogene reported, folding the note carefully.

Her mother frowned. "Odd. Both of us?"

Imogene nodded. "He says we have much to discuss."

She reached out her free hand and took her mother's. "I know you cannot feel up to company, Mother, but I think we should accept his offer, just as I plan to accept his offer of marriage, if he'll still have me."

Chapter Twenty-Two

Two days later, Vaughn stepped down from the chariot—feeling odd to be climbing from the interior for once. He'd asked the Everard coachman to drive so he could sit with Imogene and her mother.

The Devary house stood as imposing and ornate as it always had, but he got the impression the entire edifice was holding its breath. He felt as if he was holding his as well and puffed it out. Lifting his chin, he walked to the front door and knocked.

Jenkins opened the door and bowed. "Mr. Everard. Welcome."

Vaughn raised a brow. "Welcome now, am I?"

Jenkins grinned. "Assuredly, sir." Then he put on his proper footman's look, impassive gaze going out over Vaughn's shoulder. "Her ladyship and Lady Imogene are expecting you." He turned to lead Vaughn up the stairs to the withdrawing room.

Imogene jumped to her feet at the sight of him in the doorway and was hurrying across the room in a flurry of white muslin before Jenkins even finished announcing him. She took one of Vaughn's hands and pulled him into the room, walking backward as if she refused to let herself lose sight of him. "Are you all right? Is everything all right?"

With her gazing up at him, the world was a better place. "I'm fine, thank you. And I hope you'll find that everything has been resolved with a great deal more satisfaction than we'd expected." He bowed to her mother, who was seated in a chair by the fire and watching Imogene with a tender smile. "Lady Widmore. Thank you for agreeing to drive with me today."

She rose with a whisper of silk the shade of sunlight. "How could I not, Mr. Everard? We owe you a debt of gratitude."

The very air tasted sweeter in the withdrawing room. He'd feared she might blame him for revealing her husband's misdeeds and that her anger over the matter might infect his relationship with Imogene. But Lady Widmore's smile was merely sad, as if she was trying to muster her veneer of civility but struggling. He could only hope their trip today could ease some of her and Imogene's concerns.

In a very short time the two ladies were seated in the chariot across from him as the coach set off to the west. Imogene's glance kept lighting on Vaughn and lingering. Each time he felt it as a caress. He wanted to take her in his arms and help them both forget the past. But today she was owed a gentleman, and even if he had refused to honor the role, he thought her mother might have something to say about him seizing her daughter and kissing her senseless.

As if Lady Widmore had no inkling of the emotions sizzling in the coach, she sat, back straight against the leather seat, hands folded in the lap of her cerulean pelisse. "And where might you be taking us today, Mr.

Everard?" she asked as if they were out for a picnic in the country.

He might as well play along. "To a charming manor house near the Royal Gardens at Kew," he replied. "I'm hoping you will find it a diverting trip."

Imogene glanced between him and her mother, and he saw her white teeth worrying her lower lip. This was madness. He couldn't pretend to be the proper gentleman, couldn't converse about nonsense when Imogene's world had been upended. He reached across the coach and took her hands in his.

"It's all right. They've shown your father mercy. He has been declared insane, and no word of his efforts has left Whitehall. You're safe."

Lady Widmore cried out and then pressed both hands to her lips as if to calm herself. Imogene stared at him as if he were the one who had gone insane.

"Forgive me," Vaughn said, "for breaking it so baldly."

"I should think so," Imogene said with a sudden smile that drove out any concern. "For a man dedicated to the dramatic, you jumped to the conclusion of the tale remarkably fast." She leaned across the coach and pressed a kiss to his mouth. The touch was gone before he could savor it, yet he felt it lingering.

"Thank you," she murmured, drawing back.

In her gaze, he saw his future written, and the sight had never pleased him more.

"Yes, thank you," Lady Widmore said, reminding him of her presence.

Vaughn released Imogene's hands. "You have no need to thank me, either of you. We owe much of this to my cousin Jerome. He is known for having a gilded tongue."

"And for being a bit of a rogue, I seem to recall," Lady Widmore mused.

"Only until he wed, I promise you," Vaughn replied, then his gaze returned to Imogene's. "It's amazing how love can change a man."

She blushed but did not look away. "Or a woman."

He thought he heard a smile in Lady Widmore's voice. "Much as I hate to interrupt this philosophical conversation, I fear I'm a bit confused. Are you saying my husband won't have to pay for his crimes?"

Vaughn knew he had to go carefully. He didn't want to distress them further, but they had to know what to expect when they reached the house.

"He is already paying, your ladyship," he said, turning to look at her. "I fear his reason has largely left him. He has been remanded to the care of keepers, to spend the rest of his life on the estate we are about to visit. He will never be left alone, even with visitors."

She nodded, face pale. "But he can have visitors?"

"Only family," Vaughn replied. "If there are others such as your solicitor or land steward who need to meet with him, they must be approved by the War Office beforehand. The Prime Minister is taking no chances that the marquess's followers will regroup and attempt to release him."

She shuddered and dropped her gaze.

Imogene touched her mother's shoulder. "He's alive, Mother. We can be thankful for that." She glanced at Vaughn. "And his title? Our estate?"

"Safe for the moment," Vaughn assured her.

She paled, as well. "Until he dies, you mean."

There was nothing he could do to parry that blow. "I'm afraid so."

Imogene's face tightened, but Lady Widmore rallied,

reaching up to pat her daughter's hand where it rested on her shoulder. "Where are our manners, dearest? I'm certain Mr. Everard would prefer better conversation than our sad trials. How is your youngest cousin Lady Everard getting on? Is she enjoying her Season?"

Vaughn watched fascinated as Society's mask fell once more on her face, but Imogene laughed. "Oh, Mother, I fear you've shocked him." She dropped her hand and smiled at him. "Mr. Everard is used to far more interesting conversation than the weather or the state of the Season. I suggest you ask him about his horses."

As that was also a well-known conversational gambit, Vaughn laughed as well, and they were able to discuss literary interests, Napoleon's threats to England and yes, even Vaughn's pride in his matched pair before the carriage pulled into the drive of the manor.

Vaughn had already been out to the house once, but he hoped Imogene could see that everything about the place said peace, from the creamy stone walls of the two-story manor to the beautiful gardens spreading out on all sides. Inside was just as lovely, with walls of calm blue and peach-colored upholstery on the polished wood furniture. The owner of the house escorted them to a withdrawing room that rivaled the elegance of her mother's, and a burly manservant in breeches and tailcoat escorted the marquess to visit with them there.

His white hair was cut in the latest style, and he carried himself with his usual grace. But Vaughn noticed as the man took a seat on the settee next to his wife that his hands trembled and his gaze never rested, flitting from her to Imogene to far across the room as if everything held equal interest or no interest at all. His conversation was nearly as disjointed, but it was clear Lady Widmore wished to speak with him alone, so Vaughn requested a moment with Imogene, and the two excused themselves.

He took her hand and led her out to the chariot.

Imogene raised her brows. "Where exactly are you taking me, Mr. Everard?"

"I have a destination in mind," he promised. "But I thought perhaps you'd like to drive us there."

Her grin was his reward. He helped her up onto the driver's bench, then took his place beside her. As the groom released the horses into her care, she clucked to the team, and Aeos and Aethon raised their heads and set off. Each prancing step said they were as proud to be carrying her as Vaughn was to be sitting beside her.

Vaughn directed her down the road to the entrance to the Royal Gardens. The gatekeeper didn't even blink to find a lady in the driver's seat and opened the gates to them. Vaughn tipped his hat to the elderly man, who winked at him as they passed into the park.

"Along there," Vaughn told her, and she managed to maneuver the chariot to a lawn surrounded by trees. The emerald expanse, dotted with marble statues in classical poses, led down to a folly with Grecian columns supporting the domed roof. The sun was warm, the sky a clear blue. As Vaughn helped Imogene down, the breeze ruffled the collar of her muslin gown where it peeked out of her satin pelisse. It was the perfect setting for what he had to say.

"Lovely day for a stroll," he said as he set her down, hands lingering at her waist.

She dimpled at him. "Do not start with the weather again. But yes, a walk would be delightful."

They moved across the grass, the air heavy with the

perfume of the exotic species for which the park was famous.

"Are you satisfied with the resolution of our adventures?" he asked.

She nodded. "Yes. I think Father will be safe at the house, and I know England will be more secure. You and your family are a wonder for working it all out."

"Then only one thing remains." He looked to the folly, caught the light of a brass telescope pointed in their direction and nodded. A moment later, music drifted on the breeze.

Imogene stopped and gazed at him. "Is that…?"

"Your composition? Yes. At least, what I could remember of it."

She clasped her hands together as if in awe of hearing her work. "You recalled it beautifully." Then she dropped her hands and craned her neck as if to try to spy the musician. "Who's playing?"

"I asked a talented pianist to attempt it."

She relaxed back beside him with a smile. "It's your cousin Lady Everard, isn't it?"

Samantha on the piano, Richard on the telescope to watch for them, and Jerome, Adele, and Lady Claire waiting beyond with refreshments to celebrate. Or commiserate with him if Imogene refused his offer. "Do you mind?" he asked.

She shook her head. "Not at all. She plays well, and it sounds better than I imagined." She glanced around suddenly as if noticing the bucolic setting for the first time, then her look speared back to his. "All this, you planned it."

He bowed. "With great expectation."

She smiled. "Even the bluebirds flitting through the willows?"

"Ah," he said, straightening, "God supplied those, and I shall have to thank Him for it." He knelt before her.

"This isn't necessary," she said.

"It is absolutely necessary," he replied with a grin. "I am a poet, you know. I have a reputation to uphold."

Imogene shook her head. "But you already proved your love. 'Now hope flies close on gilded wing, and love can blossom in a kiss.'"

The promise of his words swept over him, made stronger by her breathless rendition. He had written the poem for her, and the thought that she returned his feelings still left him humbled.

"You aren't going to allow me to propose properly, are you?" he asked, gazing up at her.

She smiled and reached down for his hands to tug him to his feet. "No. I already know my answer. Only tell me you love me, and we are sealed."

The words trembled on his tongue. "I love you, Imogene. My heart, my strength, my devotion all belong to you."

"And I love you," she said, smile bathing him in light warmer than the day. "Every amazing thought, every spontaneous action, every leap of faith. I am honored to accept your proposal of marriage."

He took Imogene in his arms and kissed her, feeling her lips and heart responding to his. How many times had he wondered why God had made him the way he was? Now he knew. This was who he was meant to be—her protector, her supporter, the one who encouraged and loved and admired her. Nothing had ever felt so right, so true. He had come home at last.

Imogene drifted out of the kiss with Vaughn to cries of congratulations and spent the next while accepting

well wishes from all the Everards. The age difference
between her and her brother, and his loss at an early
age, had made her feel as if she'd been an only child.
Having so many people willing to offer friendship and
support was amazing, and she thought she could well
grow to love it.

Almost as much as she loved Vaughn. Watching him
as he lay on the grass, long legs stretched out, up on one
elbow, tossing challenges to his cousins, she could only
marvel that this man wanted to marry her. He held her
hand as they returned to the chariot, and she let him
drive back to the house. Her emotions were singing so
loudly she didn't think she should be trusted with the
horses just then.

She barely waited until they were on the way home
before telling her mother, who immediately wished
them happy with tears shining in her eyes. Imogene
knew they were tears of joy. She felt a similar joy knowing she would spend the rest of her life with Vaughn.
Her feelings so overfilled her that she was amazed to
find the world continued on its course.

In fact, back in London, Society moved on. Concerned with staving off a revolution, the government
had done an admirable job of hushing up her father's
treachery. All anyone knew was that the Marquess of
Widmore had fallen ill and repaired to the country to
recuperate. Although people asked after him, commis-
erated with Imogene and Lady Widmore and sent him
their best wishes, no one censured her or her mother,
particularly when it became known that Imogene had
a reason for staying in London.

She was betrothed to Vaughn Everard.

Speculation on the reasons behind that betrothal ran
rampant, but many remembered the once close friend-

ship between her father and his uncle and put her connection to Vaughn down to that. She and her mother planned for a quiet wedding at their home in late June.

But she had another wedding to attend in the meantime. Captain Richard Everard and Lady Claire married two weeks later in May. They had originally planned to wait until the end of the Season in August. That was when Adele Everard had been scheduled to present her case to the solicitor, who served as executor of the will. As Samantha's former governess, she had been designated in Lord Everard's will to prove that Samantha had fulfilled its requirements. However, Mrs. Everard had made her report a week after Imogene and Vaughn's betrothal, and the Everards only awaited the results of the solicitor's deliberation.

So Imogene sat on a gilded chair in the Everard House drawing room with her mother on one side and Vaughn on the other and watched as Richard Everard and his Claire pledged their devotion. The look in his dark eyes as he towered over his bride and the smile on Claire's face as she gazed up at him told Imogene of their love, and many a lady wiped away a tear as the vicar pronounced them man and wife.

"Beautiful," Samantha declared afterward as she and Imogene repaired with the other guests to the wedding breakfast in the dining room. Imogene's mother had gone to wish Claire happy, and Vaughn was helping Jerome with other guests. "I hope your wedding will be as lovely, Lady Imogene."

"Imogene," she insisted, trying to decide what to select from the groaning sideboard. "We will shortly be cousins, after all."

"Very well, Imogene," Samantha said with a smile and a finger point to suggest the apricot tart. "And you must call me Samantha. I still can't get used to this 'your ladyship' business." Her smile widened as Vaughn joined them. "I was just telling Imogene I expect your wedding to rival this."

"Rival?" He lifted a brow as he slipped an arm about Imogene's waist with one hand and selected a strawberry with the other. "It will surpass it by far."

Imogene laughed as he popped the fruit into his mouth. "So much for humility."

"A humble Everard?" Vaughn chuckled. "You are marrying into the wrong family if that is your expectation. Tell her, Cousin," he continued as he picked up both their plates and led them to chairs at one end of the flower-decked table. "I imagine you have similar dreams for your wedding."

To Imogene's surprise Samantha's smile faded as she seated herself on the harp-backed chair. "I'm not planning on marrying. This business of courting is too difficult."

Imogene thought she was still mourning Lord Wentworth, and her heart hurt for the girl. She took a seat beside Samantha as Vaughn set her plate on the damask cloth.

"You may change your mind when the legacy is in jeopardy," Vaughn answered, sitting on the chair next to Imogene's.

Imogene frowned at him. "Do you think the solicitor will deny her claim?"

"That's not it," Samantha answered for him. "We heard today that they accepted Adele's recommendation. The fortune is ours. I was presented to the queen, welcomed in Society and courted, just as Papa wanted."

"Congratulations!" Imogene cried. She raised the

glass a footman had put before her to Samantha in toast. Samantha blushed.

"I knew of the others," Vaughn said, fingers toying with his own glass, "but who was your third proposal?"

Samantha's face sagged. "Lord Wentworth. Jerome said he asked for my hand the day before he died. He just never had a chance to ask *me*."

"Oh, Samantha!" Imogene reached out to touch her still fingers. "I'm so sorry! Small wonder you're so blue!"

"Forgive me, Cousin," Vaughn murmured, watching her. "I had no idea matters had progressed so far."

"Neither had I," Samantha said, drawing back her hand with a smile of thanks to Imogene. "It may all have been part of the marquess's plan. Perhaps he meant merely to have Lord Wentworth distract you from pursuing him."

"Possible," Imogene agreed, but Vaughn shook his head.

"The courtship was part of the marquess's plan, but you do yourself an injustice if you think that's the only reason Lord Wentworth pursued you."

Samantha poked her tart with her silver fork. "That's why I say that courting is so difficult. Who's to say whether the gentleman is sincere?"

"Only your heart," Imogene said, gazing at Vaughn.

"Well, my heart isn't very reliable," Samantha answered. "I know the last requirement of Papa's will is for me to marry by the time I'm five and twenty or I forfeit the largest part of the legacy, but I think perhaps I'll be content with staying at Dallsten Manor, if I'm allowed to keep it. The rest of my portion of the legacy can go to charity."

"I don't believe it," Vaughn insisted. "You won't let

everything our family worked for leave us. You'll marry to save it."

Samantha raised her chin, dark gaze narrowing, and Imogene saw a similar determination building in Vaughn. She put a hand on his arm but faced his cousin.

"I think," she told Samantha, "that you will be more tempted to marry when you find the man God intended. He may not be the man you expect, and he won't be perfect, but he will be the right man for you."

"And he will love you with all he is," Vaughn said. The warmth in his voice forced Imogene's gaze to his. In the dark expanse, she saw the love she had dreamed of.

"Only love, Cousin," he added, "can bring an Everard to his, or her, knees."

He leaned over and kissed Imogene then, and the world slipped away. She rather thought if she hadn't been sitting down she might be on her knees as well, glorying in His love, thanking God for this gift. Her rake was redeemed, and neither of them would ever be the same.

* * * * *

Dear Reader,

Thank you for choosing *The Rake's Redemption*. Vaughn Everard stepped into my imagination, sword in hand, flowery phrase on his lips, more than five years ago, but it took a while to find him and his cousins the right ladies to wed!

Finding the right person for Vaughn was particularly difficult. Vaughn isn't like the other men around him—he cannot be still, he cannot stand idly by. In my house, we call these men "hunters," and both my oldest son and husband are among their number. I, however, am a "farmer," like Imogene—more content to move with the rhythms of life. We all need a hunter or two to liven things up!

Be sure to stop by my website at *www.reginascott.com* for more information on England during the early nineteenth century and news on upcoming books.

Blessings!
Regina Scott

Discussion Questions

1. The death of Imogene's brother, Viscount Charles, changed many things in the lives of her family. Her mother is devastated, her father decides to take fate into his own hands and Imogene chooses to save her family by making the perfect marriage. What are better ways to grieve an unexpected death?

2. Imogene is determined to find the perfect husband. How can we know who God intends us to marry, or if we should marry at all?

3. Vaughn initially rejected Christ's love because of the strict upbringing of his grandfather. How does the way we are introduced to faith affect the way we respond?

4. Vaughn cannot understand why he cannot behave like other men, particularly during an era when a gentleman was judged on his ability to be civil even when confronting difficulties. What other men have you known who felt compelled to act when faced with injustice?

5. The Marquess of Widmore was driven mad by his ambitions and fears for his family. When is ambition useful?

6. Samantha Everard struggles to fulfill the requirements of her father's will, particularly in winning a proposal from a proper gentleman. To what lengths

should a woman go today to encourage the man she loves to marry her?

7. Jenkins, the Devary head footman, starts out by judging Vaughn but eventually sees the good in him. How can we know someone's character?

8. One of the ways Imogene shares her feelings is to compose music, a rarity for a woman in the nineteenth century. How do you share your feelings with others?

9. Vaughn composes a poem to show Imogene he loves her. What other ways can we let others know of our love?

10. Samantha and Imogene discuss what makes a perfect wedding. What is your vision of a perfect wedding? How did you decide on the elements?

11. *The Rake's Redemption* sees the last Everard man meet his match. Which of the three Everards—Jerome, the charming rogue; Richard, the commanding captain; or Vaughn, the romantic rake, did you like best? Why?

12. The Everard men chose equally strong ladies to wed. Which of their loves—the wise and dedicated Adele, the clever Claire or the energetic Imogene, did you like best? Why?

COMING NEXT MONTH
from Love Inspired® Historical
AVAILABLE NOVEMBER 27, 2012

MAIL-ORDER HOLIDAY BRIDES
Dry Creek
Jillian Hart and Janet Tronstad
A chance at having a home and family brings these mail-order brides out west...but only love will make them stay, if they can learn that togetherness is the best way to celebrate the season.

A ROYAL MARRIAGE
Protecting the Crown
Rachelle McCalla
En route to her arranged wedding, Princess Gisela, headstrong daughter of the Holy Roman Emperor Charlemagne, is attacked. When she is rescued by a renowned healer, King John of Lydia, will forbidden love overcome the claims of honor?

A SUITABLE WIFE
Ladies in Waiting
Louise M. Gouge
With her family fortune squandered, Lady Beatrice Gregory can attend London's Season only as a companion. Attaching himself to her ruined family would jeopardize Lord Greystone's ambitions—but letting her go might break his heart.

COUNTERFEIT COWBOY
Lacy Williams
If Erin O'Grady discovers that Jesse Baker is a con artist, he knows she'll never give him a chance. Yet the more time they spend together, it seems that what started as a charade could lead to true love.

Look for these and other Love Inspired books wherever books are sold, including most bookstores, supermarkets, discount stores and drugstores.

LIHCNM1112

REQUEST YOUR FREE BOOKS!

2 FREE INSPIRATIONAL NOVELS
PLUS 2
FREE
MYSTERY GIFTS

Love Inspired.
HISTORICAL
INSPIRATIONAL HISTORICAL ROMANCE

YES! Please send me 2 FREE Love Inspired® Historical novels and my 2 FREE mystery gifts (gifts are worth about $10). After receiving them, if I don't wish to receive any more books, I can return the shipping statement marked "cancel." If I don't cancel, I will receive 4 brand-new novels every month and be billed just $4.49 per book in the U.S. or $4.99 per book in Canada. That's a saving of at least 22% off the cover price. It's quite a bargain! Shipping and handling is just 50¢ per book in the U.S. and 75¢ per book in Canada.* I understand that accepting the 2 free books and gifts places me under no obligation to buy anything. I can always return a shipment and cancel at any time. Even if I never buy another book, the two free books and gifts are mine to keep forever.

102/302 IDN FEHF

Name	(PLEASE PRINT)
Address	Apt. #
City	State/Prov.	Zip/Postal Code

Signature (if under 18, a parent or guardian must sign)

Mail to the **Reader Service:**
IN U.S.A.: P.O. Box 1867, Buffalo, NY 14240-1867
IN CANADA: P.O. Box 609, Fort Erie, Ontario L2A 5X3

Not valid for current subscribers to Love Inspired Historical books.

Want to try two free books from another series?
Call 1-800-873-8635 or visit www.ReaderService.com.

* Terms and prices subject to change without notice. Prices do not include applicable taxes. Sales tax applicable in N.Y. Canadian residents will be charged applicable taxes. Offer not valid in Quebec. This offer is limited to one order per household. All orders subject to credit approval. Credit or debit balances in a customer's account(s) may be offset by any other outstanding balance owed by or to the customer. Please allow 4 to 6 weeks for delivery. Offer available while quantities last.

Your Privacy—The Reader Service is committed to protecting your privacy. Our Privacy Policy is available online at www.ReaderService.com or upon request from the Reader Service.

We make a portion of our mailing list available to reputable third parties that offer products we believe may interest you. If you prefer that we not exchange your name with third parties, or if you wish to clarify or modify your communication preferences, please visit us at www.ReaderService.com/consumerschoice or write to us at Reader Service Preference Service, P.O. Box 9062, Buffalo, NY 14269. Include your complete name and address.

LIH11B

Love Inspired HISTORICAL

celebrating
15
YEARS

Love will find you when you least expect it.

Despite her protests, Princess Gisela, headstrong daughter of the Holy Roman Emperor Charlemagne, must enter into a diplomatic marriage. Yet en route to her wedding, her ship is attacked. Rescued by a renowned healer, King John of Lydia, Gisela recuperates at his Mediterranean castle. The handsome, widowed ruler soon has her reevaluating her beliefs on love and marriage...but only if King John could be her groom.

A Royal Marriage
By Rachelle McCalla

Available November 27
wherever books are sold.

A fractured family comes together during Christmas.

Read on for a sneak peek of
REUNITED FOR THE HOLIDAYS
by USA TODAY *bestselling author Jillian Hart,*
the exciting conclusion to the TEXAS TWINS *miniseries*
from Love Inspired® *Books.*

It was good to be home, Dr. Brian Wallace thought. The long trip from rural Texas had tired him. He missed his kids—although they were grown, they were all he had left of his heart.

He dialed his daughter's number first. A muffled ringing came from what sounded like his front porch. The bell pealed, boots thumped on the front steps and joy launched him from the couch. His kids were here? He tugged the doorknob, and there were his three children.

Maddie tumbled into his arms. "Dad, you have no idea how good it is to see you."

"Right back at you, sweetheart. I was gone a little longer than I'd planned this time—"

"A little? Dad, you have no idea what we've been through over you."

"Where have you been?" Grayson, his oldest child, stepped in.

"We've been looking for you." Grayson's hug was brief, his face fighting emotion, too. "We found your wallet in a ditch and we feared you were missing. The police—"

"I was in rural Texas. You know that. I would have gotten a message to you kids, but I lost my cell—"

"I know. We found your phone, too." Carter, his youngest from his second marriage, stepped in.

"We feared the worst, Dad," Maddie said.

"I never meant to worry you." He shut the door, swallowing hard. His illness had been severe and there'd been days, even weeks, where it hadn't been certain he would live. "I survived, so it wasn't so bad."

"This is just like you. Always keeping us out instead of letting us in." Maddie sounded upset.

He hated upsetting her. "I'm on the mend. That you're here means everything."

"Oh, Daddy." Maddie swiped her eyes. "Don't you dare make me cry. I'm choked up enough already."

"What do you mean?"

"Dad, you'd better sit down for this."

He studied Carter's serious face and the troubled crinkles around Grayson's eyes. "Something happened while I was gone. That's why you were trying to reach me?"

"It's not bad news, but it could give you a real shock. There's no easy way to say this, so I'm just going to do it. We found Mom."

*Separated for more than twenty years,
can Brian and Belle find the love they lost?*

*Pick up REUNITED FOR THE HOLIDAYS
in December to find out.*